The Britannica Junior Detectives Solve...

THE SECRET OF THE SUMMER SWEETHEART

BY GREGORY R.E. GALLAGHER

DIXON & KEEN, LTD.

First Edition

Characters and Story by

Gregory R.E. Gallagher & Corey Hickenbottom

Cover Art by

Jazz Miranda

dangerjazz.com | instagram.com/dangerjazz

All names, characters, and events in this story are entirely fictitious.

CONTENTS

CONTENTS

"*Sometimes—and this is very, very important—sometimes the bomb might explode without any warning. You may be in your schoolyard playing when it happens. Always remember, the flash can come at any time of the year day or night, no matter where you may be. Brighter than the sun, brighter than anything you have ever seen. We must be ready all of the time for the atomic bomb.*"

Duck and Cover (1951)
Federal Civil Defense Administration classroom film

Mary-Sue Welles was on a stakeout.

The Phantom of Prom

Mary-Sue Welles was on a stakeout. The teenage detective had found the perfect spot at the back of the gym, right next to the snack table and far from the crowded dance floor. She was completely inconspicuous in her shimmering blue prom dress, pretending to be just a sad girl pining for a dance.

On stage *Hap & the Upbeats* were playing a lively rock and roll number inside of a clamshell bandstand. To her left were the eighth-graders, talking and gossiping amongst themselves. To her right were the chaperones, keeping a keen eye on student propriety. Ignorant, all, of the malevolent *Phantom* who had been threatening the Bonnifield Junior High prom for the past week.

The class president had gone all out in planning the dance that year, selecting "Bon Voyage" as their theme. Cliché, true, but appropriate; in only two weeks' time, school would break for the summer and they would all be off to high school in the autumn.

Out on the dance floor, nearly two hundred students twisted and swayed to the music. There was an

unusual energy to the crowd, with nervous eyes darting back and forth between each group—but not in
fear of some supernatural specter. No, the machina-
tions of a far more sinister force had gripped Mary-
Sue's classmates: romance.

"Okay, cats 'n kittens," Hap cooed from the proscenium as the song's final note faded to silence. He
and the band had eschewed their usual yellow blaz-
ers for pressed Navy surplus uniforms. "We got one
last tune for y'all. It's gonna be a real slow one, so it's
time for you to find your sweetheart."

The drummer began a slow, cool beat. A dreamy
bass followed, then a soft saxophone and guitar. And
by the time Hap's vocals began, over three-quarters
of the kids had rushed away from the dance floor.

Mary-Sue was anxious, too—but not for some
silly dance. She flicked her eyes discreetly up to the
lighting booth where she could see the silhouette of
a figure working at a control panel high above them
all. It was the Sherlock to her Watson, the Green
Hornet to her Kato, the Lone Ranger to her Tonto.
It was her best friend in the whole world: Danny
"Britannica" Oxford.

She wanted to check in, to pull the walkie-talkie
out from her purse and ask if he had seen anything
that she might have missed, that she might have

overlooked. But couldn't risk exposing her position at the most critical moment of *The Britannica Junior Detectives'* biggest case yet.

"Good evening, my dear." Prescott Trowbridge, the mayor's spoiled son, oozed toward her in his new checkered polyester suit—the worst the *Sears Spring Catalog* had to offer. "I couldn't help but notice—"

"Buzz off, Prescott," Mary-Sue said curtly.

"Come, now." The boy sleazed his way over to the punch bowl, grabbing the ladle and stirring the half-melted blobs of sherbet round-and-round. "I realize how utterly nerve-wracking it must be to ask one's crush for a dance, so I shall do it for you: the answer is yes."

"I take it every other girl in school already said no?" she rolled her eyes.

"Of course not!" Prescott scoffed with his haughty affectation, raising a ladleful of foamy sherbet up into the air, then letting it dribble back down into the bowl below. "Simply the ones I asked."

"Get out of my hair, Prescott—I'm busy." She crossed her arms, eyes diligently scanning around the room. "I'm sure there are dozens of other girls out there who would be more than happy to turn you down."

"But none quite so lonesome as—"

"I said no, Prescott!" Mary-Sue shot the weasel a furious look. "Not if you were the last boy on Earth. Not if you were the last boy in the solar system, or the galaxy, or even the entire universe. No!"

"Very well! I take your meaning." Prescott studied her face. After a moment he leaned back against the table. "Never you mind that, I apologize for my rude demeanor. To make penance, I offer up my boutonnière—its odour is the sweetest of perfumes! If you would sample her fruits—"

"Promise to leave if I do?" Mary-Sue sighed.

"Indeed!" Prescott beamed, pushing himself away from the table. He walked over to the girl and thrust his chest out, looking down to the pink carnation on his homely lapel, arms stiff at his sides. "There she is. Enjoy, my dear!"

Mary-Sue looked Prescott directly in the eyes and smiled, then leaned down and squeezed the boy's hand as hard as she could. A long stream of water burst from the flower and splashed limply onto the ground at his feet.

"Blast it all!" He scrunched his face up. "How did you discern the true nature of my perennial prank?"

"I've seen ads for those in the back of every monster magazine I've ever read." She released his hand from her grip, then reached out, opened her palm, and raised her eyebrows. He scowled, then reluctantly handed the squeeze-box over. "Plus, boutonnières are only exchanged by dates, and I know you're here alone." She turned back to the dance floor with a shrug, tossing the contraption into the wastebin at her other side. "But what gave you away was the apology—I know you'd never do that without an agenda."

"Fiddlesticks!" Prescott kicked at the air, then walked off grumbling. "A new low, rejected even by Mary-Sue…"

"You've truly been a wonderful crew tonight," Hap said as the song wound down. He glanced backstage and nodded. "But now we've gotta hand it over to the man who made this magic happen: Principal Felding."

A smattering of applause came from the chaperones as the portly man stepped through the curtain, shooing the band offstage. He waddled up to the microphone, then grinned and yanked two bright red envelopes out from his front pocket.

Mary-Sue's heart skipped—this was it, the final chance for *The Phantom of Prom* to strike. During the royal court reveal the Prom King and Queen would be announced, they would receive their sashes and crowns, and then they would proclaim the dance to be concluded. It was now or never.

A piercing *SKREEE!* of feedback screeched out from the loudspeakers as Felding adjusted the microphone. Everyone grimaced and turned away—everyone except for Mary-Sue. Her eyes remained fixed straight ahead where she saw exactly what she had been waiting for: a shadow dashing in front of the lights above the stage.

She sprung into action, bolting toward the stage as she unclasped her purse, pulling the walkie-talkie out and extending its antenna in one smooth motion. It was nearly to her mouth when a sharp *BLEEP-BLEEP!* burst through the speaker.

"Mary-Sue, the catwalk," Danny said in his calm, authoritative tone. "I need you to head to Position Four. Once you've arrived, just wait for the signal."

"On it!" Mary-Sue said as her freckled, rosy-apple cheeks broke into a wide grin. She released the button and pushed through the stage door, then leapt up the stairs directly inside.

She dashed behind the cyclorama depicting a Naval warship battle, her neck craned all the way back, trying to catch a glimpse of *The Phantom* somewhere above. As she reached the far side, she finally spotted the specter in silhouette, creeping amongst the cables overhead.

"Now, class of nineteen fifty-nine!" Principal Felding's voice echoed across the gym. "That special time has arrived. The nominations have been made, the votes have been cast, and it's finally the moment you've all been waiting for!"

Mary-Sue found her mark right next to the wall of carefully-wound ropes and sandbags which controlled the stage's scrims and curtains. Danny had made a large X on the floor with masking tape in preparation.

"So without further ado," Felding said, pulling one card out from its envelope, "your prom queen is…" His eyes scanned across the card and his mouth broke into a huge smile. "Your class president, Sondra Fiehly!"

Everyone broke out into applause, cheering as the student body president bounded up onto the stage and gave them all a deep curtsy. Mrs. Applebaum, the pear-shaped English teacher, waddled up the side of the proscenium to place an elegant tiara on her head.

"Congratulations, young lady!" Felding gave her shoulder a pat as the crowd began to settle, then produced the second envelope. He first pulled the card out and took a private peek, then slid it back inside. "And your prom king is..." The man gave a coy smile and looked out over the crowd, who all began to titter. "*The All-American Boy*..." A chatter began. "Say it with me now! One, two, three..."

The entire crowd burst out all at once, "Danny Britannica!"

That was Mary-Sue's signal. As the rest of the student body began to hoot and holler in a wild cacophony, she grabbed the closest rope and unfastened the loop, sending the teaser's sandbag hurtling to the ground.

The crowd gasped as the curtain snapped up to the ceiling, revealing a dark figure on the catwalk above. *The Phantom* was crouched down low in the shadows next to a large plastic barrel, no doubt preparing to spring some devious trap.

From Danny's position in the booth, the beam of a spotlight burst on, then swiveled around toward the catwalk. By the time it hit the platform, however, the specter had already dashed away, nearing the rooftop exit on the other side.

Mary-Sue ran to the next taped X and grabbed ahold of a metal lever on a control panel. She yanked down hard and on stage the clamshell bandstand slammed shut, its rope quickly unfurling to drop a heavy sandbag directly in the path of *The Phantom*.

But instead of pivoting the other direction as anticipated, the specter pulled a small device out from a hidden pocket. It pushed a button and a foul, acrid smoke began to slowly roll out from the vents in the ceilings and along the walls. *POP-pop-POP! POP-pop-POP!*

The sprinklers immediately kicked in and ice-cold water rained down onto the students below. With cries of confusion and dismay, the prom-goers began to scatter and run for the exits. Mary-Sue glanced over to the booth to see Danny running from the spotlight over to the control board.

He pulled a lever down and the old industrial fan kicked in, pulling the smoke back into the vents and out through the chimney. After a few seconds the sprinklers petered out, prompting *The Phantom* to let out an otherworldly howl.

Mary-Sue turned to see it bound for the emergency stairwell on the other side. The specter flew down the stairs toward the second-story exit, pushing through the door and setting the fire alarm off with a loud *BWAMP! BWAMP! BWAMP!*

BLEEP-BLEEP! At her side, Mary-Sue barely heard her walkie-talkie beep. She swung it up next to her ear.

"Head to Position One," Danny said, calm. "I'll go to Fifteen."

"Copy!" Mary-Sue said, then tossed the chunky radio into her bag and grabbed the pleats of her dress. She bolted to the rear door, pushing through and racing down the stairwell to the lower level, which was lit only by the unsettling red light of the fire alarm.

On both sides of the hallway were long lines of lockers, broken up by the occasional classroom entrance. At the far end was a thick, steel door with grey rivets running down each side, diagonal support bars crossing its surface, and a large, red turnwheel directly in the center.

Above the door was a plaque. On the top half was a simple graphic, comprised of three yellow triangles meeting at the center of a large black circle. On the bottom half were two words printed in a simple, bold font. It read:

Mary-Sue dashed to the door and grabbed the turn-wheel. Her first tug did nothing, but she planted her feet and tightened her grip, then pulled again with all of her might. *GRRR-NKK-NKK!* The wheel began to slowly give way, and as it turned, a flurry of rust flakes rained down onto the floor.

Mary-Sue spun the wheel all the way around, then again and again until it was fully loose. She yanked, swinging the door open to the dark chamber beyond. As the red light faded in, forgotten cases of rations and supplies were illuminated, covered in a thick layer of dust. She stepped back and found the X behind the door, then slipped around to stand on it. And waited. And waited.

She wanted to call Danny, to confirm that everything was going according to plan. But her walkie-talkies were the cheap kind with a limited range—purchased with a check sent to an address in the back of a pulp magazine.

She imagined Danny upstairs, chasing *The Phantom* down. The boy had the fastest mile in the school and would have to slow his pace down to avoid giving away that he was luring the ghoul into a trap—unless, that is, Mary-Sue's suspicion that something supernatural was afoot proved true.

She heard the clattering of footsteps down the

far stairwell. As the figure reached bottom it paused, then rattled at a door handle. Locked. It grunted and ran a few yards further, then tried another. Then another and another, until it stopped, silent. Listening. Mary-Sue heard it, too: the steady, confident footsteps of her best friend, echoing closer and closer behind *The Phantom*.

Just as expected, it made a beeline toward the bomb shelter. Mary-Sue prepared herself, planting her feet against the baseboard and placing her shoulder against the crank. She tensed as the specter approached, and as it crept across the threshold the girl shoved hard, slamming the door shut behind it with a loud *KER-CHUNK!*

There was a clattering of footsteps at the end of the hall and Mary-Sue turned to see Danny dash down the stairs.

"Did we do it?" He called out, a sly smile on his face.

"We did it!" Mary-Sue broke into a wide grin.

The detectives ran toward each other, then came in for a warm embrace. The mystery had finally come to a close. *The Phantom of Prom* would soon be revealed. And *The Britannica Junior Detectives* had done it again.

"Now," Danny said, "let's find out just who this mysterious 'Phantom' really is."

PROLOGUE II   Vanquishing the Villain

"'Your prom is doomed!'" Danny growled out in his best impression of *The Phantom*, gazing out over the sea of two hundred eager faces, each waiting in the basement hallway for the dramatic reveal. "This is how it all began," he continued, "in a note slipped under our administration's door, constructed from letters cut out from the newspaper. It claimed that heartbreaking devastation would ensue unless the event was canceled."

"I was rather worried!" Principal Felding nodded.

"It wasn't until decorations began to go missing," the young detective said, pacing in front of the bomb shelter, "that *The Britannica Junior Detectives* were finally called in. My first clue was the note itself; the stock was too weighty for a simple prank. Quickly peeling each letter back, I discovered that it had been composed on official school letterhead— the use of which is restricted to faculty and staff alone. Under lock and key."

"How could I have missed it?" Felding sighed.

"This was when I knew that I had to take the case." Danny paused to adjust his crown. "My second clue came from a faculty member; during a recent rehearsal for the *The Odyssey*, Mr. Schlafke noticed that a costume had gone missing from the dressing room. Soon after, the man spotted a mysterious figure lurking around backstage. But it wasn't until a Fresnel light came crashing down that he reported these incidents to the administration."

"It's when I got worried." Felding put his hands on his hips.

"A meeting was called to discuss the merits of canceling prom," the boy continued. "From the start, nearly everyone was in favor of calling the whole affair off. But I soon convinced Superintendent Unkrich that if we gave way to the demands of *The Phantom* then, that we might never discover the villain's true identity. So it was decided that prom would continue unabated—with *The Britannica Junior Detectives* at the ready."

"We put our full faith in Danny!" Felding beamed.

"Over the following days, a series of additional clues came to light." Danny flicked his eyes over to Mary-Sue and the two best friends shared a private look. The girl clutched tightly at the fallout shelter's crank, ready at any moment for his signal. "Tax exempt receipts for fireworks, missing skeleton keys, and damaged air-conditioning vents. So as the night of prom approached, my suspect list began to shrink, shorter and shorter until only one name remained."

He scanned the crowd. Student and chaperone alike were standing up on their tippy-toes in anticipation.

"So before the promenade began, I engineered my trap." The boy let a smile pull at the edge of his lips. "And through careful and meticulous planning, I covered for any and every eventuality—until I was certain that I could outwit the *The Phantom's* dastardly scheme, whatever it might be." Danny took a breath, then turned his back to the crowd and faced the fallout shelter door. "Then it was a simple chess game, waiting for the villain to make their first move. After that, it was my turn—I spotted their hiding place on the catwalk above the stage, exposed them, then chased the fiend all around the school until I trapped them here, in the fallout shelter. Where *The Phantom of Prom* sits at this very moment."

Danny could feel the electricity of the crowd building behind him as he looked Mary-Sue in the eyes, then gave her a nod. She spun the wheel hard, yanked, and pulled it open. The gears gave a soulful

GRRRN! and a flurry of dust kicked up into the air, swirling around the entrance and obscuring its inhabitant until Danny clicked his flashlight on, directed the beam at the concrete floor within, and caught a pair of old, dirty old boots in its glow.

"Now," Danny said, "let's find out just who this mysterious *Phantom* really is."

The boy slowly raised the beam up the body, past the tattered cloak, past the tightly-clenched fists, and all the way up to the face of the *The Phantom of Prom*, concealed beneath a hood. Danny reached out, grabbed the fabric, then yanked back, causing a sharp gasp to escape each and every onlooker in the crowded hallway.

"Jumping Jehoshaphat!" Felding clapped his hand to his chest. "It's George Hudson!"

"Oi, the janitor!" Officer Doogan, the police detective assigned to the case, shook his head as the villain took a step into the hall, fingers balled up and knuckles white with rage.

"Of course it's George Hudson." Danny crossed his arms with a satisfied smile. "After all, who but the custodian would have access to the backstage, access to the letterhead, and access to the school's tax-exempt code?" Danny turned to face the man, whose dark, angry eyes stood fixed straight ahead.

"That circumstantial evidence, however, wasn't enough to convince me of the man's true identity. No, it was his character that put the cherry on top of the proverbial sundae. You see, through meticulous research I uncovered my final clue: that Hudson had been dishonorably discharged by the United States Air Force. That he had a criminal record, kept secret from the administration. That he had spent time in prison."

"George!" Felding turned to the man, shoulders slumped. "Tell me it isn't true!"

"Every word of it," Hudson growled stoically.

"That be enough for me!" Doogan stepped forward and grabbed the custodian's arms, pulling them roughly behind his back and slapping the handcuffs onto his wrists. "Now let's get down to the station, shall we?"

"Before you take him away, sir." Danny held his hand out and the officer paused. "There's just one thing that I couldn't figure out." The boy frowned as he looked into Hudson's eyes. "Why did you do it?"

Hudson stared back, jaw clenched, then looked out into the crowd. "I would have been just about your age when word came over the wireless: Oahu attacked by Japanese bombers."

"Pearl Harbor?" Danny frowned, recalling the

incident from History class. "What does that have to do with prom?"

"That's when everything changed." Hudson cast his eyes to the floor. "The next day, we declared war on Japan. As a loyal citizen, I wanted to do my duty—so I marched right up to the local Air Force recruitment office and volunteered. I was turned away for being too young, of course, so later that day I altered my documentation then headed right back into the office. The same man who had rejected me only hours before gave me an approving look, then stamped my card."

"You enlisted at fourteen?" Danny tilted his head to the side.

"Before I left Bonnifield," the man continued, "I'd had my entire life planned out: finish school at the top of my class, get a scholarship from a good university, marry the girl at the end of the street, raise a family." He paused and looked back to the floor. "Live the American dream."

"Then you really *were* the same George Hudson from our yearbook," Mary-Sue said from his other side.

"I was the greatest football player in the history of Bonnifield Junior High." Hudson nodded, gesturing to a nearby trophy case, where a huge gold football was prominently featured. The plaque beneath read:

There was a photograph of the squad, and listed below that were the names of the members, Hudson amongst them.

"I was obedient, which earned me the respect of my officers. I was intelligent, which earned me the respect of my peers. Early on, I proved a quick study in maps and charts, soon becoming a navigator on scouting missions over France. As the theatre of war moved to the Pacific, so did I, continuing to earn esteem in the eyes of the higher-ups." Hudson paused and shut his eyes. "November of nineteen-forty-four, I was approached by my commanding officer. I was handed a beige folder with a large, red *Top Secret* stamped across the front. Inside were a series of photographs marked 'Trinity.' And that's when I learned about the atomic bomb."

"You flew on the *Enola Gay*?" Principal Felding gasped.

"Of course not." Hudson shot a cruel look his way. "Despite my loyalty to this country, despite my obedience, I couldn't bring myself to be a part of such a monstrous mission. I refused the assignment and was quickly court-martialed, thrown into a military prison where I rotted for five long years."

"I—I don't understand." Danny frowned. "How did—"

"When I returned to Bonnifield, it was with visions of sock hops and malt shops, letterman jackets and picture shows. In reality, my classmates had graduated and the girl at the end of the block had already married, with two kids and a white picket fence." He tightened his fists. "With my reputation and my lack of education, I found it difficult to get good work until finally, out of desperation, I applied as a janitor at my junior high."

"But there isn't anything wrong with that." Danny shook his head. "I believe that sanitation and maintenance positions are part of the bedrock of our society."

"Try a decade of cleaning toilets for kids who won't even look you in the eye and tell me that again!" Hudson growled at the boy. "So I decided to give you sniveling brats a taste of real-world disappointment and get prom called-off, putting an end to all of your budding romance. When threats didn't work, I began to hatch a more devious scheme, not just to cancel the dance, but humiliate your best and brightest. So I stole a cloak, planted smoke bombs, and laid in wait to dump sewage onto the royal court." The man paused, directing his gaze at the detective. "And I would have gotten away with it, too, if it weren't for you, Danny Britannica."

"Gosh," Danny said, turning to Doogan. "That sounds an awful lot like a confession to me—don't you agree?"

"I reckon the boys'll take it." The officer nodded.

"Then I think," Danny grinned and turned to Mary-Sue, "that we can call this case officially closed!"

The girl nodded and opened her purse, pulling a small camera and a flashbulb out. She ran over to the front of the crowd and crouched down on one knee, screwing the bulb in.

"Sondra?" Danny looked out over the crowd and spotted his newly-crowned Queen. "Care to join me for a photo opportunity?"

The girl's eyes went wide and she ran out from the crowd and up to Danny's side. The two adjusted their sashes as Officer Doogan leaned in, yanking Hudson along with him. Mary-Sue crouched down and raised the viewfinder up to her eye, placed her hand on the button, and grinned.

"Say cheese!"

"Cheese!" the whole crowd called out.

KA-PIFF! the flashbulb exploded in a puff of smoke. Danny coughed and waved at the air as the police officer pulled Hudson away toward the far stairs, the crowd parting to let them through. Danny blinked his eyes and shook his head, causing the bright after-image to fade away.

"Now," Danny said, "there's only one thing left to do."

"The paperwork?" Principal Felding asked hopefully.

"While paperwork is important, sir," Danny chuckled and shook his head, "it can wait until Monday morning. Right now, we have something far more important to do." He looked out into the crowd, then winked. "Eat free ice cream sundaes, courtesy of Graham's Soda Fountain!"

A wild cheer burst from the crowd and they began to chant, *"Danny! Danny! Danny!"*

All around, the air crackled with an intense, stippled glow that could mean only one thing: atomic radiation.

1   The Mutant of Mercury Marsh

The scientist cowered in the far corner of his laboratory, attempting to shield himself from the horrified gaze of his onlooking family, arms in front of his face. But where once there were rugged, steel-jawed features, there was now only the grotesque, frilled stalk of a mushroom bursting forth from his neck. All around, the air crackled with an intense, stippled glow that could mean only one thing: atomic radiation.

Mary-Sue traced her finger across the murky illustration in the latest issue of *The Crypt of Mystery*—her very favorite monster magazine. It was pulp horror, printing serialized stories of the macabre from the likes of H. P. Lovecraft, Robert E. Howard, Clark Ashton Smith, and M. R. James.

The girl had found the quietest spot at the after party: the last stool at the soda shop counter in the cramped back corner of the brightly lit room. Behind her, dozens of kids were dancing on the checkered tile, with a few dozen more standing around the fringes, sitting in the booths, or perched around the counter. The jukebox was at maximum volume, set to play the latest hits from the likes of *Johnny and the Hurricanes*, *Skip & Flip*, and *The Virtues* on repeat.

Mary-Sue moved her finger down the page and felt the noise of the room fade away. It read:

18   THE CRYPT OF MYSTERY

the man with a trillion eyes

by . . . Peter Langelaan

If they looked upon the hideous horror any longer, they just might scream for the rest of their lives...!

Every revolution begins with an idea. A seed. A spore.

Man's final revolution began with a lichen—the lowest of the decomposers, the detritus dwellers of the forest floor.

The result of a mutualistic bond between two unlike species, the humble alga and fungus are able to join together for a common purpose: survival.

My epiphany came not in the laboratory, but in the bedroom. I had been absorbed all day in my most recent experiment, exposing my newly discovered lichen test subject to small bursts of gamma radiation in order to accelerate its growth.

My wife had been asleep for some time, but was awoken when I slipped into bed after midnight. Margaret accurately pointed out that I had once again worked straight through the dinner that she had worked so hard to prepare—leaving her and the children to eat alone for the third night that week.

I once again explained that my work was simply too important to be disturbed by a thing so bothersome and trivial as sustenance. But though she nodded in understanding, I saw a pout come across the woman's face as she turned to sleep without another word.

In recent days I'd begun to sense that Margaret was becoming more and more fatigued with my constant but necessary excuses. I wished that man had evolved past the need for something so silly as requiring kilocalories to operate at maximum efficiency. And at that moment I realized: if two beings could work in harmony, then why not three?

Three separate entities working as one toward a mutual goal—but instead of the instinctual survival of two mindless species, this mutualistic entity could be driven by the brilliant mind of a man dedicated to the advancement of science.

Were I to allow this new atomic lichen to combine with my own flesh, I would be able to photosynthesize enough energy to continue my work undisturbed! True, I would likely mutate into something monstrous and inhuman. But for science, I would do anything that was required of me! And thus

(continued on next page)

From her side, an errant elbow careened into Mary-Sue's sundae glass, spilling the melted concoction all over the counter. The girl quickly reached for the nearby stack of napkins, but was swiftly cut-off by the attentive hand of the best soda jerk in all of Williams County: Danny Britannica. He swooped in with his bright red washcloth and his striking blue eyes, wiping the ice cream away in one perfect swipe.

"My good man!" Prescott trilled from her side, eyes flicking down to inspect the elbow of his blazer for stains, avoiding the girl's fuming gaze. Satisfied, he pulled a quarter out from his pocket, breathed on it twice, then gave it a shine on his lapel. "My patronage awaits."

"Oh, no need for money, Prescott, sundaes are on the house tonight!" Danny beamed. "Courtesy of Mr. Graham's kind generosity. You see, he wanted to provide a safe and fun atmosphere for all of the—"

"Yes, I'm well aware." Prescott gave a smug smile. "However, I'm afraid that my palette is quite a bit more refined than an *ice cream sundae* would allow. No; a Trowbridge desires only the finest of confections."

"Ah—so the usual, then!" Danny nodded and reached for the shake machine's frosty metal cup.

"That's double-chocolate, and an extra scoop of malt, right?"

"What can I say?" Prescott chuckled, slapping the quarter down onto the now-pristine counter and sliding it forward. "I prefer them rich."

"Well in that case, I should charge you another nickel for the extras." Danny laughed and dumped the first scoop of malt into the mixing cup, then went for the second. "But seeing how this is a special occasion, I'll be more than happy to give them to you for free."

"Free? Heavens, no!" Prescott recoiled, then pulled a second quarter out. "I require no special treatment, my dear boy—nor shall I tolerate it." He gingerly placed the second quarter down next to the first. "Thus, you may consider any change your tip."

"Twenty cents!" Danny dropped the second spoonful of powder into the cup. "There's no need for such a generous offer; the only reward that I require is the knowledge that you've received satisfactory service—a job well done is my reward!"

"Regardless," Prescott turned his nose up, "I refuse to carry lower denominations, so I'm afraid that you have no choice but to accept."

"Well okay, then," Danny laughed, plopping two heaping scoops of double-chocolate ice cream into the cup, then adding a splash of milk. He turned toward the mixer, flipped the switch on, then expertly twisted and shook the concoction, whipping up a perfect malt in just a few moments. *WHRRRR!*

With his free hand, Danny grabbed a malt glass from the bar, poured the mixture in, then slid the whole thing across the counter into Prescott's waiting hand one smooth motion.

"Perfection!" Prescott smiled, lifting the drink and sucking a long sip through the straw. He smacked his lips and nodded in approval. "Nearly as good as your rousing speech from before—I think that your theatrics at the bomb shelter may have single-handedly saved the event from having been a dreadful bore."

"Gee, thank you, Prescott!" Danny shrugged. "And thank you for the charitable tip—I'll be sure to donate it to an organization in need."

"See that you mention the Trowbridge name when you do." Prescott nodded, then turned around and pushed back through the sea of bodies behind them. Mary-Sue rolled her eyes, then turned her attention back to *The Crypt of Mystery*, flipping to the next page.

"Say..." Danny placed his elbows down onto the counter in front of her, then put his chin on his hands. "Has something got you down, Mary-Sue?"

"No," the girl lied, twisting her mouth to the side. After a moment, she felt Danny's gaze still on her. She sighed and glanced back up. "How could you tell?"

"Well, gosh." Danny shrugged. "What kind of soda jerk would I be if I'd failed to notice that my very best customer had barely touched her strawberry sundae?" He gave a kind smile, then lowered his voice. "And what kind of friend would I be if I'd failed to notice that my very best pal had spent the entire party nose-down in one of her monster magazines?"

"You got me." She shrugged, looking back over her shoulder around the room. All of the other kids were laughing, gossiping, and flirting with their fellow prom-goers—as if they had already forgotten about the case. About *The Phantom*. About George Hudson.

"I apologize that I've yet to have the time to discuss the case," Danny said, "but I believe that *The Britannica Junior Detectives* just pulled off their best mystery yet. We should be celebrating!"

"No, that's not it." Mary-Sue shook her head. "I understand—you're making sure everyone has a good time."

"Hm." Danny straightened back up. "Then perhaps it's because *The Phantom* wasn't the paranormal specter that you'd hoped?" He gave her a knowing look. "That, once again, your imagination got the best of you?"

"No—though that certainly didn't help." She sighed. "It's what Mr. Hudson said that's been bothering me."

"I see," Danny nodded. "Then I'm afraid that your poor mood is my fault, entirely. I see now that I should have controlled the narrative more closely—I could have cut the villain's speech off at any point. Nobody needed to hear the ravings of that disturbed mind."

"Gosh, do you really think so?" Mary-Sue reached down and flipped the magazine shut. "You don't feel the least bit sorry for him?"

"Sorry?" Danny raised his eyebrows and gave her a wry smile. "For the convicted criminal who just terrorized a junior high prom?"

"But enlisting so early," she said with a frown, "thrust unexpectedly into adulthood, then coming back to a world that's forgotten you, only to be perpetually stuck in the place you left behind. It's a bit sad, isn't it?"

"No." Danny said, standing up straight. "Because regardless of any other factor, the man made his choices—and he has to take responsibility for those choices." He paused to consider. "But I do hope that in time Mr. Hudson is able to see the error of his ways and re-enter society a changed man. Though with his recidivism in mind, I can't imagine—"

"Excuse me, Mr. Oxford?" The austere Phil Waxman leaned in next to Mary-Sue. He was a fellow student, and a crackerjack reporter. He had the honor of being a writer for the *Bonnifield Gazette*, the youngest in their history—and a swell one at that. The boy reached up behind his ear and sharply withdrew a pencil. "If you wouldn't mind clarifying a few details for *The Gazette*…"

"Golly, Phil!" Danny gave him an incredulous grin. "You've already begun writing the story? This is meant to be a party! Is there some rush?"

"The presses begin printing at one o'clock tomorrow morning," Phil said, putting pencil to notepad. "If I deliver a finished story to my editor by midnight, then he'll have it to the typesetter by quarter-past. Saturday is our lowest circulation day, and nothing sells papers like the adventures of *The Britannica Junior Detectives*. So it truly is imperative, yes."

"Then this is serious," Danny said with a nod. "Though I think those sales are much more to do with your skillful prose and expert storytelling than any exploit of my own. Even so, how can I be of assistance?"

"I've been looking over the casefile that Mary-Sue provided, and I'm curious." The reporter narrowed his eyes. "How early, precisely, was the Bonnifield Police Department involved?"

"Well..." Danny furrowed his brow.

"You see, Phil." Mary-Sue said, clearing her throat and leaning into the boy's sightline. The reporter turned and looked down at her. "It was just before we did. The first thing Principal Felding did when he saw the note was call the police, though they dismissed it as a student prank. Still, Superintendent Unkrich wanted to cancel prom just in case. But Principal Felding insisted on consulting us first, because we helped save his skin during *The Miniature Model Mishap* last year." She straightened up on her stool, slipping the magazine into her bag. "So the BPD assigned Sergeant Doogan to the case. At first, he didn't take it seriously—but boy was there egg on his face when I found that tax-exempt receipt!"

"Interesting." Phil raised an eyebrow, scribbling

a note. "Go on."

"After school that day," Mary-Sue said, beaming, "we officially took on the case. While Danny was busy interviewing the faculty and staff, I was looking through the dumpsters to see if I —"

"Truth be told, Phil," Danny interrupted, reaching up and scratching at the back of his neck, "if it's all the same to you, then I'd prefer that those particular details were left out of the record—I wouldn't want the police or administration to come off poorly in your story—I'm sure that you understand." He straightened up, then stroked at his chin. "Why not say that I requested light police involvement, to ensure that *The Phantom* wouldn't get suspicious?"

"Yes, an astute idea." Phil nodded, crossing the previous line out and scribbling another note. He then flipped back several pages and scanned his previous scrawl. "During the reveal, Mary-Sue mentioned something about, let's see now..." The boy paused, reading down the page. "Ah, yes, here we are—a yearbook?"

"Right again." May-Sue nodded. "See, after we'd found our clues, it was time for the research phase. While Danny was interviewing persons of interest, it was my job to go through any documents, books, and records I could find, cross-referencing the names with any faculty or staff—which is how I found out there was once a student named George Hudson at BJH. Because of the mismatch in age, though, Danny didn't think it was the same person." She gave a small shrug. "I guess even *The All-American Boy* occasionally makes a—"

"Actually," Danny grimaced, "I'm afraid that I would prefer that you leave those details out as well, Phil—I wouldn't want some enterprising criminal to read about our methods in the papers to use them against us."

"Understandable." Phil nodded. "What would you prefer?"

"Hmm. Why don't you just say that we knew it was the same George Hudson the whole time?" Danny shrugged. "I think that it would make for a much more compelling narrative, wouldn't you say?"

"Much cleaner," Phil agreed, flipping back and crossing another line out. He scribbled a series of notes in shorthand. "Well, in that case, there's really only one outstanding matter: the title of the exposé."

"I can't wait!" Danny said. "You're always so good at these, Phil."

"What was wrong with *The Phantom of Prom*?" Mary-Sue frowned. "I thought I really got the hang of your naming scheme."

"While the alliteration was well-executed," Phil said, "I decided that I would need something a little more dramatic for the Saturday edition. So what do you think about *Danny Britannica Solves: The Perplexing Case of the Perilous Prom?*"

"Wow! That's real boss!" Sondra leaned in from the next stool over, a wide grin on her face. "It's catchy, too!"

"Gee, it sure is," Danny said. "Thank you, Phil, you're an incredibly gifted reporter. I look forward to reading your article tomorrow."

"Yes." Phil nodded, put pencil back to paper, then turned around, disappearing out into the crowd.

"Hello Sondra!" Danny grinned at his Prom Queen. "Would you like something to eat?" He gestured up to the menu on the wall. "A brownie sundae, perhaps? Maybe a slice of Mrs. Graham's homemade blackberry pie? Or even a simple, refreshing Coca Cola?"

"No, no, that's okay." A smile slowly spread across the girl's face. "I just like watching you work, that's all. I bet you're the best soda jerk in all of The United States of America."

"Gosh." Danny frowned and rubbed at his chin. "I don't know about that, Sondra—after all, there are likely a good number of soda purveyors who have been perfecting their craft for decades. No. No, I'm sure that I would rank well below them from any objective measure. I'll simply keep attempting to make my customers as happy as I'm able. I think the world would be a better place if we all treated others that way!"

"Now you sound like a politician," Sondra said. "You even look like one—well, like Senator Kennedy, anyway." She batted her eyes. "Perhaps this autumn you'd be interested in running for co-class president with me? I think we made rather handsome pair in front of the student body earlier. What do you say?"

"Hm. An interesting prospect." Danny nodded slowly. "However, at the moment I have to focus on the here and now. Final exams are coming up, as I'm sure we're all aware, and they'll be requiring my full attention for the foreseeable future. After they're over, I would likely be able to give the idea its proper due."

"Well if you need a study-buddy," Sondra cooed, "I'm all yours."

"Gee, thanks!" He tossed his washcloth onto his shoulder. "However I'm afraid that I have a strict, solitary regiment when it comes to my study habits that mustn't be disturbed. I'm afraid that not even

Mary-Sue will be seeing much of me for the next two weeks."

BRRNG-BRRNG! the bell above the front door chimed, barely audible over the music, and a middle-aged man stumbled through. It was Dale Brown, the town drunk, and he was wearing a plaid coat, rubber waders, and a floppy brown hat covered in fishing lures.

"Speaking of the here and now..." Danny gave the girls a look. "I'm afraid that I have to deal with this at the moment—but please, Sondra," the boy said as he began walking toward the front of the counter, "do let me know if you get a craving for anything."

"I'll try." Sondra gave a small sigh as he turned. "Again."

"Good luck," Mary-Sue chuckled to herself, reaching into her bag.

"I'll sure need it..." Sondra drummed her fingers on the edge of the counter, then turned to Mary-Sue. "So, what's next?"

"Next?" She raised her eyebrows. "What do you mean?"

"For *The Britannica Junior Detectives*." Sondra shrugged. "The two of you have another big summer mystery lined up this year?"

"Not yet." Mary-Sue pulled her bookbag onto her lap and unbuckled the straps. "Around finals, he's got no time for anything else until the last bell rings—he's purely academic."

"I'm not convinced he's ever anything but." Sondra gave a huff, then hopped down from her stool. "Well, it was nice talking to you."

"Mm." Mary-Sue nodded, turning her attention back toward Danny, who was directing Mr. Brown to the back of the shop. The man nodded, bleary-eyed, then began to shove his way across the dance floor. As he got closer to Mary-Sue, Dale made a beeline for the payphone directly behind her.

She glanced back out of the corner of her eye and saw him grab the handset and slip a dime into the coin slot, fingers shaking. The girl could smell the distinct odor of whiskey emanating as he dialed a number.

"Police, what's your emergency?" The operator asked.

"Howdy, ma'am," he said, voice wavering. "You got Dale Brown—formerly of Brown's Shoes—on the horn." He took a quick breath. "Now, I know you ain't gonna believe me, 'specially not this time 'a night, but I swear to you it's all true, y'hear?"

"Okay, sir—"

"Well, don't ya know, I got a hankerin' for some bass fishin' tonight, ya see. Went on down through the woods out to Mercury Marsh, know where I mean? Out past that old graveyard, near the lagoon."

"Yes, sir—"

"Well, let me tell you!" Dale banged his fist onto the payphone. "This thing done scared the bejesus outta me, lurkin' in the swamp all spooky-like. And it weren't like no man I ever seen before—skin all wrinkled and discolored. Hairless. Eyes big as saucers. Like... some kinda... I dunno... some kinda moleman, or, or—"

Mary-Sue perked up.

"Slow down, Mr. Brown," the operator said, "did you say—"

"Dang it, no—that can't be it, can it? Moles don't have no eyes." The man scratched at his chin. "Maybe like some kinda... mutant. Yeah, that's it—some mutated man done leaped out of the shadows 'n scared me half outta my wits."

"Dale," the operator said, "have you been drinking tonight?"

"Well I been fishin', ain't I?"

"Yes, well. I've taken a note of the incident," the operator said curtly. "Now, if I might make a suggestion—drink a glass of water, walk home, and get a good night's rest. I think we'd all sleep better knowing that you had."

CLK-BRRRNNNN! the dial-tone droned.

"C'mon now!" Dale slammed the payphone down onto the hook. "I don't need that sorta guff!" He shook his head, then stumbled back into the crowd and squeezed out through the front door. *BRRNG-BRRNG!*

Mary-Sue chewed at her lip. While Dale was a notoriously unreliable character, there had been something in his voice that made the girl think that he believed what he was saying—and Mary-Sue had a knack for reading people. She reached into her bag and pulled a pencil out, then grabbed a napkin from the counter and scribbled down the words *Mutant* and *Mercury Marsh*.

It might be nothing. After all, it was nearly eleven o'clock and he had clearly been intoxicated. But maybe, just maybe, it could be the start to their next big summer mystery.

The Dull Disaster Drill

2

The semester's final two weeks sped by in a flash. Danny had spent the intervening time meticulously and methodically memorizing every chart and diagram in each of his subject's required reading—as per usual. He had written and rewritten his notes a dozen times, poured over every word of his syllabi, utilized the office hours of his teachers, and entered the testing period supremely confident in his ability to ace each exam—plus extra credit.

Danny's fellow students sat in their homeroom seats, staring intently at the clock above the door, waiting for the bell to ring and the summer to begin, each tick of the second hand making them squirm just a little bit more. Danny's attention, however, was focused solely on the salmon-colored envelopes at his English teacher's side.

"Now class," Mrs. Applebaum trilled with perfect diction, "please do pay attention. While I'm quite certain that each and every one of you is excited for your imminent summer holiday to commence, there remains one very crucial thing to consider before you depart."

The woman reached out and picked the stack of envelopes up.

"Each and every one of you has made his or her own choices about how you have spent your time this year." She pushed herself up from her desk and began to pace across the front of the room. "Some have chosen to spend their precious education dilly-dallying, doodling, staring out the window, or passing notes to friends—while others have chosen to spend their time wisely, studying and striving for perfection."

She began to walk up the first row of desks, placing each envelope in front of each student with a precise *SWAACK!*

"But as you enter high school this autumn," she continued, stepping to the next row and beginning the process again, "you will be doing so as young adults—and I pray that each of you prioritizes your studies to arm yourselves with the tools which you will need in order to thrive."

She placed the last envelope gingerly on Danny's desk, then walked to the front of the room. One-by-one the students tentatively reached for their envelopes, cringing at what might await beyond. Danny excitedly unfastened his brad and pulled the thick card-stock out from its sheath, quickly scanning down the column. It read:

STUDENT'S REPORT CARD BONNIFIELD JUNIOR HIGH SCHOOL	
ART	105%
CIVICS	105%
ENGLISH	100%
FRENCH	105%
HISTORY	105%
MATH	105%
SCIENCE	105%

Danny stared at his English grade with a frown.

"Each choice that you make moving forward will ripple throughout the rest of your lives. I do hope that some of you take this responsibility rather more seriously than you have chosen to take your studies at this fair institution." The woman sat against the edge of her desk and crossed her arms. "Now, with the time remaining, you may all quietly—quietly, mind you—discuss your final grades amongst your—"

There was an immediate cacophony as a dozen students turned and began loudly chattering to their neighbors. In front of Danny, Mary-Sue swiveled around in her seat.

"So," his best friend said, giving him a look, "I assume you—"

"Danny!" Francine Maxwell called out from the next row, pulling the boy's attention away. "You were right."

"About the test?" He raised his eyebrows.

"Yeah!" She beamed. "That exam was a breeze—plus, Ms. Schiffer really liked my sculpture. So… I wound up with an A-plus, like you said! Hopefully," she said with a cartoonish grimace, "for my folks it'll balance out my B-minus in French."

"My sculpture was a hit, too," Mary-Sue leaned in, "but memorizing the names and dates gets me every time—but my A-plus in Math should make my mom pretty happy ."

"Simpletons!" Prescott chortled from behind them. "Wasted effort, I'm afraid; your As and Bs are no different than my Cs and Ds."

"What're you yammering about, you reprobate?" Mary-Sue turned and scrunched her nose up at the boy.

"You… aren't aware?" Prescott crossed his arms with a smug smile. "Grades don't carry over to high school; as long as one receives a passing mark, one will begin with a clean slate in autumn. Universities don't even look. So at this point in our lives, poor grades don't matter, as long as one doesn't get held back."

"We should be so lucky," Mary-Sue stuck her tongue out.

"So you see," Prescott continued, unabated, "all energy spent fussing over exams would have been better put toward constructive purposes."

"Okay, I'll bite." Mary-Sue rolled her eyes. "Like what?"

"I myself spent the previous two weeks studying the permit exam in preparation for the brand new motor scooter that Father purchased me for my graduation," he said. "While you brainy buffoons are on your bumpkin bicycles this summer, I shall be free to go anywhere that I please atop my gasoline chariot."

"Why do you care?" Mary-Sue sighed. "Weren't you bragging about how you're spending your summer in the Hamptons?"

"Indeed." Prescott grinned. "And now it shall be with a pretty little New York socialite perched on the back as we wind around the pristine white coves."

"See, Prescott," Sondra called out from the boy's other side, chipper, "I actually got my permit this week as well—but I also aced my exams. So I think that maybe you're just—"

wrrmm! Wrrmm! WRRMM! The entire class groaned and sank down into their chairs as the air-raid sirens began to warm up.

"Under your seats, my dears, under your seats!" Mrs. Applebaum stood up and banged a hand onto her desk. The students grumbled. "No complaints this time. I will remind you that the Department of Education requires that these bi-weekly duck-and-cover drills be done for your and my safety. The last day of school is no excuse for foolhardiness."

Every student reluctantly slid out from their desks and crawled onto the floor, many slipping a folder or bookbag onto the dirty tile first. Mrs. Applebaum joined them, taking the time to carefully smooth out the folds of her dress before crawling under her own desk.

But instead of placing their foreheads on the floor, interlinking their fingers behind their necks, and taking a solemn moment to contemplate their mortality—as the Federal Civil Defense Administration suggested—the students simply turned to each other and resumed their conversation.

"Assuming that the Soviet Union doesn't drop the bomb tomorrow," Sondra said with a grin, crouched underneath her cramped desk, "what's everyone up to this summer?"

"Well, Father plans to purchase a cozy little yacht for—"

"Anyone but Prescott," Mary-Sue growled.

"Nothing!" Francine grinned. "Absolutely nothing. I'm just going to relax. Go to the soda fountain, go bowling, maybe go to the beach—I hear surfing is all the rage up North. How 'bout you, Sondra?"

"Movies!" Sondra leaned onto her hand. "Cowboys, ghosts, jungles, monsters, romance—you name it, I'll be at the drive-in. What about you, Danny?"

"Hm?" The boy looked up from his report card. "Oh! I really haven't given it any thought, yet. The only thing that I have planned is afternoons lifeguarding at the pool. Plus weeknights at Graham's, of course."

"Employment?" Prescott rolled his eyes. "A bore!"

"I think it's swell!" Sondra shrugged. "It's just like Mrs. Applebaum said—we're young adults. Getting a head-start on those responsibilities is admirable."

"Not everyone has a trust-fund, Prescott," Mary-Sue said. "And, not that anybody asked, but…" She looked at Danny with a mischievous smile. "I've got a big secret project in the works, and if all goes according to plan, you'll be reading about it in the papers soon enough."

WRRMM! Wrrmm! wrrmm! Outside, the air-raid sirens wound down, causing the students to immediately shuffle out from beneath their desks and look at the clock above the door.

"Class!" Mrs. Applebaum pulled herself up from the floor. "I remind you that school is not yet out. Please sit back down until—"

BRRIIINNG! the final bell rang out, causing everyone to jump up and stampede toward the door. Summer had officially begun.

"So," Sondra said, leading the group out into the hallway, "are we all going to the pool, then, under Danny's watchful eye?"

"I'm in." Francine nodded. "I'll be the one on the lounge chair."

"Indeed," Prescott said, walking over to a nearby wastebin. The boy unzipped his bag, then unceremoniously dumped his textbooks in. "I'm itching for a bit of sport, myself."

"Not me." Mary-Sue shook her head, looking over her shoulder to see Danny lingering at the classroom door. "I'll be too busy putting the finishing touches on… well, you'll see."

"See you when I see you, then," Sondra said and

gave a wave as she and Francine began walking the other way, closely followed by Prescott.

"We still on for tonight?" Mary-Sue raised her eyebrows at Danny as the last of the students filtered through the classroom door.

"Yes. Yes, of course." He nodded, fiddling with the report card in his hands. "I'm excited to see what you've got in store. I'll see you after my shift—seven thirty, my house?"

"On the dot!" The girl beamed. "See you then."

Danny nodded. Mary-Sue gave him a knowing look, eyes flicking down to the report card, then turned away and bounded out the exit. He waited until she was out of sight, then stepped back into the classroom.

Inside, a pleasant peppermint scent now wafted through the air. Mrs. Applebaum had her feet resting up on the edge of her desk and she was tipping a small, metal canteen into her coffee mug.

"Excuse me, Mrs. Applebaum?"

"Oh!" The woman lurched, startled, then recognized Danny and put a hand to her chest. "Of course, Mr. Oxford," the woman sighed. "What an unexpected surprise." She put the canteen down and took a long sip of coffee. "Presumably you are aware that summer has begun?"

"Yes, of course!" Danny nodded and approached her desk. "But I'm afraid that I've uncovered a matter of some great importance." He lifted his report card up. "I'm sorry to say that there's been an error—"

"School's out, Danny." She raised her mug up. "Shouldn't you be off with your friends?"

"Absolutely!" The boy nodded. "But I wouldn't be able to have any fun with such a serious issue weighing on my conscience." He pulled the card out from the envelope. "I'm of course referring to this silly mixup of gerunds and gerundives that we keep coming back to—"

The woman immediately picked a red pen up and grabbed the report card out from Danny's hand. Without a second thought she corrected the grade by five-percent and handed it back.

"There!" She put the pen back down. "Are we happy?"

"Oh!" Danny frowned. "No, I apologize if I wasn't clear, but my own grade wasn't where my concerns lay. Countless other students—"

"While I do admire your convictions," Mrs. Applebaum said, putting her feet back up onto the desk, "I'm afraid that it's a moot point—nobody failed the class, Danny, and junior high marks don't carry over to high school. So, in the grand scheme of things, it simply doesn't matter."

"But what about—"

"On your way." The woman rubbed at her temples. "And for all of our sake, Danny, please, have a relaxing summer."

3   Collating the Casefile

Tossing her bicycle onto the ground, Mary-Sue dashed up the stairs of her mother's duplex home, heart pounding hard. She swung the front door open, kicked her shoes off, and dashed through the kitchen where, as expected, there was a handwritten note stuck to the refrigerator door. She didn't need to look in order to know what it said. It read:

Darling—
Took a second shift tonight, I'll be working late. Dinner's in the fridge, I'll see you at breakfast.
Love you, Mom

It was a wonder that her mother wrote a new note every time. The girl spun her bookbag around, pulled her report card out, and slipped it beneath the magnet. She took off down the hall and threw her bedroom door wide open. Inside, the room was a mess, with piles of dirty clothing everywhere, ignored for nearly two weeks.

The girl tossed her bag onto the bed and ran to her desk. Its cluttered surface was covered in newspapers, magazines, and library books. There was *The Founding and History of Bonnifield*, a treasure-trove of knowledge about the town's past. There was *Mythology and Folklore Around the World*, a robust encyclopedia of every creature imaginable. And there was *The Wonderful Wildlife of the American Marshlands*, a more grounded tome on the animals living in swamp ecosystems.

Then there were the dozens of horror pulps. *The Crypt of Mystery* and *Nightmares of the Imponderable*, of course. The newest *What If…? Quarterly*, naturally. And finally, *Terrors of the Shadow Realm* and *The Haunt of Fate*. But Mary-Sue brushed them all aside to find what she was really after: a plain manilla folder with a title written in attractive bubble letters—her secret project. It read:

It was the first mystery that the girl had researched on her very own. While Danny was nose-down in his studies, Mary-Sue had been building a case for *The Britannica Junior Detectives* to pursue an investigation of what might just be their next big summer mystery. All that she had to do now was to convince Danny of its veracity.

She threw the folder open to the first page. It contained a sketch of the mutant as described by Dale Brown on the night of prom, with large, black eyes and wrinkled, hairless skin—plus a few additional flourishes, courtesy of Mary-Sue's artistic interpretation.

She flipped to the next page, which was a list of every known nuclear power plant in the United States. According to her research, if there was a mutant wandering somewhere out in the world, then there was a very good chance that it had been created by atomic energy. While no nuclear plant was located near Bonnifield, there was always a possibility that the contamination might have occurred elsewhere, and that the mutant could on a rampage across the countryside. It was even possible that a barrel of nuclear waste could have carelessly fallen off of a military truck, only to later be discovered by a hapless passerby.

The following page was a hand-drawn map of Mercury Marsh, the spruce-dotted wetland out on the edge of Chautauqua Park. On one side was Greenleaf Lagoon, bordered by the swamp. On the other side was the old Civil War graveyard, abandoned after the Stillwater Dam was built and the whole area had turned into a bog. There was also a marker for a steamboat which had run ashore but, abandoned for over a century, it had long since rotted away. Notable, nonetheless.

Mary-Sue rifled through the rest of the papers to find the section in the rear titled *Possible Related Incidents*. She reached into the front pocket of her dress and pulled out the three pieces of folded paper that she had collected on her way home. She laid them out and smoothed the wrinkles away. All three were fliers for missing animals—each posted within the past two weeks. A single incident would be tragic. Two incidents would be a coincidence. But three? That pointed to a pattern.

She slipped the fliers inside, then closed the folder shut. It was done. Finally, her casefile was as complete as it was going to be. And for the first time in over two weeks, she took a deep breath and relaxed, leaning back into her chair.

On the wall in front of her was a massive corkboard, still covered in notes and photographs of suspects from *The Perplexing Case of the Perilous Prom*. Beneath that were a number of framed editions of *The Bonnifield Gazette*, featuring Danny and her greatest adventures.

The newest edition featured her photograph of Danny and Sondra in their King and Queen attire, standing in front of the scowling George Hudson. Underneath that was *The Trail of the Technicolor Thief*, which had turned out to be a smuggler transporting stolen jewelry in emptied film canisters. Then, there was *The Sterenbourg Stamp Scandal*, which had turned out to be a former art forger turning to the lucrative world of philately. Then, in *The Peculiar Pen Pal Predicament*, a disgruntled postal worker had devised a scheme to plunder a widow's inheritance. Then, *The Miniature Model Mishap*, in which a prized dollhouse collection on display at their school had been pilfered by a model train enthusiast for his toy village.

Finally, there was the first case of *The Britannica Junior Detectives*. The picture at the top was of Danny standing next to Mayor Trowbridge, once again taken by Mary-Sue. The man was giving Danny the key to the city. She leaned in to look at the article. It read:

The Counterfeit Currency Conundrum

YOUTH-SLEUTH BUSTS NATION-WIDE NETWORK

by Phil Waxman

BONNIFIELD—Danny Oxford, 9, may look like an 'all-American boy,' but there was far more on display than his good looks, athletic prowess, and irresistible charm this past weekend when he became a hero and received the city's top honor his first week in town.

A case that baffled even the Bonnifield Police Department, it all began with a $100 bill. Danny's schoolmate, Philip Lyle, had been attempting to settle his debts with the school cafeteria. Unable to make change for the big bill, however, the kitchen staff sent the boy out to ask his fellow students if any if them had more diminutive denominations.

When approached with the gigantic greenback, Danny noticed several minute printing errors on the fringes. Suspecting a forgery, the prodigious private-eye confiscated the problematic paper and began an inquest into its illicit origins.

On the 14th of April, the boy detective's investigation led him to Grandview Care Center, home of Albert J. Stevens, 78—Philip Lyle's geriatric grandfather. Along with his new sidekick, Danny uncovered the suspicious septuagenarian's history as a convicted counterfeiter in Chicago's prohibition past.

But after Philip went missing, Danny uncovered a nation-wide network of criminals blackmailing former frauds to create foolproof fakes, eventually leading him to the warehouse headquarters of Joe "Bixby" Wilson, James "Fritz" Weatherford, and Sy Millbank, a group of greedy gangsters.

Through his wits and will, Danny saved the kidnapped kid and stopped the outlaw operation, then gave his evidence to the Secret Service, who in return gave him their appreciation and admiration for a job well done.

The boy's remarkable encyclopedic-knowledge of every subject under the sun quickly earned him the nickname Danny Britannica amongst his peers, and he has reportedly begun an amateur agency under the name 'The Britannica Junior Detectives,' which is, as of this printing, calling for clientele.

When reached for comment, Britannica said, "Counterfeiting is a felony and could cause major problems to the country's economy if it were to get out of hand. I'm simply glad that I was able to stop this devious operation before anyone was harmed."

The treacherous trio are expected to face proper prosecution in the coming weeks—a thrilling trial that you can be sure we'll be covering with great gusto. For more adventures of The Britannica Junior Detectives... watch this space!

The story's publication was one of the proudest moments of her life. The next morning, Danny had showed up on her doorstep, insisting that her research skills and her insight into the criminal psyche had proved invaluable in leading him to the counterfeiters.

Right then, he had asked if she would be interested in accompanying him on all of his future adventures—if she would be interested in being his permanent sidekick. She had, of course, agreed without question.

And the rest was history.

4   Lesson for a Lifeguard

The bright ray of sun broke through scattered clouds, causing each of the teenage sunbathers at the poolside to relax into their lounge chairs. One-by-one each rolled onto their backs to even out their budding tans. Behind them a powerful *SWAAAAKK!* rang out from a scrubby patch of grass and echoed off of the brick walls of the changing rooms.

Prescott stood on the makeshift handball field, craning his neck back to watch the foam ball soar to its apex.

"Run, you moron, get it!" The pitcher cried out, causing him to slowly step back, then take off across the field as the small, spongy sphere began to descend.

Prescott swerved toward the sunbathers and leapt over lounge chair after lounge chair, causing each sunbather to cry out in alarm. He cleared the last chair and his feet hit the cold poolside tile, then slid to a stop just underneath the ball. He extended his arm and opened his fingers as—

PREEEP! a piercing whistle shrieked out from

his other side, pulling Prescott's attention away at the last second and causing the ball to rocket straight into his face, then bounce harmlessly off onto the ground. The agitated sunbathers all burst into laughter.

"Mr. Trowbridge!" Danny scolded from high atop his lifeguard chair a dozen yards away, sunglasses down at the end of his nose. "How many times do I have to tell you: no running inside the yellow line."

"Indeed." Prescott scowled, leaning down to grab the ball. "Perhaps next time, my good man, you might wait until after I've caught it."

"I know that you think of me just as one of your peers," Danny said, folding his arms sternly, "but I've taken an oath to enforce the regulations and rules of this facility—which includes blowing the whistle as soon as I see any misconduct. I know that you wouldn't want me to get in trouble with the management, and I certainly know that you wouldn't want them to reduce their strict safety standards. So let's make sure that there isn't a next time, shall we?"

"Naturally." Prescott rolled his eyes, then began to walk back toward the handball field as all of his teammates snickered.

"Thank you, Prescott!" Danny pushed his sunglasses up, then turned back to the deep end where Sondra was treading water. "I'm sorry about that, you were saying?"

"Golly! I can't even remember." She giggled, gazing up toward him in her frilly white bathing costume. "You just have such a commanding presence. Have you ever considered going into acting?"

"Acting?" Danny scrunched his nose up. "I've never given it serious consideration before—though I have been able to assist in technical work on a number of productions over the years. And while I do admire the talent of our thespians, I doubt that I could ever match their prowess."

"Well don't rule it out." The girl smiled. "I can easily imagine you up on the big screen. Heck, you even look like a movie star—well, like Paul Newman, anyway."

"While it certainly is an interesting idea, I've already got my hands a little too full to take on a new vocation." Danny scanned his eyes across the pool. "Between the soda fountain, lifeguarding, and mystery-solving, there just isn't enough time in the day to study the necessary techniques that I would require to be satisfied with my performance. No, I'm afraid that I'll have to leave the acting to the professionals."

"Maybe you're better suited as an audience member. Like... maybe tonight at the drive-in with me?" She gave him a coy look. "There's a real spooky-looking double-feature on at the Co-Ed. What do you say?"

"While I'm certain that the films would be quite engaging," Danny said, eyes on the pool, "I'm afraid that it's out of the question—*The Britannica Junior Detectives* have a meeting tonight."

"More work?" She pouted. "All that you ever do is work. Why not go out with me and have a bit of fun?"

"While a night with a pal at the pictures does sound swell—"

"Danny." Sondra swam up to the poolside and furrowed her brow. "Can you really be that clueless? Can't you see that I'm trying to flirt with you? Aren't you interested in dating?"

"Dating?" Danny scrunched his nose up. "I've never given it serious consideration before." He slowly pulled his sunglasses off, then looked at the grinning girl. "But... you and me?"

"Why not?" The girl bit at her lip. "Prom King and Queen, out at the pictures together? The gossip column headlines write themselves! I could even drive us, if my dad promises to stay in the parents' lounge."

"Gee…" The boy took a breath. "Aren't we a bit young for that?"

"Young?" Sondra rested her elbows on the cool tile. "Jim and Marsha have been dating for, what, two years, now?"

"Gosh." Danny nodded. "Of course, I think that you're swell and all, but we have the next four years to become interested in romance. What's wrong with enjoying our youth?"

"Youth? Danny, you're literally working right now. On the first day of summer!" She laughed. "Besides, it's like I said earlier." Sondra raised an eyebrow. "We're adults now."

Danny swallowed, his throat strangely dry. Sondra was a kind friend and an astute leader. As the class president, she had pushed for a number of fair and practical initiatives with the school administration, including the construction of a healthy salad bar at lunch and a vending machine in the student lounge. The girl was an honors student, a gifted cheerleader, and a charming presence. Plus, she was very pretty.

"W—well, golly," Danny stammered.

"So?" She shook her head. "All I need is a yes or—"

KA-KRAK! Prescott collided with an empty lounge chair to their left, sending the boy careering out of control over the yellow line and falling head-first into the deep end of the pool. Danny snapped up from his chair, placed his sunglasses down, then grabbed a life-preserver as Prescott sunk beneath the surface.

"I'm afraid that you'll have to excuse me once again, Sondra."

Danny crouched down, then sprung forward with perfect technique, leaping over the girl's head into the cool water beyond. There was barely a splash as his sleek form slipped into the water. A dozen yards ahead he could clearly see Prescott panicking, shirt wrapped around his head, his arms and legs flailing in a barrage of bubbles.

With a powerful kick he thrust himself forward, closing the distance in a few short seconds. He hooked his arms beneath the boy's shoulders, then dragged Prescott the rest of the way down to the bottom, crouched, and launched both of them upward, rocketing to the surface.

As they broke through, Danny could feel Prescott's body go limp in his arms. He quickly slipped the life preserver around the boy's neck and paddled them to the pool's edge. He shot up the ladder, then dragged the boy's body onto the tile.

A crowd had formed at the edge of the concrete. They moved back as he laid Prescott flat, feeling himself begin to shake as he squeezed the boy's nose, pulled his mouth open, and leaned in. Danny took a deep breath, put his mouth against Prescott's, and blew hard, transferring the oxygen from his lungs into the other boy's. After a moment he raised up, took a second breath, and prepared to repeat the process once again.

Before he did, however, Prescott convulsed and coughed a gurgling stream of water up. He took a gasping breath, groaned, then rolled onto his side. As his eyes fluttered open, the crowd burst out into a cheer.

"No…" Prescott took a breath. "Running inside… the yellow line…"

Danny looked on, still shaking, breathing hard himself. The two boys exchanged a meaningful look before the onlookers rushed forward and began to tousle their wet hair.

"That was amazing, Danny!"

"Incredible!"

"Astounding!"

"Please, everyone." Danny managed to choke out, grabbing the other boy's hand and helping him to his feet. "Let's give him a little room."

Danny steadied Prescott as the boy got his bearings, but was forced to release him to the crowd. They pulled him in, then began to shuffle off toward the grass, leaving Danny at the poolside, dripping.

For a moment, he just stared at the ground and took ragged breaths, feeling his elevated heart-rate begin to return to normal. When he finally looked back up he saw Sondra at the poolside nearby, eyes wide.

"Are..." She placed a hand gently on his arm. "Are you okay?"

"Y—yes, I think so," he said, wiping the stinging chlorinated water away from his red eyes. He looked up at Sondra's worried face and gave her a small smile. "The answer's yes, Sondra; I'd love to go to the double-feature with you tonight."

5   # Atomic-Age Anxieties

Mary-Sue sped her bicycle down the long road toward the Victorian mansion looming at the end of Sunset Drive. It was nestled amongst the evergreens, a single turret jutting out above the surrounding branches. A thick, wrought-iron fence snaked across the front yard, disappearing back into the woods on either side.

As the road's pavement turned to gravel, she gripped her handlebars tight and pushed back on the pedals, skidding to a stop just at the edge of city limits. She hopped down from the seat, then wheeled the bicycle the remainder of the way to the fence.

The top was lined with razor-sharp barbed wire, and along its length the fence was adorned with ominous signs like *BEWARE: 50,000 VOLTS* and *DANGER: ELECTRIC SHOCK*. At the top of the gate was a warning light, glowing a bright, ominous red.

Mary-Sue looked back over one shoulder, then the other, then all the way down the fence until she was certain that nobody was watching. She walked up to a metal pylon and pulled a compartment aside to reveal a small keypad. She punched in the secret code: *8A3C-B259*.

The red light blinked off. With a halting *GGR-RUUKK!* the heavy gate began to slowly pull to the side, inch-by-inch. Mary-Sue waited until the gap was large enough to fit through, then pulled her bicycle inside. The gate came to a halt at the far end, tremorred, then began to reverse course automatically. With a loud *KER-CHUNK!* it closed behind her and the red light blinked back on.

Mary-Sue flipped her kickstand down, propped her bicycle up at the edge of the lawn, then took off across the woodchip-covered path and up the stairs to the front door. She squeezed her hand into a fist, gave three sharp knocks, and waited. And waited.

With a frown, she looked down to her wristwatch: seven-thirty, on the dot. She then reached out to the small, round button next to the door and pushed it in. But instead of the pleasant chimes of a doorbell, there was only the sharp hiss of a radio intercom.

"Mary-Sue Welles?" A man's deep, rich voice asked over the speaker hidden somewhere nearby. The girl looked all around the porch until she spotted the closed-circuit television camera tucked away behind a sconce. She gave a small wave. "Come around back."

Mary-Sue turned and hopped down the stairs, taking off around the side of the house. In the center of the backyard, where an ordinary family might have a sandbox, playhouse, or vegetable garden, the Oxford family had a concrete, windowless building topped by a glass geodesic dome.

A chill ran down Mary-Sue's spine as she approached the rivet-lined steel door. She flipped the compartment aside and once again punched in the access code. The door slid to the side to reveal a small room beyond. She carefully stepped in, squeezed her eyes shut, then pressed the button on the far wall.

KA-TAM! The exterior door slammed shut and a large vent began to blow cool, sterilized air around the room. After a moment, it petered out and the interior door creaked open. Mary-Sue fixed her messy hair, then stepped inside.

No matter how many times she had been inside of the laboratory, it always gave her the creeps. The overhead lights were dim and the walls were lined with a computer array, its magnetic reels spinning endlessly as a thousand lights blinked off and on in some indecipherable pattern.

To the girl's right were several long, formica workstations covered in dozens of chemical beakers bubbling red liquid into yellow and yellow into purple. To her left were several towering machines with miniature bolts of lightning crackling up and down a pair of metal coils. And from somewhere nearby there was a constant clicking. *TK-tk-TK-tk-TK-tk!*

Directly ahead of her, a dark figure sat hunched in a lab coat, holding a set of small tongs, a glittering yellow crystal within. It gave off an eerie, stippled glow, illuminating the scientist from underneath and casting the entire area into harsh highlights and shadows.

The scientist lowered the tongs into a bubbling chemical bath, and as the the crystal touched the surface, the liquid began to fizzle until the whole thing popped in a bright flash. Mary-Sue thrust her hands in front of her eyes, turning away. When she looked back, the light had faded and the crystal sat at the bottom of the beaker, clear and inert.

TK-tk-Tk-tk-tk-k...

"D—Dr. Oxford?" She stuttered out. "Is that you?"

The scientist whipped around toward her, his face distorted by a pair of huge, black eyes. Mary-Sue took a step back in horror, but the scientist quickly pulled his black welding goggles down around his neck to reveal his normal visage, then broke out into a wide grin.

"Greetings, young lady!" Dr. Oxford stood up and waved her over, a good-natured glint twinkling behind his piercing blue eyes. The scientist slipped his black rubber gloves off and rubbed his clammy hands against his spotless white lab coat.

Her best friend's father was steel-jawed and handsome, sporting a broad, athletic frame. His bronze skin was more taut than that of most men his age, which was apparent only by the two shocks of grey hair running across his temples. He sat down on his stool as she walked over.

"Now, to what do I owe the pleasure?" The man pulled a pipe and a box of matches out from his pocket.

"Agency business, sir," Mary-Sue said, patting at her bookbag.

"Business?" The man raised his eyebrows and chomped down on the end of his pipe. "Could it be that the legendary *Britannica Junior Detectives* are on the cusp of yet another exciting summer mystery?"

"I sure hope so." Mary-Sue smiled. "But we were supposed to meet here at seven thirty and Danny—"

"Well, I'm afraid that you've just missed him."
The man shrugged. "The lad left not fifteen minutes
ago in some boat of a car. I remember, now, yes..."
He patted at his various pockets until he found a
small piece of notebook paper and pulled it out. "He
asked me to give you this."

Mary-Sue reached out and took the note. It
read:

Hi Mary-Sue!
I tried to call, but you may
have been on your way over.
I'm afraid that an unexpected
matter has come up. Rain
check for morning? Let's say
at 10:30 — I'm looking
forward to hearing about the
secret project!
Your pal,
Danny

"Oh, I see." Mary-Sue slumped her shoulders.
"Well, I guess I'll see you in the morning, then, sir."

"Now..." The scientist raised his eyebrows. "It isn't all bad news!"

"No?" Mary-Sue looked up as she crumpled the note, then tossed it into a nearby wastebin.

"Look at it this way." Dr. Oxford pulled his pipe out from between his lips and grinned. "Morning means breakfast, and breakfast means a heaping stack of my famous chocolate-chip waffles—now there's a thing to look forward to!"

"I guess," Mary-Sue gave a half-hearted chuckle. "I was just excited to tell Danny all about..." She trailed off as her eyes moved all around the laboratory. "Y—you're an atomic scientist, aren't you, sir?"

Dr. Oxford struck a match on the side of the box. A bright yellow flame burst from its head, filling the room with the sickly sweet smell of sulfur.

"Well," the man said, giving a few short puffs to let the flame catch the tobacco, "technically I'm retired."

"Technically?" The girl eyed him with suspicion.

"Well." Oxford shook the match out. "I still tinker here and there, for the right project. What makes you so curious?"

"Have, uh..." Mary-Sue cleared her throat, looking down to the floor. "Have you had any lab accidents lately?"

"Of course not!" He gave a hearty guffaw. "What a silly question that is. Tell me, young lady, what exactly are you getting after?"

"I'm sorry." She grimaced. "It's got to do with this mystery that I'm putting together, that's all."

"Oh?" The man raised his eyebrows. "I'm all ears."

"Well..." A mischievous look flashed in her eyes. "Don't tell Danny yet, but there's been a report of a mutated man wandering around in the swamp—and according to my research, atomic radiation causes all sorts of mutations."

"And you imagined that I might be the cause?" The man pursed his lips as Mary-Sue nodded. "Hmph. I suspect that you got that idea from one of your science-fantasy magazines, yes?"

"Yes that's right," Mary-Sue said, swinging her bookbag around. She unbuckled the straps and rifled through its contents until she found the latest issue of *The Crypt of Mystery*, then pulled it out and offered it over to the scientist.

He took the magazine and studied it for a moment, letting a trail of smoke slowly drift out from his nostrils. The cover illustration was from *The Man with A Trillion Eyes*, the story which Mary-Sue had nearly finished reading. It depicted a mushroom-headed scientist hanging from a radio tower in the middle of a thunderstorm, a battalion of gun-wielding soldiers at his feet. Dr. Oxford handed it back to the girl.

"You heard that ticking sound when you entered, yes?" He took a drag from his pipe and raised his eyebrows.

"Yes." She nodded enthusiastically.

"Well." The man patted a dull green box on the table next to him. "That was from this Geiger counter, a device used to detect and measure gamma rays."

"I've heard of gamma rays!" She grinned. "They're what turned *The Indestructible Ionauts* into super-beings when they stole the government's rocket ship and took it on a joyride into space!"

"Mmph. The unfortunate reality is," the scientist said, dropping the spent match down onto the linoleum and grinding it into a streak of ash with his heel, "the sort of mutation that gamma rays encourage is strictly the deadly kind—like in Hiroshima and Nagasaki."

"Oh." Mary-Sue grimaced, turning her gaze to the floor. "Of course; we learned all about what happened in history class."

"History class?" The scientist gritted his teeth. "And what, pray tell, did our public school system teach you about the bombs?"

"They were part of the Second World War, in the Pacific." Mary-Sue slipped the magazine back into her bookbag. "Japan wouldn't surrender, so we had to drop the bombs and try to save as many lives as we could. It was that or invasion, which would have killed more people."

"Is that what they told you?" He chewed at his pipe. "Tell me, have you heard of The Manhattan Project?"

Mary-Sue shook her head.

"I thought not." The man sat straight up and crossed one leg over the other. "It was a group of scientists who designed and developed the first atomic warheads—the same that were dropped onto Japan. Before that, however, the purpose of the project was to research the long-term effects of gamma rays on human beings." His gaze drifted off into the distance. "Radiation sickness, gamma burns, crippling anemia, a dozen cancers—and who knows what else in generations to come?"

"I—I didn't know that." Mary-Sue raised her eyebrows. "Those poor Japanese people!"

"I wasn't referring strictly to Japan." He shook his head.

"What do you mean, sir?" Mary-Sue frowned.

"Are you... certain that you want me to continue?" Dr. Oxford raised his eyebrows. "I'm afraid that the answer is rather disturbing."

"I'm sure," she said. "Wasn't Japan the only county we bombed?"

"No, not exactly." The scientist sneered. "You see, the most gamma-radiated country in the entire world is The United States of America."

"Huh?" She twisted her face up.

"Each and every time our military wants to test her newest, shiniest atomic bomb," the man said, gesturing with his pipe, "the same deadly particles created at Hiroshima and Nagasaki drift around this country's air and water supply for hundreds of miles in every direction."

"My gosh!" Mary-Sue gasped. "Why would they let that happen?"

"Well, that depends on how you look at it." Dr. Oxford stroked at his chin. "In the minds of our government and military, those tests represent an acceptable risk to maintain technological superiority over the Soviet Union. It's what the media has labeled a 'nuclear arms race.'"

"To... see who has the fastest missiles?"

"To see who has the deadliest." He raised his pipe and stared down at the glowing red embers in the chamber. "And the most."

"How..." Mary-Sue felt goose-pimples run down her arms and legs. "How many do we have?"

"Tens of thousands." The man took a deep drag from his pipe, held it in for a few moments, then let a rolling cloud of smoke out. "And every time the Reds begin building a newer, deadlier bomb, our Army recruits its best and brightest scientists to get to work on an even larger one. It's what some opponents call 'mutually assured destruction.'"

"But that's... that's..." She was lost for words. "That's crazy! Insane! What on earth is the point?"

"It's just the beginning, I'm afraid." He pulled a second match out from the box, then struck it on the side. But instead of bringing it back up to his pipe, he just held it out and watched the flame slowly burn down. "Our military has now built atomic warheads with more than ten times the destructive force of Nagasaki."

"Surely..." Mary-Sue took an instinctive step back, a knot forming in her stomach. "Surely that's biggest they can get?"

He shook his head.

"The Reds have a hydrogen bomb nearly a thousand times deadlier." He dropped the charred match onto the floor, then pressed his toe firmly down.

"And if our current intelligence can be trusted, then they'll soon have a bomb nearly thirty times that size."

"But that could destroy the whole country! Or, or…" She cast her eyes down to the matches on the floor. "Or… even the entire world."

Dr. Oxford turned his gaze up through the geodesic dome.

"*And with my wrath I shall cleanse the land—sweep beast from plain and fowl from sky and fish from sea. Tear kingdoms to ruin. I shall scour mankind from the face of the earth.*"

Mary-Sue's eyes were fixed on the matches. Just dead, grey ash.

"I'm sorry for saying so, sir…" Mary-Sue said softly, arms wrapped around her torso. "But that's stupid. A bigger bomb doesn't sound like any kind of a defense to me."

"Hmph." The scientist pulled his head back down from the heavens, mouth twisted to the side. "From the mouth of babes."

Mary-Sue's eyes drifted to the tray of yellow crystals.

"Are… you trying to win the nuclear arms race, sir?"

"Win?" Dr. Oxford tightened his jaw. He stood

up from his stool and tapped his pipe out into the wastebin. "While the details are classified, I can say that I'm working on something which I hope will end the nuclear arms race once and for all."

Mary-Sue nodded, took a step back, then another, and another until she reached the door. The scientist just stared at the yellow crystals. With a knot in her stomach, the girl stepped out into the airlock and pushed the button.

Their dripping proboscises jabbed to-and-fro.

6   ## The Social Scene Shocker

Keeping low, Barbara carefully crept along the rosebushes out to the front of her quaint suburban home. As she emerged, a look of pure terror washed over the recent widow's face. Strewn across the cul-de-sac as far as the eye could see were dozens of lifeless, emaciated corpses, drained of their bodily fluids.

Then, she heard it. At first, just a high-pitched whine, an irritating buzz that seemed to come from everywhere all at once. Soon, however, it got deeper and deeper until from above she saw them burst through the low-hanging clouds: dozens of impossibly massive mosquitos, swarming her way.

Barbara clutched at her face and gave a horrified scream as the ugly irradiated monsters approached, closing in while their dripping proboscises jabbed to-and-fro. But just as she cowered, tensing for the inevitable, the woman heard the roaring rumble of an engine in the distance.

The hovering beasts turned as the Humvee sped around the corner, a white cloud of smoke billowing out behind it, filling the air with Dr. Van Gutenberg's miraculous insecticide. The wings of the horrible creatures began to twitch and falter until one-by-one they tumbled down from the sky onto Barbara's front lawn, shuddering in a horrible death knell.

The Humvee pulled into the driveway and Sergeant Mansfield threw the door open, then dashed into Barbara's waiting arms. The man placed his hand on the small of her back, gently stroked at her comely face, then leaned in and gave her a fiery, passionate kiss. The music swelled and the screen faded to black, then two words faded in. They read:

Danny watched on wide-eyed from the passenger seat of Sondra's roomy Bel Air, sporting his best cardigan and pressed slacks. The girl sat on the opposite side of the front seat as he leaned forward, eyes glued to the screen as the final frames of *Curse of the Emaciating Swarm* sputtered through the projector.

"Gosh!" Sondra cooed. "Those creatures sure were scary, huh?"

"Boy, you can say that again," Danny agreed, looking down into the box of Milk Duds grasped tightly in his hand. He rattled the last piece of candy back and forth. "Gee, I, uh…" The boy cleared his throat. "I really have to get out to the pictures more often—that one sure was swell!"

"I wonder." The girl inched across the plush leather seat toward him. "How they make those beasts look so real? So terrifying!"

"Well, gee!" Danny perked up. "It really isn't too surprising once you know how it's done!" He popped the last chocolate-covered caramel into his mouth. "You see, it's a process called 'stop-motion animation.' What happens is that the filmmakers create miniature puppets out of metal and latex. They then move the model by a tiny increment, take a photograph, and repeat the technique until the scene is finished. After that, it's really just a simple matter of—"

Sondra gathered the folds of her skirt up and slid all the way over to him. The boy's eyes shot down to their fingertips, millimeters apart on the seat.

Danny wasn't entirely unfamiliar with dating protocol—the boy was nearly fifteen, after all. Just that autumn their physical education class had been presented with an instructional short film titled *The Do's and Don'ts of Dating* which broke down the common mores of the activity.

It had been highly informative, and coupled with knowledge culled from popular film, television, and printed media, Danny felt as if he had a good sense of what the sociological aspects of dating should entail.

"Of, well…" He swallowed. "Of filming—I mean, of creating a matte and… then double exposing the negative and… uh…"

"Actually…" Sondra cooed, stroking his pinky finger with her own, "I didn't really want to know—I was only trying to get you to put your arm around me."

On the screen, a line of cartoon snacks danced from right to left.

"Say, I—I'm pretty hungry." Danny pulled his

hand away to grasp at the door handle. "The next film won't begin for another ten minutes, so if you're feeling peckish, I can get us something from the concession stand. Popcorn, perhaps? Or... a hot dog, if you're famished?"

"Right now?" Sondra raised an eyebrow.

"It's the best time, if I don't want to miss any of the next feature." He attempted a casual smile. "Besides, my blood-sugar levels feel a little low. I wouldn't want to become fatigued part-way through our date. We have a, uh..." His throat went dry. "A long night ahead of us, still."

"Sure." She sighed and leaned back into the seat, folding her hands on top her lap. "I'll take some Raisinets."

"Swell!" Danny pulled the handle and quickly slid outside. He shut the door behind him and pushed himself up against the side of the car for a moment, feeling the cool night air on his flushed cheeks.

As his heart rate began to slow, Danny pushed off and began to walk through the maze of vehicles back toward the concession stand at the rear. From the corner of his eye, he noticed that inside many of the vehicles were teenage couples, holding each other close—a few even necking.

The boy's cheeks flushed crimson and he sped his pace up, averting his eyes as best he could. He finally emerged from the last row of cars, only to see a wild throng of kids flocking toward the tables in front of the concession stand. Each major social group appeared well-represented: the jocks, the rockers, the surfers, the hayseeds, and lurking on the fringe, a lone greaser.

Danny squeezed into the throng, attempting to push his way to the concession stand. The energy around him was electric, with everyone chattering and laughing, reveling in the excitement of the first evening of summer. From behind him, a hand grabbed his shoulder, then spun him around.

Standing in front of the boy was Jack Hardy, the star pitcher of the Bonnifield High Hurricanes.

"Hello, Jack!" Danny gave a nod. "How's the arm?"

"It'll be off in the mornin'," he said coolly, tapping at his signature-covered cast. "Right in time for the start of the season."

"That's real swell to hear," Danny said. For a moment, Jack stood in silence, staring at him, expectant. Danny pointed his thumb back over his shoulder in the direction of the stand. "Well, I'm just—"

"So…" Jack raised his eyebrows. "What case are the *Junior Detectives* workin' tonight?"

"What makes you think that I'm working a case?"

"Come on, kid, be real with me." Jack grinned. "You're out at the pictures, so there's gotta be some kinda mystery afoot. Yeah?"

"No." Danny shrugged. "I'm just here on a date."

"Hot damn!" Jack whistled. "Then it is true!"

"What's true?" Danny tilted his head to the side.

"Guess that girl bagged ya, after all." Jack smiled. "They tried to tell me, Britannica, but I just couldn't believe it."

"I'm confused." Danny narrowed his eyes. "Why—"

"You're full of surprises, kid." Jack shook his head, incredulous. He took a step back and gave the boy a funny look, then turned around and walked over to his friends, pointing his thumb back over his shoulder.

Danny scrunched his nose up, turning back around. He took a step forward, but was swiftly cut off by a server whizzing by on roller skates holding a tray of soft drinks. She skidded to a stop, then spun to face him with a look of disbelief.

"Is this a dream?"

"I'm not sure, Nancy." Danny cleared his throat as she stared. "Are you all saved up for your big French trip yet?"

"After tonight." Nancy nodded slowly. "Thanks for remembering." She shook her head. "Say, it's good to see you out and about."

"I'm just here on a date." He twisted his mouth to the side.

"Yeah," she said, studying him up and down. "I heard."

"Is that really so unusual?"

Without answering, she bit her lip, spun around, then pushed off the other direction, waving back to him over her shoulder.

Danny twisted his face up, then pushed his way behind another set of friends in the direction of the concession stand. He managed to get just a few steps before getting cut off once again, this time by Phil, pencil and notepad at the ready.

"I've already prepared tomorrow's new gossip column headline," the reporter said. "*Super Sleuth's Social Scene Shocker*—care to comment, Mr. Oxford?"

"I don't know about that, Phil." Danny said flatly. "My guess is that your column space could be utilized for something more notable than my social life."

"I assure you, Mr. Oxford," the reporter said with a serious expression, "there's nothing more notable happening in Bonnifield tonight."

"Even so." Danny scowled. "I'd prefer that you not run the line."

"Hmph." Phil frowned, then snapped his notepad shut. "Very well, then, I'll just have to run with my other story: *Lionhearted Lifeguard Lifts Lifeless Louse from Liquid Lamentation.*"

"I look forward to reading it." Danny pursed his lips and gave Phil a stiff pat on the arm, then turned and walked away. He stepped around yet another group of teenagers, only to find himself a few feet away from the concession stand.

Behind the window was Judy Birchmore, a recent high school graduate. The girl was leaning down on her elbows and staring straight at him, eyebrow cocked. She blew a huge pink bubble. *POP!*

"Danny Britannica." The girl chuckled, world-weary. She leaned her shoulder against the wall and shook her head. "I always hoped someday you'd come walking up to my snack counter."

"Geez, Judy!" Danny huffed, then scratched at the back of his neck. "A date at the drive-in isn't so unusual. Everyone goes out to the pictures every now and again."

"Not Danny Britannica." Judy crossed her arms.

"I was here just a few months ago," he insisted.

"Hot on *The Trail of the Technicolor Thief*, if I recall."

"You're not wrong," Danny said. "But please, tell me—why does my social life seem to be of concern to everyone else?"

"Come on, detective, get a clue." Judy rapped her fingers on the edge of the counter. "You're the biggest *it boy* this dinky little town has to offer. National hero, captain of the football squad, junior high Prom King? It's just that…" She shrugged. "Everyone kinda had you pegged for a bit of a dork."

"Square?" Danny narrowed his eyes. "Correct me if I'm wrong, but that's not exactly a term of endearment, Judy."

"C'mon." She raised her eyebrows. "Valedictorian, chess champion, volunteer Safety Supervisor?"

"Yes, what of it?"

"Well…" Judy blew another large, pink bubble. *POP!* "Around your age, brainy kids like you, well…" She studied his face. "They either start wearing pocket protectors and stop going outside, or they kinda mellow out and grow up, y'know?"

"I…" Danny gave a small nod. "I see."

"Plus, y'know, the detective thing." She gave

him a strange look.

"What do you mean by that?" He frowned.

"Ugh." Judy grimaced, as if realizing that she had said too much. "I just mean, no offense or anything, but that mystery-solving junk is kids' stuff. People kinda figured you'da grown out of it by now."

Danny's stomach tightened.

"Don't get me wrong," Judy continued, raising her hands in defense, "I'm not saying you're, like, a dork or anything, but a catch like you? I figured you'd be going up to Lover's Lane already."

"Lover's Lane?" Danny asked. "What's that?"

"Seriously?" Judy chuckled. "Okay, maybe you actually are a bit of a square." She blew another bubble, but this one misfired and she chomped it back in. "See, Lover's Lane is where everyone goes after the pictures to make out, let loose, have a beer."

"You mean… high schoolers?" Danny's eyes went wide. "Drinking alcohol?"

"Sure!" Judy burst out laughing. "It's, like, the place to get in a bit of trouble, y'know?" She paused, then cracked a wicked smile. "Say, I think you and your date should head up after the next flick—I'll introduce you to the gang."

"O—oh." Danny's cheeks burned. "W—well… Sondra only has her permit, so, unfortunately, well, I don't think that her father…"

"Too bad." Judy sighed. "I'm off to college in the fall."

"P—perhaps next time," Danny said, clearing his throat. "But I'll just take a box of Raisinets, Jud'." He glanced back over his shoulder toward the screen, where the previews for coming attractions were playing. "I—I think the next feature is about to begin."

Judy ducked down beneath the counter, then sprung back up with a box of Raisinets and a raised eyebrow.

"It's a real spooky one." She placed the candy onto the counter. "See, there's another planet exactly like ours—but in Dimension X. When this lab accident goes wrong on our world, it tears a hole in spacetime and their Earth winds up in our solar system, just on the other side of the Sun. Anyway, their government sends a bunch of goons on a rocket to try and take over our world. It gets so creepy when they try to switch places with their twins to infiltrate the Pentagon. So, y'know, that date of yours may need a big strong arm to hold her close." The girl slid the box into Danny's hand. "It's on the house, kid. Don't let her down."

"I need to ask your customers a few questions."

7   # The Soda Shoppe Scuffle

At the counter of Graham's Soda Fountain, Mary-Sue sat reading *The Crypt of Mystery*. All around her were groups of teenagers, talking and laughing as they sipped their soft drinks. Everyone enjoying the first night of summer to the fullest— everyone except for Mary-Sue.

Her stomach still felt tight from Dr. Oxford's ominous words. There was a strange nervous energy running through her body which made the back of her brain tingle. She could barely hear the noise of the other kids as her eyes drifted down the page. It read:

---

the man with a trillion eyes

(continued from page 125)

"Don't shoot! My God, don't shoot!" The sergeant below cried out as I scaled the radio tower, barely able to keep my footing in the intense gale of the gathering storm. "If you kill Dr. Murhammer, you kill us all!"

As I reached the zenith, a bolt of lightning burst across the sky and illuminated my monstrous visage for all to see. In the soldiers' shock and horror, they didn't hear the man's warning—or perhaps couldn't fathom letting me live, too abhorred by their instinctive, visceral reactions to my new and magnificent form. Too limitead by their solitary sentience to understand the astonishing potential of my mutualistic coexistence.

And as the thunder-crack hit, the first trigger was pulled and I immediately felt the cold lead of a machine gun bullet rip through my chest. Then came another, and another, and another, until all the men were firing—including the sergeant himself.

But as my flesh was torn asunder and as I screamed out in righteous agony, a strange thing began to happen. An... unusual thing. A thing beyond the human imagination!

It was as if a dozen new eyes had suddenly opened in my mind. And then a hundred, and a thousand, and a million, and a billion. And before the dry, shredded husk of my body hit the ground, I had been freed from the prison of my own flesh, my intelligence equally spread amongst my brood of a trillion spores.

Through the fractured and crystalline facets of my new vision I saw myself blown by the hurricane toward the soldiers, onto their bodies and into their mouths and down their throats and through their lungs and into their very flesh! And then, I felt myself begin to gestate inside each of them—inside each of us.

And at the same moment I saw myself carried off by the wind. Across the military base, across the woods, across the land and sea. Toward every human being on the surface of the Earth. Toward the next stage of the species. Toward a bright and hopeful new future.

THE END...?

It was about mutually assured destruction. She was nearly certain. It served as a metaphor for the tensions between the United States and the Soviet Union as they continued to grow their nuclear arsenals. It was the idea that a careless move on the part of either faction could result in the total destruction of the human species.

Her casefile was fiction. It was a fantasy created by her overactive imagination, dreaming of mutants and atomic superheroes. But out in the world there were real terrors; at any time and from anywhere, the bombs could come—she had heard the idea before in her classroom safety drills, but for some reason, this time she understood just how dire the situation truly was.

"Can I get ya a refill, darling?" The girl looked over to see the elderly figure of Dalton Graham wiping the counter with his pristine, red cloth. As always, he was sporting his spotless whites and starched red bowtie.

"Thank you, Mr. Graham…" Mary-Sue pushed her empty malt glass forward, leaving a long trail of condensation in its wake. "But I'm okay for now."

"Hmph." The man put his fists on his hips. "Not with that frown on your face, you're not. I think I reckon I know what's goin' on here…" The man glanced over one shoulder, then the other, then right back to Mary-Sue. "I do believe you've got a serious case of *the ice cream headaches*," he whispered in mock secrecy. "I get 'em, too, sometimes. But not to worry: as soon as the sugar rush hits, you'll be ready for another in no time."

He waggled his wispy eyebrows up and down. Mary-Sue shrugged.

"Hm. Or perhaps not." Mr. Graham tossed the washcloth up onto his shoulder and leaned in with a frown. "Somethin' got ya down, kiddo? I know you folks would prefer Danny workin' on the weekends to boring ol' Mr. Graham—but, hey!" He winked. "I'd be sad if I was stuck with me instead of him, too."

"No." She sighed. "You're perfectly wonderful, Mr. Graham."

"Well if it's not that, then…" The elderly man's eyes drifted down to *The Crypt of Mystery*, where an illustration depicted a screaming soldier's head splitting into two frilled mushroom stalks. "These kinds of stories… they disturb the sensibilities, upset one's sensitive constitution, promote delinquency. Little ladies like yourself shouldn't be reading—"

"Thank you," she said, clenching her jaw. She took a deep breath, let it out, then looked up with a cheerful expression on her face. "But it's not that, really! You were right: just a bit of an ice cream headache."

Mr. Graham's smile returned, bushy mustache spreading out over his upper lip. He reached out and grabbed her glass, slapped the washcloth down, then wiped the condensation away in one quick swipe.

"There we go! That's the peppy young lady I know." He gave her a pat on the shoulder. "You've gotta be careful how fast ya drink 'em. I'll swing back 'round here in a little while and check in, see if ya might need one more strawberry malt—or maybe a double? Though, I'd advise ya to pace yourself a little better next time!"

He gave her a nod, then chuckled as he shuffled away.

Mary-Sue's smile quickly faded. She shut the magazine then slipped it down into her bag. The girl thumbed through the rest of the reading materials and pulled *Young in Love* out, a romance comic book that had come free with another purchase. Not her typical fare, but anything other than nuclear war sounded good at that moment.

Mary-Sue flipped it open. The first story in the anthology was that of a beautiful teenage girl who had to make a heartbreaking choice between two perfect but opposite boys. The second was about a boy-crazy student who wanted a new boyfriend every week. The third was about an elderly woman remembering back through the great loves of her life. And just as the tingle at the back of Mary-Sue's brain began to fade, a terrible racket broke out at the table behind her.

She turned around to see the detestable Prescott leaning over a booth packed full of girls. Francine had pushed herself into the back corner and put her feet up as a barricade to keep him out.

The boy was sporting a preppy blazer and a pair of wool slacks. But his typically slicked-back hair was sticking out messily in every direction, and his shoes and pant cuffs were splattered with mud. Looking down to the floor, Mary-Sue could see that he had made a blotchy trail all the way from the front door table to Francine's table.

"Please, my dear." Prescott attempted to push the girl's legs to the side. "I'm quite certain that you, in fact, *are* interested in dating."

"Yeah, jerk!" Francine growled. "I just said I didn't wanna date you, specifically!"

"Hmph!" Prescott straightened up and brushed his arms off. "I hope that you aren't holding out for *The All-American Boy*—I heard that Sondra finally knocked some sense into the fellow and convinced him to take her to the cinema. Those two are peas in a pod, so why not settle for second best, my dear?"

Mary-Sue nearly fell down from her stool.

"No, Prescott! No, no, and no again." Francine stuck her tongue out. "And for the last time: no."

"But have you considered, my dear—"

"Shut up, Prescott!" Mary-Sue shouted. "And please, for our sake, go away! Nobody likes you."

Prescott whipped around, incensed. He straightened his blazer, then took a step forward, glancing down toward the comic book. His mouth turned up into a cruel smile.

"Says the spooky girl reading romance rags alone on Friday night?" He chuckled. "I'm afraid not, my dear—you're just jealous that your only friend finally went girl-crazy and failed to seize upon you."

"It's not like that, Prescott—and you know it." Mary-Sue jumped up from her stool and took an assertive step toward the boy. "I have half a mind to tell your mother what you just said."

"Oh no!" Prescott clutched at his chest. "Not my mommy! Whatever shall I do?" He stepped even closer, leaning in. "Please, why don't you just sit back down and mind your own—"

SWAACK! Mary-Sue slammed her palm down

onto the counter.

"Or maybe you'd prefer I tell your mother that you snuck out of the house while you were grounded to go to the soda fountain?"

"W—what the..." Prescott's eyes went wide. "How did you...?" The boy shook his head, then straightened his shoulders. "What I mean to say is, that isn't true."

"Oh no?" Mary-Sue raised an eyebrow and gestured outside. "Then why didn't you drive your new moped here, Prescott? You couldn't wait to bring up your permit this afternoon—yet I can't help but notice it's not parked outside! It... couldn't be that your parents took it away when they saw your poor grades, could it?"

"I..." Prescott hesitated as the other tables began to look their way. "I had the butler drop me off, that's all. I didn't want to risk letting my baby get scuffed before we arrived in the Hamptons."

"Did the butler drop you off before or after you trudged through the swamp?" Mary-Sue gestured down. Prescott looked to his cuffs, then looked back up, panicked.

"I didn't mean it!" He began to plead. "I—I take it back, yes? You... you and Danny, you're just friends. And everyone knows that it's purely platonic. And I'm sure that you have many other friends, as well. Just… if Father finds out, then I'm done for!"

"Oh no!" Mary-Sue pouted. "Whatever shall you do?"

Prescott glanced around as several of the on-lookers began to chuckle. He huffed, scowled, then stomped off toward the restrooms, brushing at his muddy pants.

BRRNG-BRRNG! the front bell chimed as the door swung open and a tall, stiff man in a black suit and sunglasses stepped inside. He stopped, carefully scanning his eyes around the soda fountain, then paused at the footprints on the floor. He pulled a notepad and pen out from his inner pocket, wrote something on the page, then walked up to the counter.

"Well, howdy, stranger!" Mr. Graham began to shuffle over, wiping his hands on his apron. "You know, sir, I've seen that look in a fella's eye before—it's a banana split you're after."

"No." The man pulled his sunglasses off, then reached into his side pocket and pulled out a case. He snapped it open, then gently placed the glasses inside and put the case back into the pocket.

"Ah! I see—a hamburger man, of course! Or maybe…" Mr. Graham hesitated, studying the other man up and down. "Or maybe you're a hot dog sorta fella…"

The man clenched his jaw, reached into his inner pocket, and pulled out a billfold. He held it up, then flipped it open to reveal a golden metal badge inside.

"Agent Ford with the Federal Bureau of Investigation." The man said tersely. "I need to ask your customers a few questions."

"H—has someone done something wrong, sir?" Mr. Graham asked.

"I'm looking for information." Ford flipped his badge shut, slipping the billfold back into his inner pocket. As he did, Mary-Sue spied a pistol holstered over his shoulder. "About an incident which just occurred out in Chautauqua Park."

"W—well, of course, sir!" Mr. Graham looked rattled. He cleared his throat and turned toward the customers. "Listen up, now! This man from the government is gonna need to you ask y'all a few questions. Be of any assistance you can, now, y'hear?"

The FBI agent gave Mr. Graham a sharp nod, then looked around the room once again. He flipped his notepad back open and took a few steps toward a group of teenagers in the nearest booth.

Behind Mary-Sue, there was a quiet *thwump-*

thwump! The girl turned and found the source: the kitchen doors, swinging ever so slightly. As if someone had just discreetly snuck through. And Mary-Sue was going to find out why.

Her eyes shot back over to the agent, who was busy with his interrogation, then glanced around the room to make sure that nobody was looking her way. She slid off from the stool, quietly lifted the flip-top counter up, then ducked underneath and slipped quietly into the kitchen and out through the back door.

In the dim, orange light of the alley Mary-Sue could just see Prescott standing next to a row of metal trashcans, leaning his back up against the brick wall and breathing hard.

"Don't you move one inch, Prescott Trowbridge!" she hissed.

The boy froze, then recognized her. He breathed a sigh of relief.

"Thank heavens! It's just you."

"What are you doing out here, you worm?" Mary-Sue hopped down the steps onto the grimy concrete, walking his direction.

"Getting a bit of fresh air." Prescott turned his nose up.

Mary-Sue stomped closer and closer, backing

the arrogant boy into the corner of the alley.

"That man," she said, eyes narrowed, "he's after you, isn't he?"

"What's it to you?" Prescott asked quickly, avoiding eye contact.

"If you don't tell me," she said, planting her hands firmly onto her hips, "then I'm going to march you right back inside by the scruff of your neck and toss you at his feet."

"Fine!" Prescott gave a huff. "I admit it: you were right. After Father saw my poor marks I was grounded for the night. However, after I had a harrowing brush with my own mortality this afternoon, I simply wasn't able to remain imprisoned in my own bedroom all evening." The boy's eyes shot back toward the door and beads of sweat began to form on his forehead. "Now, Father has had me tailed by a Federal agent, so I simply must return to the manor before—"

"Come on." Mary-Sue rolled her eyes. "Tell me the truth."

"That is the truth!" Prescott frowned, serious. "Father said one more transgression and he shall be forced to leave me in Bonnifield all summer—with Aunt Gladys! Clearly, he's quite serious about the matter."

"I don't think the FBI deals in truancy," Mary-Sue sighed.

"I knew it!" Prescott shook his head, ignoring her. "I knew that I was being followed."

"Followed?" She raised an eyebrow, glancing down to his muddy pants. "Since when?"

"Perhaps eight-thirty," Prescott said, eyes fixed to the door. "When I took a shortcut through Chautauqua Park, in order to avoid detection by any nosy neighbors." He chewed at his cheek. "But... around the old cemetery, I began to feel..."

"What?" Mary-Sue leaned in.

"Uh, well," he said, embarrassed, "spooked, I suppose."

"The old cemetery? That's just where..." Mary-Sue's eyes went wide. "Spooked by what, Prescott?"

"Well..." He gestured back to the soda fountain. "By that agent. Through the mist, I spied an unusual red glow. At the time, my mind went to more... chilling explanations. Now, however, I see that it was simply my imagination."

"You came straight here?" She crossed her arms. "That's it?"

"That, as you say, is it." Prescott straightened his blazer. "I arrived, and then ten minutes later a Federal agent showed up. Case closed."

She studied Prescott's eyes. The boy was a known liar, but a bad one, and there was something in his voice that told her that he believed what he was saying—true or not.

"Go home, Prescott." She uncrossed her arms and took a step to the side, gesturing out toward the street. "But take the sidewalks this time—no short-cuts."

"Scout's honor," Prescott said, rolling his eyes. He looked back at the door, then took off, sprinting down the alley and out into the street.

Goose-pimples shot down Mary-Sue's arms. There was no way that the Federal Bureau of Investigation would bother tailing the mayor's son for sneaking out of the house. But whether or not Prescott really had been followed, he had seen something in Mercury Marsh near the Civil War graveyard, just like Dale Brown—and that was too much of a coincidence to ignore.

Maybe, just maybe, there was something to her mystery, after all.

The harrowing image of an atomic explosion burst onto the screen, towering thirty feet high above them.

8   Monster Movie Madness

Danny tightened his grip around the Raisinets, crumpling the flimsy cardboard in his hand. The boy's shoulders were tense and his eyes were cast down to his feet, which dragged over the gravel as he sulked around the edge of the concession stand crowd.

Judy's words echoed in Danny's mind. The mature girl had said that mystery-solving was for kids, which made no sense to him. After all, police detectives and private investigators were given extremely serious crimes to pursue—an adult responsibility to be certain.

True, many of the mysteries solved by *The Britannica Junior Detectives* had somewhat low stakes—missing stamps, stolen jewelry, pilfered toys. But they were solving real criminal cases nonetheless. And true, he had started the agency when he was nine years old.

But now he was fourteen, a young adult with grown-up interests—and he was going to prove it. He was going to march right back over to Sondra's car, sit down next to her on the front seat, throw his arm around her shoulders, then give her a kiss right on the lips. Just like one might do at Lover's Lane.

"There ya are!" Jack called out, emerging from the sea of bodies as Danny approached the far edge of the crowd. "I've been lookin' all over for ya, Britannica."

"I'm sorry, Jack," Danny said, side-stepping the boy, "but I'm afraid that I have no time for social niceties; I have to get back to my date right away."

"Then you're headin' the wrong direction, pal." With a wicked glint in his eye, the high school boy jammed his good thumb over his shoulder toward the other side of the crowd.

Danny paused, then pivoted on his heel. "Pardon?"

"Yea." Jack raised an eyebrow, a smile pulling at the edge of his lips. "That pretty little blonde in a pink fuzzy sweater, right?"

"Yes." Danny narrowed his eyes.

"Then some fella's been mackin' on your girl for, like, five minutes." Jack pointed across the sea of bodies. "Over yonder. Real bad lookin' guy. Some greaser-type. Some... outsider."

Danny peered across the crowd and spotted Sondra's tight pony tail swishing back and forth next to a tall, handsome Asian boy in a leather jacket. Without thinking he took off, running along the edge of the crowd and around the bend. He slid to a stop just a few yards away, kicking a cloud of dust up and causing everyone nearby to look his way—everyone except for the greaser.

"Oh, there he is!" Sondra pointed right at Danny.

The greaser looked coolly over his shoulder. He appeared to be a few years older than Danny, perhaps seventeen or eighteen, with a good four inches and forty pounds on the younger boy. He was sporting a slicked-back pompadour, and beneath his leather jacket was a tight white t-shirt, tucked into a pair of grease-stained jeans. He sized Danny up with a mild curiosity, loose cigarette hanging out from between his lips.

"What, cardigan-and-buzzcut, over there?" The older boy chuckled, turning back to Sondra. "Yea, makes sense."

"Excuse me," Danny said, eyes narrowed, "but I believe that you're talking to my date. If you'd please be on your way—"

The older boy paused, pulled his cigarette out from his lips, then let a gentle, rolling cloud of smoke tumble out. Slowly, he turned his full body toward Danny.

"The hell ya say to me, kid?"

"It was a simple request, sir—there's no need for language." Danny reached his hand out in friendship. "Now, I fear that we perhaps got off on the wrong foot. My name is Danny—"

"Sir was my pop." The greaser glared at Danny's outstretched hand, making no move to meet it. "My name's Ace. And I ain't goin' nowhere."

"My pop taught me a little bit about manners." Danny retracted his hand with a frown. "Perhaps it's different where you come from, but here in Bonnifield, it's considered rude to court the date of another man."

"Where I come from?" Ace gave a wry chuckle, raising his eyebrows. "Now, what could ya possibly mean by that, smart stuff?"

Danny turned his hands out. "Now, I didn't mean—"

"Where I come from—California, mind you," Ace said, beginning to slowly walk toward Danny, "ain't nobody callin' kids like you men."

A low murmur began amongst the surrounding teenagers, and from his periphery, Danny could see the crowd starting to shift, spreading out to get a better view. Circling up.

"I—I think," Danny gulped, taking a step back, "that there may have been some kind of a misunderstanding—"

"Now, boys..." Sondra attempted to step between them. "Please—"

"You callin' me stupid?" Ace sidestepped the girl, thrusting a finger toward Danny.

"N—no, of course not!" Danny thrust his hands up into the air. "A misunderstanding is when two people have opposing viewpoints on—"

"One more condescending word outta you," the greaser said, hands tightening into fists as he stopped a few feet away, "'n the only viewpoint you're gonna have is an eyeful'a gravel—dig?"

Danny looked across the crowd, all eyes on him. Judging whether or not he was going to back down. Whether or not he was just a scared kid.

"No," he said, standing up tall. "I don't 'dig' in the least—I'm afraid that the intimidation tactics used by you people won't work on me."

"Mm-hm. There we are again..." The greaser flicked his cigarette at Danny. It bounced harmlessly off of the boy's chest, bursting into ash and ember, then falling down to the gravel. "Now, what else ya know about *my people*, kid?"

"Once again, you mistake my meaning." Danny

looked down to his cardigan, brushed the ash away, then looked up directly into Ace's eyes. "I refer not to your heritage, but to your brutish nature. I simply meant that you're a trouble-maker, a juvenile delinquent, I'm left to assume—a public charge who would find himself more at home in a prison cell than in a civilized society. As opposed to my type," Danny narrowed his eyes, "who uses our words to solve our problems."

"Only problem I see," Ace said, stopping a few feet away from him and shrugging his leather jacket off, "is standin' right in front'a me."

He tossed it to the ground beside them, then rolled the sleeves of his white t-shirt up, revealing a faded tattoo on his left bicep. It read:

BAD LUCK

"I…" Danny said, clearing his throat. "I know a bully when I see one. And your type is nothing but empty threats."

"Wanna test that theory, smart stuff?" Ace cracked his knuckles.

"Come on, Danny!" A voice yelled from the far side of the circle. He looked over to see Jack with a grin on his face. "You can take him."

"Yeah!" Another voice yelled. "Kick his butt!"

"Please." Danny looked around the crowd. "There's no need to—"

"Fight!" Someone else yelled. "Show 'im what's what!"

"Yeah, fight 'im!" Another voice echoed.

And all at once, the crowd began to chant. First low and steady, then louder, and louder, and louder, *"Fight! Fight! Fight! Fight!"*

"Whaddya say, square?" Ace's eyes scanned the crowd. "You wanna give these good people what they're askin' for? I'll even let ya throw the first punch, kid."

"Fight! Fight! Fight! Fight!"

"I am not a kid," Danny growled, pushing his sleeves up. "And I'm not a square!"

"Fight! Fight! Fight! Fight!"

Without thinking, Danny charged forward,

throwing a wild punch at the greaser's face. The crowd exploded as he lunged, but Ace was ready, leaning back and letting Danny fly past, stumbling across the circle.

"Good follow-through." The greaser smirked, crouching down into a boxing stance. "A natural. Just gotta work on your aim, kid."

"You're a ruffian. And a cad." Danny stared the boy down, breathing hard. "And I refuse to let you get away with your poor behavior."

Behind Danny, the projector's light flickered off for just a moment, then sputtered back to life with a deep drumroll, followed by the sharp and menacing sting of a full orchestra. The next feature had begun—but nobody was heading back to their cars.

Ace took a step to the side. Then another, and another, beginning to stalk the perimeter of the circle like a caged animal. Danny followed suit, studying the more experienced boy's every movement.

Behind Ace, the screen flashed a brilliant white, throwing the greaser into dark silhouette against the screen. A deep, unsettling roar rumbled out from the car speakers as the harrowing image of an atomic explosion burst onto the screen, towering thirty feet high above them. Slowly, the title faded in.

It read:

Taking advantage of the momentary distraction, Ace barreled right at Danny, hurling a powerful left hook directly at the younger boy's face. Danny's instincts took over and he ducked beneath the punch then slid across the gravel, kicking a spray of dust and rocks out into the crowd.

They cheered as the boy pivoted and charged back toward Ace, this time attempting to aim for the greaser's ribs—but again, the older boy was too fast. He leaned back and let Danny charge past once more, but the younger boy managed to swing his elbow around and make contact with Ace's cheekbone.

He skidded to a stop, then quickly spun around to see the other boy charging at him, shoulder first.

Danny braced for impact as Ace slammed into him, sending the smaller boy tumbling down to the ground, dozens of razor-sharp rocks cutting at his exposed arms. He quickly flipped onto his back to see the greaser slowly stalking toward him, a fire in his eyes.

"Excuse me! Pardon me! Out of my way, now!" A shrill voice called out from the crowd, causing Ace to stop in his tracks. From the other side of the circle, Mr. Orpheus, the proprietor of the theatre, pushed through the sea of teenagers, followed by a group of concerned parents—Sondra's father amongst them.

"What precisely is going on here?" Mr. Orpheus shouted as his eyes flicked back and forth between the two boys, stopping on Danny's blood-streaked arms. "My word, Mr. Oxford! Are you injured?"

He pushed himself up onto his elbows. "It's just a scratch, sir."

"I don't know precisely who you are," Mr. Orpheus said, turning to Ace with his nose thrust high up in the air, "but trouble-makers like you have no place at The Co-Ed Theatre."

"This kid…" Ace jutted a finger toward Danny, still breathing hard. "Threw the first punch."

"I doubt that very much, young man!" Mr. Orpheus scoffed.

"Just ask any one 'a these mooks." The greaser gestured around to all of the staring onlookers. Nobody moved to concur.

"I know the content of Mr. Oxford's character." The man put his fists on his hips, studying Ace. His pompadour. His tattoo. His face. "But you, young man, appear to be some sort of an outsider—a juvenile delinquent. Who is hereby banned from this picture-house, for life!"

"Outsider." Ace gave a wry laugh and shook his head, grabbing his leather jacket from the ground. "I see how it is, old man."

"Leave here at once, or I shall be forced to call the police." The man pointed toward the exit. "At once!"

Ace shrugged the jacket on and made a beeline for his motorcycle, the crowd parting as he approached. The greaser then threw his leg over the motorcycle's seat, flipped the kickstand up, and thrust a key into the ignition. He paused, pulling a cigarette out from his pocket and slipping it between his lips. He flicked his lighter on, held it up to the end, then looked right at Danny.

"This ain't over, kid."

He turned the key. *VRRRRMM! RM-RM-*

Rm-Rm-m... The boy revved the engine twice then took off, peeling out and spraying the crowd with rocks and gravel.

"Typical!" Orpheus huffed, watching as the motorcycle disappeared from view. He turned and glared at the crowd. "And you lot should be ashamed, watching on. That only one amongst you came to tell an adult," he said, gesturing to Sondra whose eyes were cast down to the ground, "is a mark against your whole generation. Now, back to the picture— or I shall begin to take names."

The group dispersed as the man herded them toward the cars. Of the crowd, only Sondra and her father remained. Danny looked up at them from his place on the ground, propped up onto his elbows.

"Come, darling," Mr. Fiehly said, shaking his head. He put his arm around his daughter's shoulder. "It's time to go home."

Sondra nodded sadly and turned, following her father into the maze of cars and leaving Danny alone on the gravel. On the screen ahead, there was a group of men in black suits sitting around a shadowy council table, gesturing to a map of Arlington, Virginia.

"First fight, daddy-o?"

KA-TINK! the sharp sound of a lighter flicking

shut rang out from the concession area behind Danny. He turned to see a teenage girl leaning back on a picnic table, a cigarette between her lips. She looked to be about his age and was sporting a black shirt, black pants, and a red kerchief around her neck. She was sharp-featured with a mole on her cheek, and her long, dark hair was pressed straight.

"How could you tell?" Danny gave a wry chuckle.

"Well, you're on the ground." She took a drag and tossed the lighter back into her purse. "Bleeding."

"That's inductive reasoning, I'm afraid—an educated guess made on partial evidence." Danny pushed himself up onto his feet, arms stinging. "I may have lost many fights in my time, for all you know."

"Mm." The girl nodded, looking off in the other direction. "So that buttoned-up, yet rough-and-tumble type—a little breaking and entering after school for fun, but home for supper by six."

"I'm afraid that you have me all wrong." Danny raised his arms to examine his injuries, which were only surface level scrapes. He pulled the sleeves of his cardigan back down. "I'm not the criminal type. Rather the opposite."

"Yeah, I'd induced that." The edges of the girl's lips curled up into a hint of a smile. She shook her head, then took a drag. "Still, you did okay—there's a fire in you, man, just waiting to get out."

"Pardon?" Danny looked at her, a funny feeling in his stomach.

"Y'know—passion. Spirit. Verve." Her eyes drifted back toward him. "*The only people for me are the mad ones, the ones who are mad to live, mad to talk, mad to be saved, desirous of everything at the same time, the ones who never yawn or say a commonplace thing, but burn, burn, burn...*"

"What is that?" Danny cocked his head to the side, words echoing in the back of his mind. "A riddle?"

"Something like that." She laughed and reached into her purse, then grabbed a small, silver canteen and held it out toward him, bouncing it back and forth. "C'mere. You seem like you could use it."

"Thank you very much," Danny said, walking over to her. He took it and unscrewed the cap. "After all of that exertion, my throat is rather dry."

He threw his head back and took a large swig—but instead of a cool, refreshing mouthful of water, Danny was met only with a sharp, burning sensation.

"This…" he coughed, holding the flask out. "This is liquor!"

"Tell the whole neighborhood why don't you?" She grabbed it back, then glanced over each of her shoulders before taking a swig herself and returning it to her purse. She zipped the bag shut, then slid forward and hopped down from the table. "Well, thanks for that crazy scene, daddy-o. Only exciting thing I've seen since I got to this one-horse town." She gave a small wave over her shoulder. "Anyway. It's been cool."

"You're leaving already?" Danny frowned, suddenly feeling anxious. In many ways the girl was his opposite—relaxed, casual, cool. But there was something about her that intrigued Danny immensely. Perhaps because of that fact. "We've… we've just begun to get to know each other. Besides," he said, pointing back over his shoulder toward the screen, "the picture's barely begun."

"Nothing in that flick is gonna top the action I just saw." She swung her bag over her arm, then began to walk toward the exit. "Plus, I wanna get up early for this morning shindig."

"Wait." Danny held his hand out. She paused, looking back over her shoulder as a wispy trail of smoke curled around her head. "I—I didn't get your name. Who are you?"

"You're the detective." The girl raised her cigarette and took another drag, batting her eyelashes demurely. "Figure it out, gumshoe."

9   **The Belated Breakfast**

In the soft mid-morning light, the Oxford mansion now looked like a fairytale castle nestled amongst the evergreens, rendered in pastel shades of lavender and dandelion. Miniature gnats and specks of pollen danced in and out of the sunbeams around Mary-Sue as she skipped up the front path in the dappled shade.

After a good night's sleep and a good deal of revision on her casefile, the girl was now feeling renewed in her purpose. *The Mutant of Mercury Marsh* had two corroborating witness reports of unusual activity near the Civil War graveyard—plenty to convince Danny of its import.

She had even found a new clue that very morning; unable to sleep in, she had rushed down to grab the early edition of *The Gazette* at the crack of dawn, pouring over the newspaper in her excitement. And there, in the middle of the police blotter, was a new lead.

It read:

FRIDAY—At 10:28 p.m., a troop of
Adventure Scouts reported a vandalism
incident at Camp Chautauqua after
returning from a hike. There are no
suspects and no arrests have been made.

˙˙˙˙˙˙ p.m., a raccoon was
' back yard. The
al control

According to her hand-drawn map, Camp
Chautauqua was less than a mile away from the
cemetery, which wasn't likely a coincidence; all roads
seemed to lead back to Mercury Marsh.

She hummed a few bars from *Sunny Side of the
Street* as she hopped up the front steps, then curled
her hand into a fist. But before she could even
knock, the door swung open to reveal a flour-dusted
Dr. Oxford standing in the entryway, a grin pushing
deep dimples into his cheeks.

"Right on time, little miss!" The man stepped
aside and gestured her in with a greasy spatula, a
wisp of flour drifting from his bright yellow apron as
he moved. "Chocolate-chip waffles are in the iron!"

"Good morning, sir!" She returned the smile,
then stepped inside to be hit with the scent of frying
butter. "Smells delicious!"

Off to her left, the kitchen was all pastels, formica, and bright lights with modern, Scandinavian accents. At the center of the room was a large dining table piled high with every breakfast dish imaginable: milk, coffee, tea, orange juice, toast, eggs, cereal, jello salad, and hash browns. Like a scene from an upscale housekeeping magazine.

Perched at the far side of the table was Danny in his red cardigan, surrounded by stacks of books, posters, and folders of all types. He was nose-down in the previous year's *Quill Annual*, running his finger across each page, then flipping to the next and repeating the process. Mary-Sue was all too familiar with the look—he was absorbed in a conundrum. An enigma. A mystery.

"Missing school already?" Mary-Sue dashed over to the table, then slid down into the next chair over.

"Pardon?" Danny looked up, startled. "Oh, good morning!"

"Why the yearbook?" she asked. "First day of summer and you're already nostalgic for junior high?"

"No, no." Danny shook his head. "It's just…" He flipped to the last page, scanning his finger across each row of students. "I'm afraid that I'm having the most difficult time figuring out the simplest thing."

"Let me guess." Mary-Sue's eyes lit up and she scooched her chair in closer. "You've stumbled upon some new mystery!"

"I'm afraid so." Danny shut the yearbook and rapped his fingers on the edge of the table. "But leads have proven hard to come by."

"I can relate," Mary-Sue said, "that's what I called this meeting for! My secret project: a new mystery!" She paused, then narrowed her eyes, looking at all of the mess in front of him. "Gosh! You don't think that…" She perked up in her chair. "Maybe it could be the same mystery?"

From across the room, Dr. Oxford gave a hearty laugh. He turned from the stovetop and gave the girl an amused look.

"I doubt that very much, little miss."

"Oh?" Mary-Sue tilted her head to the side. "Why?"

"You see…" Danny's father chuckled as he flipped one last waffle onto the stack at his side. He turned the burner off, picked the tray up, and walked in their direction. "The only mystery that Danny is trying to solve this morning is that of the feminine mystique."

"Huh?" Mary-Sue said, then turned back to her

friend, whose cheeks were flushed a bright crimson. She frowned. "Oh. It's about your big date with Sondra?"

"You heard?" Danny cringed.

"I take it that went well?" She put her elbows up onto the table.

"W—well…" Danny looked away. "Not precisely. It's a bit of a long story, but…" He scratched at the back of his neck and sank down into his seat. "I actually met another girl after the date."

"Another one?" Mary-Sue pushed her cheek down into her hand. As unreliable as Prescott was, it appeared that the boy was correct about one thing: Danny had gone full-on girl-crazy.

"It seems," Dr. Oxford said, placing the tray of golden, crispy waffles down, "that the boy has finally developed a crush."

"I'm lost," Mary-Sue sighed. "What exactly is the mystery?"

"Unfortunately," the man chuckled, tousling his son's hair, "our boy detective failed to get the identity of the young lady in question."

"I do have a few clues." Danny shrugged. "You see, she implied that she had just moved to town, but she knew that I was a detective. This led me to think that perhaps she had moved from a neighboring town, or had just enrolled in a local school other than our own—hence the yearbooks."

"Sure." Mary-Sue nodded.

"She also quoted a rather unusual phrase that I didn't understand," he said, sitting up straight in his chair. "So I went to the library first thing this morning and repeated it back to the librarian as best I could recall. She directed me to this." Danny picked up a book from the table, titled *On the Road*. "It was written by an unusual fellow named Jack Kerouac. When I perused it, the work appeared to be nonsensical rambling—but according to further research, the author is a beatnik."

"Uh-huh."

"My final clue was in the girl's enigmatic exit." Danny stroked at his chin and picked a flier up from the table, advertising a local dance. "She had mentioned that she needed to wake up for a party this morning, but despite perusing all of the bulletin boards in town, I couldn't seem to find a record of any such event." He slumped down. "So I'm left at a bit of an impasse."

"That's a shame." Mary-Sue said, swinging her bookbag around. "It sounds like you tried everything short of asking the EARS."

"That's it!" Danny shot back up. "Of course—

how did I not think of that? Somehow they always seem to know what's going on in town."

"I was joking." Mary-Sue raised an eyebrow, unbuckling the straps on her bookbag. "With those crackpots, you're far more likely to wind up in a three-hour discussion about the predictions of Nostradamus or about the secret cure for cancer the government doesn't want us to know about. But, if you want to put that energy toward a real mystery," she said, pulling her file out and onto the table, "just wait until you see what my case is."

"Yes, yes, of course…" Danny nodded, drumming his fingers on the edge of the table and staring out the front window. "I would wager that there isn't a party in Bonnifield that the EARS don't know about…"

"Danny—"

"In fact," the boy said, pushing his chair out and standing up. "If I were to leave now, I might just be able to catch the tail-end of this party."

"But—"

Danny dashed into the entryway and began to slip his sneakers on. From the other side of the table, the boy's father cleared his throat.

"Pardon me, young man." Dr. Oxford crossed his arms. "Aren't you forgetting something?"

"Of course, Pop—and thank you!" Danny tied his laces, then stood back up. "But no need to worry: I'll be more than happy to eat leftovers tonight. My nutrition will have to wait just a little bit longer."

"No, no..." The scientist took a sip of his coffee and gestured over to Mary-Sue. "I mean your commitment to your friend, here. She's come all the way across town to meet with you—don't you have a responsibility to her?"

"Oh. Oh! Yes, Mary-Sue. Well..." Danny nodded, his fingers tapping at the door handle. "I am interested in your mystery, too, Mary-Sue, but mine is rather time-sensitive, you see." He perked up. "Of course, you're more than welcome to join me, we could discuss along the way!"

"Thanks." May-Sue pursed her lips. "But I think I'll pass."

"Well," the boy said, twisting the knob, "it'll have to be another rain check, then, I'm afraid. Are you free tonight for supper?"

"Yes, but—"

"Great!" Danny swung the door open. "Graham's at six o'clock. I'll see you there!"

"Oka—"

SLAM! Mary-Sue watched through the window as Danny pulled his bicycle off from the side of the house and dashed down the driveway.

"Young romance." Dr. Oxford twisted his mouth to the side, turning his gaze down to the casefile on the table. "I can imagine that you're more than a little disappointed; I know how excited you were to tell the boy all about your atomic mutant."

"No," Mary-Sue lied, shoulders slumped. She was disappointed, of course—though felt as if she shouldn't be. Danny was allowed to pursue girls if he wanted to, after all. She would just have to try again another time. The girl slid the folder off from the table and put it back in her bag. "It's fine. I just—"

"You know, I was a boy detective myself." The man reached into his pocket and pulled his pipe out. "A lifetime ago."

"Yes, sir, I've heard." Mary-Sue gave a glum smile. "With *Rocket the Wonder Dog*, right?"

"Yes, a remarkable companion." He nodded, pulling a matchbox out from his pocket. "Have you ever heard the term 'confirmation bias'?"

"I don't think so." She shook her head, tearing a small piece off from the edge of a waffle.

"It's something that I wish that I knew about during my adventuring days." He struck a match and brought it up to his pipe, then took a few short puffs. He shook it out and placed it into a nearby ashtray. "Confirmation bias is a common error in inductive reasoning."

"You're talking about the scientific method, aren't you?" Mary-Sue asked.

"Yes." He nodded. "When one begins with a strongly held belief in their hypothesis, one tends to interpret all subsequent evidence through the lens of that belief—even if, from an objective standpoint, the nature of that evidence is actually ambiguous. Often this leads to missed opportunities and incorrect conclusions."

"And..." She popped the waffle piece into her mouth. "That's what you think my mutant is?"

"In scientific circles," Dr. Oxford said, champing at his pipe, "instead of attempting to prove our hypotheses, we often find far more success in attempting to disprove them. To challenge our own biases."

"You sound like Danny," the girl said, chewing. "He's always saying I need to get my head out of the clouds, that my imagination gets the best of me—like with *The Phantom of Prom* just being a man in a costume."

"Now, there's nothing wrong with imagination!" Dr. Oxford broke out into a wide grin. "After all, it's how I've begun most of my scientific breakthroughs—by daring to dream." He took a long puff from his pipe, then pushed his chair out and stood up. "But it's also important to try to remain objective and open to all possibilities, both rational and seemingly irrational. That's the scientific method—have an observation, construct a hypothesis, gather your evidence, then analyze the results against your hypothesis. If the data supports it, then you have a theory."

"So, what you're saying is…" Mary-Sue swung her bookbag over her shoulder, grabbing the rest of the waffle as she stood up. "Is that I should investigate my mystery as if there both is and isn't a mutant?"

"That way you can uncover all of the evidence, whether or not it fits into your pre-existing hypothesis." The man nodded, wandering toward the door. "In fact, why don't I lend you my Geiger counter? That way you can prove conclusively for yourself whether the answer to your mystery truly is an irradiated man or not."

"Gee, really?" Mary-Sue perked up, following the scientist out into the entryway. "I'd like that very much, sir."

"Swell!" Dr. Oxford grinned, opening the door and gesturing the girl outside. "To the lab, then."

Mary-Sue dashed out through the door. The scientist shut it behind them and the two walked gingerly down the front stairs, across the path, and around the house.

"You know, sir." She took another bite of the waffle. "Now that you mention it, there is one thing that I'm not quite sure fits into my mutant theory."

"Oh?" The man's eyes brightened as they approached the laboratory. "What's that, now?"

"This agent from the government," Mary-Sue said, mouth full. "He was looking for Prescott after the guy took a shortcut through the woods, but I'm not really sure why. Maybe he really was the one following him, and not the mutant after all."

"Government agent?" Dr. Oxford paused at the airlock and frowned. "Of what sort?"

"The Federal Bureau of Investigation." Mary-Sue shrugged.

"I see." The scientist punched in the secret code: *8A3C-B259*, then cleared his throat. "Young lady, unfortunately I've realized that there's much work to be done—and no time to waste. So let's get that Geiger counter and get on your way."

10   # Radio Reconnaissance

Danny propped his bicycle up against the massive oak tree behind the new suburban development on the far edge of town. He gazed up the towering trunk, where a series of pine boards were hastily nailed into its surface. They led all the way up to a wooden clubhouse hidden amongst the branches, covered in dozens of peculiar metal antennas pointing out in every direction.

It was the headquarters for the Electronic Amateur Radio Society, or EARS. Officially, they were a group of electrical engineering enthusiasts of all ages who gathered to discuss new trends in radio technology. But unofficially, they were a group of fringe conspiracy theorists, obsessed with scanning the ionosphere for secret government communications.

They had intercepted the signals of Sputnik, Explorer, and Pioneer, they had listened in on classified Air Force pilot training, and they were convinced that the Soviet Union had already sent a man into space—with disastrous results. They also claimed that all of the evidence was covered up by the communists to avoid embarrassment.

But an unintended result of their hobby was picking up radio signals from all around Bonnifield. To them, the signals were a minor annoyance, noise which they had to filter out in order to achieve their true goals. To Danny, however, they were an opportunity.

He gripped onto the first board of the makeshift ladder and shook it back and forth, testing its construction. Satisfied, he put his weight on it and reached for the next board, then the next, and the next until he found himself peeking over the treehouse platform. Danny pulled himself to his feet, walked over to the knotted door, and balled his hand up into a fist. *KA-TONK! KA-TONK! KA-TONK!*

The peep slot shot open. A second later, a pair of Coke-bottle glasses peeked up into view, studied Danny, then the slot slid shut again. Inside there were muffled shouts and whispers, then total silence. And after a few moments, the door slowly swung open to reveal Kat Lewandowski, the most precocious fourth-grader that Danny had ever met.

Behind her stood more of the members: Hugh O'Murphy, a freckled, corpulent high schooler sporting some unfortunate orthodontic headgear,

Pierre Truffeau, a former member of the French Resistance with a faded Cross of Lorraine tattoo poking out from his half-unbuttoned shirt, and Gloria Lombardi, the elderly proprietor of the town's fabric store. Each of them stood in the doorway, arms crossed and noses turned up.

"Well, well, well..." The little girl shook her head with a smug smile. "Look who finally comes crawling up to beg for a membership."

"Membership?" Danny raised his eyebrows, taken aback. "No, I—"

"Ze boy is bashful!" Pierre cooed in his gentle accent. "He does not want to admit his, how you say, defeat."

"The poor, poor darlin'." Gloria sighed. "But at this point, I'm afraid it won't be nearly so simple as beggin'."

"Begging?" Danny asked. "But—"

"That's right." Kat lisped, pulling a stack of index cards out from the front pocket of her overalls. "If you wanna be a member, you're gonna have to prove your passion, dedication, and commitment. We have a real tough gauntlet of questions ready to test your knowledge."

"And your intentions!" Pierre said. "Zis way, we can know zat you are not a spy sent from ze government, attempting to shut our operation down!"

"A snitch!" Gloria growled, wide-eyed.

Danny tilted his head to the side. "Wait, why—"

"That's right, Gloria!" Kat placed her fist onto her hip. "So you better hope you answer every question right, Britannica. We won't tolerate any snitches around here."

Danny frowned. "But you know me—"

"Spies may be anyone." Pierre shook his head. "From anywhere."

"And this one looks like a rat to me." Gloria narrowed her eyes.

"Well, golly, folks! I'm confused." Hugh scratched at the side of his head and pointed back over his shoulder. "I thought we were keeping an open desk just for him?"

All the other members groaned and threw their arms up into the air, breaking away from each other and shooting Hugh a dirty look.

"Oh." Hugh cringed. "He wasn't supposed to know that, was he?"

"Please, fellas." Danny finally managed to get out. "Tell me, what's this all about?"

"I guess the ruse is up…" Kat sighed, then gestured him in. "See, to us it's always been obvious that as a fellow seeker of knowledge, you'd eventually figure out that we're the wisest people in town."

"Zis is right." Pierre put an arm on Danny's shoulder, then tapped at the boy's head. "For some time now, we have known that ze boy with the encyclopedic brain will desire ze answers to ze true mysteries of ze world!"

"The ones they don't want you to know," Gloria narrowed her eyes and looked around the room with suspicion.

"They?" Danny cocked his head to the side.

"Yes, yes. Come!" Pierre led the boy through the door. "Your home away from home awaits!"

Inside, the clubhouse was a mess of electronic components, frayed wires, and deconstructed radio units. The walls were lined with large metal panels covered in lights, buttons, and switches, cobbled together from what appeared to be a dozen or more sources.

Against the far wall, separated out from the chaos, was a single desk completely free of clutter. On top was a large, shielded box with a half-dozen knobs, three indicators, and a huge tuning dial. Danny broke away from Pierre and walked over to it.

"Y'know what that is, don't ya?" Kat waggled her eyebrows up and down. "I can see it in your eyes."

"Military right?" Danny asked, studying its construction. "Yes... yes, unless I'm mistaken, I believe that I've seen similar devices before in the pages of *Popular Electronics*."

"United States Navy surplus." Pierre nodded, a mischievous grin on his face. "Ze most powerful radio one can acquire."

"I see. Yes, of course..." He leaned in closer to examine the dials. "It's an..." He snapped his fingers. "An... RBC unit, right?"

"That is correct, darlin'." Gloria nodded, eagerly rubbing her hands together. "We've been poolin' up our spare change for some time, now."

"I knew you'd know it!" Hugh smiled and patted Danny on the back.

"We've been looking forward to this since I was in Kindergarten." Kat stared at the radio, chewing at her lip. "This baby's gonna be what we use to listen in on the Martians."

"The... Martians?" Danny frowned and turned back toward them. "I hate to break it to you, but according to the latest scientific observations, the surface of Mars has been dead for millions and millions of years—at least." He shrugged. "The only thing you'd be likely to pick up from that dusty old rock is radioactive interference."

"Unless," Pierre said, tapping his own head, "ze Martians, zey are living in ze canals, yes?"

"I'm afraid not, Pierre." Danny shook his head. "The canals of Mars are a myth—"

"Or a cover-up by our government!" Gloria barked. "Trying to hide the truth from the people. Like always!"

"Unfortunately, Gloria," Danny said, "the effect is simply an optical illusion created when using low-quality telescopes. If you'd like to know the science behind it—"

"Ze Venusians, then!" Pierre huffed. "Or ze Mercurials."

"Or moon men!" Hugh nodded.

"Or the moon men." Kat agreed, then gestured to a nearby workable with a small radio on top. "Now, this is where you'll be sitting. I've built a basic quartz IMP unit to get you started, all you have to do is—"

"Well golly!" Danny whistled, walking over and running his fingers across the handmade radio. "It's been a long time since I've seen one of these—I made one just like it when I was in the Adventure Scouts!" The boy paused, then turned around with a frown. "But I'm afraid that there's been some sort of a misunderstanding. Unfortunately, I'm not here to join the EARS."

"You're not?" everyone asked at the same time.

"No." He shrugged. "But I am here seeking a very important piece of information that I think you all might be able to help me with. You see, I'm looking for a girl—"

"Sacré bleu!" Pierre gasped. "A missing persons case!"

"A kidnapping!" Kat immediately began to pace, stroking at her chin.

"Or arrested, hidden away by the government in one of their secret cells!" Gloria placed her hand over her heart. "That poor darling…"

"Or maybe she was eaten!" Hugh shivered. "By the creature…"

"Creature?" Danny asked, skeptical. "What creature?"

"You haven't heard the rumors?" Hugh asked. "Up at camp?"

"No." The young detective shook his head. "I can't say that I have."

"Over the past week, a bunch of campers up there got spooked," Kat said. "Claimed that something was making lots of noise out in the bushes and trees. Pretty much everyone skedaddled."

"Zis is right," Pierre confirmed. "And while ze campers claimed zat ze culprit was a greaser boy causing trouble, we believe—"

"It's the Sasquatch!" Gloria's eyes went wide. "A deadly swamp ape roaming the American marshlands. Teeth like razor blades!"

"Enormous feet!" Pierre cried out, curling his fingertips. "And claws like daggers!"

"Surely you jest?" Danny said, scanning their faces, mouth pushed to the side. "If all of the witnesses said that it was just a juvenile delinquent, then what cause is there to doubt it?"

"I suppose," Pierre sneered, "zis, too, is a possibility, yes."

"Well I think I know just the greaser. And I'm inclined to agree with their conclusion." Danny reached down to his ribs, feeling the sting of the bruises from the night before. "But I'm afraid that you have it all wrong; There's nothing so serious as a kidnapping—I was just hoping that in all your scanning of the airwaves, you'd heard about a party this morning. I just want to find a girl that I met last night, that's all."

"Ah! A matter of ze heart…" Pierre nodded knowingly, twisting at his mustache. "What could be more serious zan zat?"

"Is that all?" Kat rolled her eyes. "Well, at least it'll be a good test for the versatility of our new network. Society? Gather up."

"New network?" Danny raised an eyebrow.

"Pierre," Kat said, pointing to a metal panel on the wall, "make sure emergency channels are clear. Hugh, switch the system over to twenty-seven megahertz. Gloria, grab me the new mic. I'll jump onto the eleven meter band. Good? Good. Break!"

Kat jumped into a rolling chair and slid over to the RBC unit while Gloria and Hugh dashed to opposite sides of the clubhouse. Pierre ran to a large panel on the wall, slipped a pair of headphones on, then began to twist a dial back-and-forth.

"The eleven meter band?" Danny frowned. "I thought that was for industrial, scientific, and medical services—"

"And some remote control devices!" Hugh chimed in, securing the last wire and closing up a large metal panel.

"Correct, Hugh." Kat gave him a proud nod. "But at this time of day, that whole part of the spectrum is clear of any real interference."

"Clear for what?" Danny crossed his arms, intrigued.

Pierre took his headphones off. "Emergency channels are open."

"Might we try Wheels first?" Gloria shuffled

over to the radio. "That sweet old man is almost always tuned in, and he's got a brand new IMP that should have a clear signal no matter where he is."

"Gloria, you're incorrigible." Kat smiled, then cleared her throat and leaned down into the microphone. She depressed the broadcasting lever. "Break one-one for Wheels, this is Pipsqueak with a hot request from HQ. Do you copy?"

KSSSSHK! a brief burst of static came through the speaker, followed by a strong voice with a heavy Northern accent.

"Copy, ten-four, this is Wheels. Whatcha need?"

"Is that Ed Pearce, the milkman? Wouldn't he be in the middle of his route at the moment?" Danny asked. All of the EARS turned toward him and grinned. His eyes went wide. "Of course! A portable, electronic radio transceiver inside of his delivery truck. That's how you always seem to know what's happening in Bonnifield!"

"He's just the start." Kat winked and turned back to the microphone. "Wheels, what's your ten-twenty?"

"Out near the old mill." *KSSSSHK!* "What's the word?"

Gloria leaned in. "Have you seen anythin' around town this mornin', you sweet dove? Parties, shindigs, hoedowns?"

"'Fraid not, young lady!" Pearce chuckled. "Just a quiet morning on my end. Might wanna check with Buoy, haven't been to the East side yet. Over."

"Ten-four."

"A citizen's band radio network?" Danny frowned. "I thought those were illegal."

"Just because something's not legal, doesn't make it wrong, darling." Gloria reached out and pinched his cheek. "You really should loosen up a little, son."

"Break one-one, Pipsqueak to Buoy, Pipsqueak to Buoy, copy?"

"Indeed, I copy." A sophisticated voice came through loud and clear. "Though do I wish that you had not broken my serenity, you know how I enjoy my quiet morning contemplation."

"Giuseppe DeCicco!" Danny shook his head. "The ferry captain!"

"Apologies, Buoy! But we were wondering if—"

"I heard. However, the unfortunate reality is that the portside of old Stargaze has been caught up in a patch of seaweed all morning. I'm stuck South-east of Holiday Island, so all I've seen today is quite a bit of fog."

"Ten-four, Buoy, hope you get out soon. Over.

Treetop, you on?"

"All I've seen this morning," a woman's voice said on the other side, "is a nest of baby eaglets hatching. Over."

"Copy." Kat frowned and depressed the lever once more. "Anyone else on this morning? Anybody read?"

"Come again?" A muffled voice came through, partially obscured by loud background noise. "Oculus, here. Got a ten-one, can't hear a thing."

"Ten-one?" Danny asked.

"Receiving poorly." Kat nodded. "That means there's some kind of a distortion or noise on his end."

"Noise?" Danny jumped in and leaned down, pushing the call lever himself. "What's going on, Oculus? Where are you?"

"There's, well, some kind of a shindig down here in Harper's Cove. Buncha strange kids, weird music I never heard before. I'm off until this whole thing quiets down. Over and out!"

"Of course!" Danny stood up straight, shaking his head. "The beach! What other sort of party would be on a Saturday morning?"

He spun around and dashed over to the door, swinging it open then sliding across the platform. The boy grabbed the railing and started down the ladder, but stopped and peeked his head back up over the lip.

"Thank you all!" He beamed, then quickly began to descend.

"Bon voyage, monsieur!" Pierre called out. "And bonne chance!"

In front of the barn, at the end of a long trail of scarred earth, was the smoking wreckage of a circular craft.

11   Scouting the Scene

Mary-Sue pedaled up the steep hill near the entrance to Chautauqua Park, looking forward to the wind whipping through her hair as she sped down the other side. But as she crested the peak, the girl pushed back on her breaks and came to a full stop.

On the other side of the hill, marching her direction, was a long line of Adventure Scouts in their brown uniforms, dull yellow kerchiefs, and small pointed hats, each sporting a large backpack filled to the brim with camping gear. And at the head of the line was a rigid scoutmaster.

"Excuse me, ma'am." Mary-Sue waved her down. "I was wondering if you could—"

"Scouts halt!" The woman barked out at the top of her lungs, causing the entire line to straighten up and clap their boots together. "How may the Adventure Scouts be of assistance, civilian?"

"I'm curious, ma'am," Mary-Sue said, eyes drifting down the line of kids. "When I was in Scouts, we would stay for the whole first two weeks of summer. But it looks like you're leaving camp early?"

"Right you are, civilian," the scoutmaster replied curtly.

"Is it… is it because of the vandalism incident?" Mary-Sue raised an eyebrow. "The one I read about this morning in *The Gazette*?"

"Right again, civilian." She gave a sharp nod. "It pains me to go, but there's no badge for dealing with juvenile delinquency, I'm afraid."

"The vandal… was a kid?" Mary-Sue slumped her shoulders.

"At twenty-two hundred hours, the troop set out for our hike around the loop." The woman frowned. "And approximately thirty minutes later we returned, having completed the full trail. However, our meticulously constructed campsites had all been vandalized—torn apart by a drunken teenage hoodlum."

"That's terrible. Though…" Mary-Sue cocked her head to the side. "I thought the police blotter said there were no suspects?"

"Hmph!" The scoutmaster turned her nose up. "That boy might have fooled the police, but he can't fool me. I know a bad seed when I see one, and that juvenile delinquent needs more than a little discipline. All of this morning…" She paused, looking back over her shoulder down the line of increasingly antsy children, then lowered her voice. "He filled my Scouts' heads wild stories to get them riled up, to misbehave and—"

"What sort of stories?" Mary-Sue interrupted, eyes narrowing.

"Some fantastical nonsense." The scoutmaster rolled her eyes with a sigh. "Monsters and other science-fiction stuff."

"Monsters?" A chill ran down her spine. "What did they look like?"

"I can assure you, civilian," the woman said with a frown, "the only monster at that campsite is—"

"Big and hairy like an ape!" A Scout chirped out near the front of the line. "But with a space helmet!"

"Darryl!" The scoutmaster whipped her head back around. "Now, I said no more of that—"

"No, it was eight feet tall and made of metal!" A girl called out.

"Nuh-uh!" A boy yelled, giving her a shove. "It had big claws and its brain was on the outside!"

"No way!" Another whined. "It was scaly like a lizard!"

"No, it looked just like us, only different!"

"It was a crawling eye!"

"It was invisible!"

The entire line of Adventure Scouts quickly

broke out into chaos, all of the kids arguing, wrestling, and hitting each other.

"Atten-tion!" The scoutmaster yelled out at the top of her lungs, but nobody seemed to pay attention. She broke from formation and ran back to the line, grabbing two of the closest Scouts by their collars and pulling them apart.

"Cut this nonsense out right this minute!" she growled, struggling to keep the kids from swinging at each other.

"Is he still there?" Mary-Sue asked over the din. "The delinquent?"

"Indeed he is, civilian." The woman hoisted one of the kids over her shoulder and slipped the other under her arm. "And probably patting his own back about getting the entire campgrounds to himself."

The Scout under her arm opened his mouth then bit down hard on the scoutmaster's wrist, causing her to let go. The boy dashed away and the woman chased after, the other Scout bouncing on her shoulder.

"Why you little—"

"I'm sorry if I caused you any trouble!" Mary-Sue called out, failing to suppress her giggle. She gripped the handlebars tight, then pushed off on her bicycle. "Thanks for your help!"

"You're welcome!" A little girl called out, waving after.

Mary-Sue waved back, then sped down the hill and through the park entrance. She pedaled down the long, winding road beneath the dense canopy of Spanish moss hanging from old-growth trees. She zoomed past the picnic shelters, past the historic log cabin, and past the park ranger's looming watchtower.

She tensed her body as the pavement turned to gravel, then raced up the hill at the very end of the park, coming to a stop at the sign for Camp Chautauqua. Beyond was a large, circular clearing surrounded by spruce trees, with a dozen landscaped campsites around a central garden.

Not a single person was in sight, but on the near side of the clearing was a lone pup tent. Next to it was an old black-and-chrome motorcycle glinting in the late morning sun.

"H—hello?" Mary-Sue called out, tentative. "Is anybody there?"

CLANG-K! From the other side of the motorcycle, a wrench bounced to the ground. It was followed by a grunt, then the scuffling of boots on gravel. After a moment, a figure stood up, emerging in a sun-soaked cloud of dust.

It was a young Asian man, nearly six feet tall with straight, dark hair greased up into a windswept pompadour. He had a deep purple bruise across his sharp, left cheekbone and an unlit cigarette hung from between his lips. The left sleeve of his grease-stained t-shirt was rolled up to hold a pack of cigarettes, showing off a tattoo on his muscular arm.

He had the distinct look and swagger of a greaser, the sort of lawless, devil-may-care teenager that she had been warned to avoid countless times in films and on television. Rebels who race the wind on wheels, traveling from town to town without a thought or care for anyone else in the world. A lone wolf, living on the edge of danger.

"Excuse me, sir—"

"Sir was my pop." The boy turned his disaffected gaze away, wiping the glistening beads of sweat from his brow. "My name's Ace."

"Hello, Ace." Mary-Sue hopped down from her bicycle and extended her hand. "My name is Mary-Sue Welles, I'm with *The Britannica Junior Detectives*. I was hoping to ask you—"

"Detectives?" Ace tensed up, then took a step back and narrowed his eyes. "I ain't got nothin' to say to no pig I ain't already said."

"Pig?" Mary-Sue shook her head. "What do

you mean?"

Ace studied her face for a moment, then let his eyes drift down to her pastel bicycle. He relaxed his shoulders, then pulled an old Zippo lighter out from his jeans and flicked it on, igniting the tobacco at the end of his cigarette.

"Small town cops recruitin' kids now?" Ace slipped the lighter back into his pocket.

"I'm not a kid—I'm sixteen," she lied, straightening up as tall as she could. "And I'm not with the police; *The Britannica Junior Detectives* are an independent investigation agency."

"Sure, kid." Ace turned his attention away from her, wandering over to a nearby picnic table. He pulled a rolled-up magazine out from his rear pocket, hopped up onto the table, and laid down on his back, opening the dog-eared periodical.

"No, really," she said, flipping her kickstand down and taking a step toward him. "We specialize in different types of cases than the police do."

"Yea?" The boy asked idly, flipping through the magazine.

"Yes." Mary-Sue marched up next to him and planted her feet as the boy began to read. "The sort that nobody else will believe."

Ace paused, then flicked his eyes up to hers. He

slowly sat back up, curling the magazine into a tight roll, then pulled the cigarette out from between his lips.

"Okay, Red," he said, eyes drifting to her auburn hair. "Talk."

"I spoke with the Adventure Scouts." Mary-Sue pointed back to the entrance of the park. "They said that you saw something out here, in the woods. I was hoping to receive your account for a case."

"Case?" The greaser eyed her with suspicion, taking a long drag and letting the smoke tumble out from his mouth. "What's it about?"

"A monster." She narrowed her eyes. "My first witness said he saw a horrible mutant out in the swamp. My second said he was being followed in the same area. At first, I thought it was a man transformed by some atomic experiment gone awry, but now I'm keeping an open mind."

"You got the right idea, Red." He studied the girl for a moment, then hopped down from the table. "But you got the wrong monster."

"Oh?" She looked him right in the eyes.

Ace nodded and handed his magazine over to Mary-Sue. She stared at him as she unfurled it, then glanced down to the cover. The illustration depicted a burning farmstead, bright orange flames cutting through cool blue night. In front of the barn, at the end of a long trail of scarred earth, was the smoking wreckage of a circular craft. And directly at the center of the cover was a terrifying green monster with massive, black eyes.

She looked at the title of the magazine. It read:

SIGHT MAGAZINE

TRUE STORIES OF THE WEIRD AND THE MYSTERIOUS

May 1959
35¢

"True stories?" Mary-Sue raised an eyebrow.

"Ripped straight from the headlines, every word." Ace nodded and shoved his hands into his pockets. "See, this here's the only place printin' the truth anymore—saucers, psychics, Ouija…" He shrugged. "You name it, they tell ya straight."

Mary-Sue looked back down at the cover. Listed along one side were a dozen headlines teasing fantastic articles within, each purporting to be true—from Biblical prophecies to zombies to time travel. And at the very bottom, it read:

THE TRUTH ABOUT ROSWELL
A SAUCER, A FARMER, AND "LITTLE GREEN MEN"

"Wait…" She shook her head. "You mean to tell me… you saw—"

Ace reached out and tapped at the creature's gaunt, blank face. At its empty, black eyes—just like the ones that Dale Brown had described. The eyes of an extraterrestrial being.

"That." Ace said, deadly serious. "I saw that."

12   # Beach Blanket Bohemians

A blue Volkswagen bus sat at the entrance to Harper's Cove. On the scrubby ground in front of it were two teenagers with long hair, unkempt beards and wrinkled clothing. They were reading tattered books and smoking funny-smelling cigarettes.

Unusual, discordant music drifted over the sand dunes beyond. The avant-garde melody was precisely what Danny had always imagined '*free jazz*' to be. Of course, the boy had never listened to such racket himself—that sort of noise was exclusive to the radical set. The anti-authoritarians. The disillusioned. The beatniks.

"Salutations!" Danny cleared his throat. "I'm, uh, here for the party."

"Eh?" The first boy looked up, sleepily. "Right on, man."

"I hope that it's okay," Danny said, "but I don't have an invitation."

"No need, daddy-o," the second boy cooed without looking up. "All you gotta bring is an open heart and an open mind."

Danny gave the two boys a curt nod, then wheeled his bicycle past them toward the quaint, red lighthouse at the entrance to the cove. As he descended the path through the dunes, the boy spotted a large bush. He paused, glanced over his shoulders, then wheeled his bicycle behind it.

He quickly slipped his cardigan off, folded it neatly, and placed it on the seat, then unbuttoned his sleeves and rolled them up as he continued down the path past the final dune to the beach beyond.

The scene could hardly be called a party at all. Sitting near a bonfire at the surf were a dozen teenagers, none of whom Danny recognized, playing an eclectic variety of musical instruments. To his right, a smaller group sat with paper and charcoal in hand, sketching a young woman posing in front of them with her back arched. To his left, another small circle of teenagers were gathered, absorbed in a spirited discussion of politics.

On the far side of the cove were a half-dozen more teenagers, sitting on blankets, driftwood, or the sand itself. All were enraptured by a girl standing in front of them, reading from a booklet in her hand. Danny was drawn unconsciously toward the performance, and as he approached he realized that she was the one that he was searching for—the girl from the drive-in.

"...and if the absence of sunlight has got you down, then you'll have a blast with our new line of soft-as-sable blushes, transforming your pale, languid skin into a sun-kissed vision for that recently-emerged-from-the-shelter glow. Radiation burns? No problem—with our new foundation's breakthrough scientific formula, you can smooth those pesky complexion flaws out with our complimentary beauty puff!"

A smattering of chuckles came from the crowd.

"Competition from neighboring tribes of survivors threatening your love life? Bring those lashes out with our magic mascara's patented spiral brush, separating and darkening each individual lash. All of your hair singed off in the big boom? No need to fret! Our line of false lashes look and feel exactly like yours used to—only without the pesky upkeep!" The girl glanced up from her paper to look around the crowd, then stopped as she locked eyes with Danny. A sly smile pulled at the edge of her lips. "Your eyes burn out of your skull? Skin melt over your face? Birth defects start you out without any eyes at all? Don't you fret—we've got you covered, too. Our new easy-on, easy-off false eye-appliances fool even the most discerning man—especially if he's using them, too!"

All of the other onlookers began to snicker and laugh.

"So celebrate your survival with a luminous, glowing radiance—just not *that kind* of radiance." She shut the booklet. "So remember: buy, buy, buy Containment Cosmetics today for a brighter to-morrow!"

She pulled her eyes back to the crowd and gave a short bow. Danny reached his hands out to applaud, but paused when he was met by a soft *CLICK-click! CLICK-click!* as the rest of the audience simply snapped.

"That one really had some gas, huh?" A tall, lanky boy with a scruffy goatee stood up from the crowd and took the girl's place. She stepped away from the makeshift stage and walked around the crowd to Danny's side.

"I guess..." Her eyes flicked up to his. "You solved the riddle."

"Yes." Danny looked down at the booklet in her hands. "Kerouac."

"Good." She raised her eyebrows. "So... you fig-ured out who I am?"

"Yes." He nodded, eyes narrowing. "A beat."

"If you gotta put a label on it, sure." She

shrugged, then turned and began to walk toward the far end of the cove where large, algae-speckled boulders were piled high against the rocky cliffs. "Yet you still came?"

Danny watched her go for a moment, then jogged to catch up.

"That piece back there," he said, reaching her side as she climbed up onto the first boulder. "That... poem, I suppose. How can you be so light-hearted about such a dark subject?"

"How can you be so serious?" She pulled herself to her feet, looking down at him. "It's absurd, don't you think? That we're all supposed to live our lives as if nothing is wrong? As if we don't know that at any moment, it could all be gone? *Ker-boom-boom.*"

Danny scaled the boulder as she continued to climb, leading them up and around the dense colonies of mollusks to the rocky cliff above. At the very end of the bluff she sat down, dangling her legs out over the edge of the water. The boy pulled himself up, hesitated, then sat down beside her on the narrow ledge, their bodies pressed together.

"I'm Violet," she said after a moment, gazing off over the calm water.

"Pleased to meet you." Danny reached out for a handshake. "Danny Oxford."

Violet chuckled and rolled her eyes, then returned the gesture.

"I've heard." She allowed her fingers to linger for a moment, then slipped her hand away from his. "Or... is that Danny Britannica, *The All-American Boy*?"

"Whichever you prefer." He shrugged, cheeks flushing crimson. He pulled his eyes away from her and looked back down to the beach. "You know, I've never been to a beatnik party before. Or, uh, whatever it is that you prefer to call yourselves."

"I'm shocked." She laughed.

"At the entrance, those two boys..." Danny frowned. "They... were smoking drugs, weren't they?"

"Nah." Violet shook her head. "Despite what the media says, beats don't mess with smack." She shrugged. "Probably just grass."

"It didn't smell like grass," he said.

"No," she laughed, "I mean, tea-sticks."

"Tea-sticks?" He cocked his head to the side.

"Yeah, y'know." She unzipped her purse and reached inside, pulling a hand-rolled cigarette out. "Dope. Ditchweed. Marihuana."

"O—oh..." Danny twisted his mouth to the side, eyeing the cigarette with suspicion. "I didn't realize that wasn't drugs." He cleared his throat. "You know, amongst the other kids at school, I'm apparently known as a bit of a square."

"I bet they're a bunch of oblongs." She bumped her shoulder into his. "But what were you expecting to find, here? Gidget?"

"I suppose so, yes." He shrugged. "Surfing, volleyball, barbecue… That sort of a thing."

"Kid's stuff, daddy-o." Violet pulled her lighter out from her purse, flicked it on, and held it up, letting the flame lick the end of the cigarette. Danny breathed a sigh of relief as the toasted scent of tobacco drifted out. She took a drag, then held it out to him.

"No thank you," he said. "I don't smoke."

"In actuality," she said, snapping the lighter shut and tossing it into her purse, "the counter-culture movement is about living in the moment. Examination and the exploration of the ideas that scare you—right here, right now."

"You know," Danny said, watching the wisps of smoke curl around Violet's head, "leading studies show that tobacco is harmful to health."

"Oh yeah?" She raised an eyebrow and took another drag. "Wonder why all those cats think you're a cube?"

"Hmph." Danny huffed. "I don't see what's so

square about ensuring your future health."

"And…" She let out a long stream of smoke. "If there isn't a future?"

She offered the cigarette out once more.

"I take your meaning," he said, staring at the burning tobacco. Violet had a point. Plus, he didn't want to appear a square in front of her. After a moment, Danny reached out and took the cigarette, tentatively holding it up to his mouth.

"All you have to do is breathe."

Danny nodded, then inhaled, his throat filling with noxious, burning smoke. Immediately, he began to cough, his body attempting to hack the terrible tasting smog up from his lungs.

"So," she laughed, plucking the cigarette out from his fingers, "want your own, then, I suppose?"

"I, uh…" Danny cleared his throat and pounded at his chest. "I think I'd better leave it at just the one puff for now." He waved the smoke away from his face, eyes drifting back down to the beach. "Why haven't I seen any of you before? I thought that I knew everyone in town."

"Maybe we didn't want you to know us." She studied his grim face, then shrugged. "Or maybe we're just drifters."

"Runaways?" Danny asked.

"Nomads." She said. "Coming and going as we please."

For nearly a minute the two sat in silence, looking out over the calm water as the seagulls dipped and swayed.

"It's funny." Danny broke the silence. "All that I've ever heard about beats is that they're strung-out heroin users, or they're in violent street gangs, or they're lewd sexual offenders. But... I haven't seen anyone like that here. Mainly artists of one sort or another."

"Everyone has an agenda." Violet took a final drag, then stubbed the cigarette out on the rock beside her. "The media only claims those things because they're scared. Scared that the status quo is changing. Scared that the next generation is going to hold them accountable."

"For what?" Danny asked.

"Building a propaganda machine." The girl scowled. "Perpetuating McCarthyism. Stoking the flames of the Cold War. Cramming the nightly news with doom and gloom. Making every one of us live in fear that each moment could be our last. And—"

"May I... hold your hand?" Danny interrupted, eyes wide.

"I was beginning to think you'd never ask." Violet laughed, flicked her eyes over to his, leaned in, and pressed her lips gently against his. For a moment he tensed up, confused, but after a few more seconds he relaxed into it. His first kiss.

After what felt like a very long time, she pulled away.

"Maybe you're not such a square after all, daddy-o."

13   # Clues at Camp Chautauqua

"You're telling me an extraterrestrial is running around the woods of Bonnifield?" Mary-Sue stared at the greaser with suspicion, gripping the issue of *Sight* tightly in her hands.

"What, monsters ya buy—but Martians're a step too far?" Ace asked, his eyes narrowing. The boy took a drag of his cigarette, then pushed the smoke out from his nostrils in two long columns. "I'm just tellin' ya what I saw with my own two eyes, Red."

"Yes, of course. I'm just…" The girl's eyes were drawn to the treeline behind him, scanning across the deep shadows. "I'm just trying to remain skeptical. I've been prone to… fantastical thinking in the past."

"Yeah, well—ain't so fantastic to me." Ace gritted his teeth. "Thing's been out here every night, rustlin' around in the bushes, makin' these… I dunno, noises and such. Tore up the whole damn camp last night."

"Yes, about that…" May-Sue frowned and snapped her eyes back to the greaser. "The scoutmaster claimed that was your handiwork."

"Yeah pigs, too," he spat. "But I shut 'em up real good."

"You proved your own innocence?" She raised an eyebrow. "Beyond the shadow of a doubt?"

"That look like I did it?" Ace asked, gesturing over to his tent. There was a large tear in the side, flapping gently in the afternoon breeze. "That ain't proved it to 'em enough, though. Said I tore it up myself, makin' it look like I was innocent. So I showed 'em this."

Ace reached into his pocket and pulled out a pink ticket stub, then handed it over to Mary-Sue. It read:

"Told 'em the story to the whole first flick. Told 'em to ring the place if they ain't believe me, check the ticket number." Ace shrugged. "But I skipped out on the second flick, so they says I coulda come back to camp 'n still messed it up. So I showed 'em this."

Ace then pulled a folded-up sheet of paper out from his pocket and opened it up, holding it out for the girl to see. It was a bowling scorecard with four rounds marked out, time-stamped to ten thirty-six the previous night.

"That's almost the exact same time the police report was filed for the vandalism incident." She nodded. "It's an air-tight alibi."

"Yea, sent 'em packin' with their tails between their legs." He huffed, folding the paper up and slipping it back into his pocket. He took a final drag of his cigarette then flicked the spent butt down to the gravel. "Now ya believe me?"

"About last night, of course." Mary-Sue nodded. "But I still need to hear about your sighting to understand what you saw."

Ace reached up to his sleeve and unrolled the pack of cigarettes. He shook it back and forth until a single cigarette poked out, then put his lips around it and yanked the pack away, offering it over to Mary-Sue. The girl shook her head and Ace shrugged, placing the pack back against his sleeve and rolling it up, exposing his tattoo once again. Bad Luck.

"It was like this, see?" He pulled his lighter out

and flicked it open, holding it up to the cigarette in his mouth and taking a few short puffs. "Rolled into camp little over a week ago." He flicked the lighter shut and put it back in his pocket. "Place was hoppin', got me the last site." He looked out over the campgrounds. "But these squares, they ain't liked the looka me from the get-go."

"I see." Mary-Sue nodded with excitement. "Go on, go on."

"They're hasslin' me, so I head out yonder for a little peace 'n quiet." He gestured to the far treeline with his cigarette. "Down the hill, over the trail, find a nice little bench in an ol' graveyard. Soon the fog starts rollin' in, and I see some weird glow, out past the trees."

"A light?" Mary-Sue's eyes went wide. "A red light?"

"Yea, that's right." Ace gave her a funny look, then turned his eyes back toward the woods. "But ain't just that. Somethin' else was out there, reflectin' it back. Somethin' big. Silver. Like a damn flyin' saucer I swear to you." He took a deep drag. "So I start headin' towards it, 'cause I know I gotta be wrong, else I'm goin' nuts, when..." *KA-PKT!* Ace snapped his fingers. "All 'a sudden the thing disappears like that. And a minute later, well, that's when I seen the thing."

A chill ran down Mary-Sue's spine.

"The extraterrestrial?" she asked, holding her breath.

"Just like on that cover, there." He gestured down to the magazine. Big eyes, space suit, helmet, the works."

Ace shook his head, as if he couldn't believe his own words.

"That's fantastic." Mary-Sue shook her head. "What did you do?"

"High tail it outta there. I ain't stupid—gettin' abducted ain't on my to-do list." He turned to face her. "So I try warnin' the rest of 'em back at camp, but they think I'm nutso—first night, at least. 'Cause by the next, everyone's on edge. Hearin' noises, seein' shadows. Tell 'emselves it ain't nothin', but I see 'em packin' up. Over the next couple days they all head outta camp 'til it's just me left."

"Incredible." Mary-Sue stared down at the cover of *Sight*.

"That's where them kids come in, them Scouts. Show up yesterday. The ol' bag starts givin' me guff straight away, callin' me all sortsa things; punk, rotten, low—subterranean, see? So I shut my mouth 'n scram for the night, let 'em work it out for 'emselves. Catch a creature feature at the outdoor. The first flick, the *Emaciatin' Swarm* sequel, gets me real on edge, see? So intermission, 'gainst my better instincts, I talk with some 'a these local yokels." Ace held his cigarette out and watched it burn. "This kid gets the whole place riled up against me, crowd callin' me all kindsa things—coded language, y'know? Typical small town stuff. He throws a punch at me, I hit back. Then they kick me out, ban me. Outsiders, they say." He gave a wry laugh. "I knew what they meant."

"I'm so sorry." She pulled her eyes away from the magazine. "That's awful."

"Yea, well. Used to it." The greaser shrugged. "But I head to bowlin', kill some time 'n clear my head, cool off. Works alright. After a bit I get tired 'n head back here. But the whole place is nuts—kids yellin' and screamin', camps torn up, cops everywhere, that lady's pointin' a finger right at me. Pigs interview me, get my alibi. That's it, whole story." He turned and looked her in the eyes. "Any questions, detective?"

"A few hundred. But the first one is," she said, chewing at her lip, "why, if that thing scared all the other people away..." Her eyes flicked over to his tent. "Why did you stay?"

"Dunno 'bout these parts," the greaser said, eyes darting away, "but Martians ain't exactly common where I come from—feel like I gotta see it again, make sure I ain't nuts. Be part 'a somethin' big, yea? See this thing through."

"I see." She nodded, smiling. "I feel the exact same way, Ace."

"So... ya believe me?" He squinted. "Martian, saucer, whole deal?"

"I believe..." She took a deep breath. "A good detective must remain objective until the mystery is solved, to avoid confirmation bias. I believe proof is necessary to reach any conclusion. And I believe all outcomes are plausible. So, while I don't have the authority to officially accept your case right now, I can say I'll be recommending it to my higher-ups for the utmost consideration."

"My case?" Ace raised an eyebrow.

"Sure." The girl shrugged. "Every case needs a client—and with *The Mutant of Mercury Marsh*, that's you."

"Look," the greaser said, hooking his thumbs into the pockets of his jeans and looking off, "I ain't really got no scratch to speak of..."

"What, you mean money?" Her smile turned into a grin, dimples deep in her freckled cheeks.

"Then I guess you really aren't from around here—everyone knows *The Britannica Junior Detectives* act as a community service. We don't charge a single cent!"

"That so?"

"That's so." She nodded. "And if the case is deemed acceptable, the two of us will be back here in no time to investigate."

Mary-Sue held the magazine back out toward him.

"Read that thing back and forth a dozen times." Ace shook his head. "Keep it—ya might learn somethin', Red."

The girl looked back down to the cover. To the crashed flying saucer. To the little green man in its bright orange spacesuit. To its massive, cold, black eyes.

And then she smiled.

14   A Widening Worldview

"How can you not have an opinion about the election?" Violet asked, frowning at Danny as they walked hand-in-hand along the scrubby knoll on the water's edge. "Ike's out after this term, so it's Nixon or Rockefeller on that side—an oligarch or a McCarthyist. They say Kennedy is going to run on the other side—a wealthy socialite. It's as if the entire nation's soul is in the balance and nobody cares enough to do anything about it."

"To be honest," Danny said, "I don't know much about politics; I've always considered that to be an adult matter."

"Claimed at the drive-in you weren't a kid?" Violet gave him a look.

"W—well…" Danny frowned. "True. Yes, I do suppose it's a matter on which I'll need to educate myself. Historically, I've simply deferred to Pop's stances."

"You always do what your dad says?" The girl squinted, stopping at the top of the ridge and looking out at the late-afternoon sun over the calm ocean beyond. They had been talking for nearly four hours.

"Why wouldn't I?" Danny shrugged, feeling the warmth of the girl's fingers between his. "He's an educated man, after all—a scientist, with a lifetime of wisdom that I've yet to experience. It would make sense that his opinions would be far more informed than my own, even if I were to put in a good amount of research."

"You have to question all authority figures." She turned to look him straight in the eyes. "Governments never have our best interests at heart—only their own."

Danny frowned and shook his head. "But in a democracy—"

"There's no such thing, in practice." She pulled her hand away from his and crossed her arms. "Governments are run by small groups of men in dark rooms—never by the people. Each of those men has their agenda, their priorities which reflect their political opinions. And the more power a person gains, and the longer they're in power, the more their priorities shift away from the people and toward their agenda. It's why I question the opinions of everyone in power, regardless of their supposed intent."

"Including parents?" Danny twisted his mouth to the side. "Is that why you ran away from home—

to rebel?"

"I didn't run away from home." The girl shrugged and turned back to the sea. "I ran away from the orphanage."

"Oh." He reached up and scratched at the back of his neck. "I—I'm sorry, I didn't know. That's terrible." The boy glanced over his shoulder toward Harper's Cove, now miles behind them. "Who did you learn all of this from, anyway?"

"Lots of people—talking to anyone I could." She unzipped her purse. "And by reading as much as I could."

Violet pulled the booklet out of her back pocket and handed it over to him. It was a dozen sheets of mimeographed paper, amateurly folded and stapled together. On the front was a cartoon character with no mouth, and in large, bold letters underneath, it read:

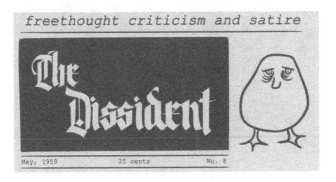

Danny flipped it open and thumbed through the pages within. There were letters from readers, editorial columns, comics, poems, and essays. He stopped at a relevant page. It read:

Kerouac Elected to White House
By P. Krassner

November 9, 1960--The meteoric rise of the Beat Generation has been nothing short of astounding. Only last year these wisened whiz-kids were political pariahs, operating out of coffee houses in San Francisco and jazz clubs in Greenwich Village.

Yesterday, they secured a historic victory over establishment candidates from both the Republican and Democratic parties when their founder and de-facto messiah, Jack Kerouac, was elected to the highest office in the land.

Only recently a decentralized movement of disparate voices and opinions, this brand new political party is now a lean and focused organization proving itself as a major power player both on Wall Street and in Washington, quickly establishing a new status quo.

While not yet sworn in, President Kerouac released a statement committing to uphold his campaign promises, though has admitted that some of the more outlandish aspects of his platform—such as rejection of materialism, exploration of alternative religions, use of mind-altering substances, and freedom of speech—may need to be put to the side in favor of more pragmatic ideas.

Campaign manager Maynard G. Krebs toasted the victory with an expensive bottle of champagne in the party's Madison Avenue headquarters, followed by lunch at Trader Vic's in the Savoy-Plaza Hotel. When reached for a quote, Krebs said:

"Look, daddy-o, I been hearin' a few squawks from the long-time cats, gettin' guff about some of the changes over the past year. But they gotta get with it, see? Hear this: in '59, I wasn't yet hip to the way things worked in the real world. I mean, I actually believed all that jazz about the human condition. Can you imagine? Craazy!"

Time will yet tell how the rise of the Beat Generation within the power structures of the United States will change our world, but the shifts are sure to be seismic. And one thing is for certain: these are the hepcats who will save the world from total annihilation.

"Okay." Danny gave a smirk and looked back. "I get it. That's pretty funny."

"No." Violet shook her head, then sat down on the grass, folding her legs together and leaning back on her hands. "It's tragic."

"What do you mean?" Danny narrowed his eyes. "It's a warning to the reader, isn't it? About not selling out your personal ideals?"

"No," the girl sighed. "It's a premonition, about what will happen to the entire radical set. They'll grow up, meet someone, and have a family. To provide? Well, you've got to compromise. Soon enough, one of us will be the one with a finger on the button—and when push comes to shove? They'll push. *Ker-boom-boom*."

"That's defeatist," he said, gently sitting down next to her.

"Wrong, again." She shook her head. "It's deterministic."

"What's the difference?" Danny plucked a piece of grass up from the ground, then tore it into smaller and smaller pieces.

"Defeatism is accepting the inevitable—giving up," Violet said. "But knowing it'll all be going up in smoke just makes the time we have more precious. Pushing back against the system, that's our chance to live in the here and now."

Danny looked out over the water as the sky began shifting to pastel shades of pink and blue.

"I have to go," he said, letting the grass blow off in the wind. "I want to stay, to spend the whole evening talking to you, but I'm afraid that I have a prior commitment which I've been putting off."

"I'm heartbroken…" Violet flicked her eyes over to his, then turned her lips up into a smile. After a moment, she leaned over and gave him a kiss on the cheek.

"Can I see you again soon?" He reached out and grasped her hand.

"No, I'm sorry," she said with a frown. "I'll be busy; see, I have this really important business meeting tomorrow, and then the whole gang is planning to fly to Ibiza for June, take some time to sail in the—"

"I get it," he laughed. "But how can I contact you? I don't even know where you're staying."

"Don't worry, detective." The girl gave him a sly look as she stood back up and brushed the dust from her slacks, then held her hand out to help him up. "This time, I'll find you."

15   A Disappointing Dinner

For the third time in two weeks, Mary-Sue found herself in the back corner of the soda fountain reading a magazine. But unlike her standard monster fare, *Sight* was non-fiction; true accounts of the stories which the mainstream press failed to cover— or perhaps, were too afraid to. The girl scanned the featured article. It read:

THE MEN IN BLACK SUITS

■ Longtime readers of Sight will be familiar with the story of WW Brazel, the hapless farmer who discovered the wreckage of the flying saucer in Roswell, New Mexico on the 14th of June, 1947. What even the most dedicated UFOlogist may not know, however, are the events which occurred nearly one month later.

On the 12th of July, three government men in black suits arrived on Brazel's doorstep and flashed their badges. Unlike his previous visitors who had come only seeking information about his incredible experience, these men had come with a story of their own—one of foil weather balloons, rubber crash-test dummies, and a grand, elaborate misunderstanding.

They had come to change the official record, to bring doubt to this innocent farmer's mind, to intimidate the man, to make him disbelieve his own eyes. To cover-up the most spectacular scientific find of the 20th century.

Since that day we have seen reports from insiders at Area 51

25

SIGHT MAGAZINE

that not only confirm Brazel's original story, but expand upon it. Rumors run rampant about tests on those extraterrestrial corpses, terrifying genetic experiments gone awry, and astounding aircraft that incorporate bizarre alien technology to surpass even the Soviet Union's most experimental prototypes.

All of this simply confirms that there is something inside that base. Something our government doesn't want us to see. And ever since Roswell, these men in black suits have plagued the people of the UFO community who look only to expose the American public to their own government's lies, secrets, and cover-ups.

These men have silenced witnesses, they've destroyed evidence, and they've crafted a systematic campaign of misinformation by posing as officials from other government agencies to gain access to the latest intelligence on UFO phenomena.

When reached for comment, Col. George P. Freeman, Pentagon spokesman for Project Bluebook, personally assured me: "No Air Force officials were present at these incidents. Whoever these men were, they acted outside of the military's official investigation into saucer sightings."

So perhaps Brazel was simply one of the lucky ones, choosing to comply with the requests of these men in black suits and change his own story—and perhaps those who refused were not so lucky.

What of dedicated UFOlogist Dr. Richard H. Pratt—missing since early last year? And what of regular Mystery in the News contributor John Sherwood—silent now six months? And what of countless readers, witnesses, and contactees who drop out from the community without a word?

And who will these dangerous men target next? Your humble editor, exposing their lies and deceptions to the world? Or maybe your favorite pen pal, found in the personals section of this very magazine? Or even, dear reader, maybe you yourself know just a little bit more than they want you to. So stay sharp, stay safe, and stay out of their hands.

—R.A.P.

Mary-Sue tried to take a sip of her strawberry malt, but was met only with the disappointing *FSSHHH!* of an empty glass. Reluctantly, she tore her eyes away from the magazine to flag Mr. Graham down for another refill, only to spot Danny dashing past the window and through the front door. *BRRNG-BRRNG!*

The boy looked around, then spotted her and quickly rushed back to her corner and hopped up onto the stool next to her.

"I'm sorry that I'm late," the boy said, short of breath. "I hadn't quite realized how far away I'd gotten."

"Are you late?" Mary-Sue looked up at the clock behind the counter, then shrugged. "I guess I lost track of time."

"As did I," Danny said, looking toward Mr. Graham, shuffling their way. "Have you ordered yet? I'm famished—I haven't eaten all day!"

"No, not—"

"Well hello there, son!" Mr. Graham smiled, his mustache spreading out over his lip. "What can I get ya? The usual—toasted cheese on rye?"

"I think it's time for a change, sir." Danny shook his head. "Perhaps something a bit more substantial is in order. Let's say..." He looked up to the menu on the wall, rapping his fingers on the edge of the counter. "A turkey club, with the works. And a side of french fries!"

"My, we are hungry today!" The man winked, then turned to Mary-Sue. "And for you, little miss?"

"I'll just take another refill, sir." She shrugged, then turned to Danny. "As long as you're okay with me eating a few of your fries?"

"Please!" Danny nodded. "Happy to share."

"Well okay, then! Comin' right up." Mr. Graham nodded and turned away, shuffling off into the kitchen with a jaunty whistle.

"Too absorbed in your mystery to remember you had to eat?" Mary-Sue cocked an eyebrow.

"Mystery?" Danny cocked his head to the side.

"Your mysterious crush from the drive-in." She rolled her eyes. "Or have you already moved on to someone else?"

"Oh! Yes, yes of course. The answer was rather simple," he chuckled. "Despite your cynicism, the EARS were able to help. They've made this wild new citizen's band radio network across the whole town and have eyes on any location at any time."

"You didn't answer the question." Mary-Sue raised her eyebrows. "Who was the girl?"

"A, uh…" Danny gave her a bashful look. "A

beatnik."

Mary-Sue laughed, then realized that he was serious.

"Aren't beats a little, I don't know, off-center for you?" She asked. "I would have thought Sondra was more your type."

"Sondra's swell and all," Danny said, shrugging, "but Violet, well…" He stared out through the window. "She's worldly. And political. Whip-smart. Funny. Challenging!"

"And pretty?" Mary-Sue pressed her cheek into her hand.

"E—enough about me." Danny's face began to flush crimson and he turned back toward her. "We've put it off long enough. Right now, I want to hear all about your secret project. The floor is yours."

"I thought you'd never say so!" She perked up, then reached down into her bookbag. "It's a good thing we waited, because this very afternoon I uncovered some new, exciting leads."

"Oh boy!" Danny grinned.

The girl pulled her casefile out and slapped it down onto the counter. Danny's eyes scanned across the bubble letters.

"Mutant…?" The boy asked, giving her a funny look, then flipped the folder open to see her gruesome illustration of the creature.

"Well..." She flipped it over to the next page, containing drawings of flying saucers. "I'm not so certain it is a mutant, now. My newest witness believes he saw an extraterrestrial—a Martian, he says. But I'm trying to remain objective until it's solved— if we take the case, that is."

"A Martian?" Danny scrunched his face up, then eyed the magazine on the counter, open to an illustration of an extraterrestrial corpse laying back on an operating table. "Like, from one of your fantasy magazines?"

"No, not this time!" Mary-Sue grabbed the issue of *Sight* and handed it over to him. "*True Stories of the Weird and the Mysterious*—everything in there is real! That's what he saw, lurking in the woods of Bonnifield."

"I see." Danny flipped the magazine shut and studied its cover with a skeptical look, then glanced back up. "You know, I've heard about this case, too."

"You have?" The girl's eyes went wide and she leaned in.

"That's right." He placed the magazine back down onto the counter. "The EARS were talking about this morning. They called it a 'Sasquatch.' And what did you call them, again? Crackpots, was it?"

"W—well," Mary-Sue stammered, "that doesn't mean there isn't any truth to it, just because they believe it, too."

"They also mentioned that they were planning on using a terrestrial radio to listen in on Martians." Danny sighed, tapping at the cover. "I'm afraid that this a conspiracy rag, Mary-Sue. Nothing more."

"But *Sight* isn't where it came from." She pushed her lips to the side. "Back on prom night, do you remember when Dale Brown asked to use the telephone, right over here?"

"Sure." Danny raised an eyebrow.

"Well, he was filing a police report. He had just been out in Mercury Marsh and had seen a monster with huge, black eyes."

"I wouldn't rely on the testimony of Dale Brown if I were you."

"I get it—not the most reliable witness." Mary-Sue turned her hands out. "But then Prescott saw something in the same area as well!"

"Prescott…"

"I know, I know…" The girl shook her head. "But now, I have a third witness who swears he saw a Martian and a flying saucer in—"

"Flying saucers don't exist." The boy crossed his arms. "I've looked into this myself; despite the thousands of reports, Project Bluebook found no compelling evidence that isn't better explained as misidentifications of natural phenomena. Lenticular clouds, soaring birds, lights reflecting off of cockpits, and over-enthusiastic hoaxers. No—I'm afraid that UFOs are nothing more than the product of an overactive imagination."

"You're dismissing a firsthand witness account?" Mary-Sue frowned. "When Ace was out near the old Civil War graveyard—"

"Ace?" Danny balked. "What, you mean that greaser?"

"You know him?" Mary-Sue tilted her head to the side.

"I'll say..." The boy clenched his jaw. "He assaulted me at the drive-in last night!"

"Wait." Mary-Sue frowned. "You're the one he got in a fight with?"

"So he bragged about it? Unbelievable. My ribs are still bruised!"

"No, he didn't brag," she said, "but he did say the other boy started the fight."

"Hardly!" Danny scoffed. "He harassed Sondra, he antagonized me, then he riled the whole crowd up! When he invited me to hit him, I had no choice but to comply."

"Wait, Sondra?" Mary-Sue narrowed her eyes. "So you did start the fight, over a girl? Like you abandoned your commitment to me because of a girl? Twice?"

"Abandoned? It's barely been twenty-four hours, Mary-Sue!" Danny said, taken aback. "But regardless, you shouldn't be associating with that delinquent. He's dangerous. He has no character. And, if I had to harbor a guess about your case, then I'd say that the brute made the whole thing up as some malicious prank." He slammed the folder shut. "Besides, the subject is childish, and beneath *The Britannica Junior Detectives*. If we're going to continue solving mysteries, then we should focus on grounded, factual, adult crimes—not the delusions of some greaser living out in the woods. So, no, I'm afraid that we won't be pursuing your *secret project*."

"If?" Mary-Sue narrowed her eyes. "What do you mean by—"

"I said no." The boy folded his hands. "It's my detective agency, and it's my decision."

THWUMP-THWUMP! Mr. Graham pushed through the kitchen door holding a tray of food. The man shuffled over, then placed the sandwich and french fries down in front of them.

"Now, if you'll just give me one moment," he

said, "I'll get that malt whipped up in a jiff. I know how y'all like to dip your fries in—"

"Don't bother." Mary-Sue yanked her bookbag up from the ground, then grabbed the casefile and magazine off of the counter and dropped them inside. She pulled two quarters out from her pocket, then slapped them down onto the counter, glaring at Danny. "I'm leaving."

"Mary-Sue, please! Be reasonable," Danny said, incredulous. "Surely your best friend is more trustworthy than a stranger?"

"That doesn't matter!" Mary-Sue balled her fists up tight. "There's something happening out there, something really weird, and you're too blinded by your newfound obsession with girls to realize it!" She hopped down from the stool. "So if you won't help me, then I'll just have to solve this case myself. Goodbye."

The furious girl swung her bag back over her shoulder, then stormed out through the front door. *BRRNG-BRRNG!*

16   # The Secretive Scientist

The geodesic dome over the Oxford laboratory pulsed with an eerie yellow glow, beckoning Danny around the side of the house and into the back yard. He trudged up to the keypad, punched the secret code in, and waited as the automatic door slid to the side.

The boy marched into the airlock, pushed the red button, and tapped his foot as the sterilization process commenced. After a moment, the air stopped and the interior door creaked open. Stepping into the laboratory, Danny saw his father standing at the far end wearing a rubber apron and welding goggles, holding a blowtorch up to a smooth, metal sphere.

White-hot sparks burst out in all directions and the boy instinctively threw his arms up to shield his eyes. After a few seconds, the sound from the torch faded.

"Ah, there you are!" His father said. "Just who I was hoping to see."

"Hi, Pop." Danny lowered his arms and opened his eyes, attempting to blink the bright after-image away.

"Now that you've arrived…" The man yanked his welding goggles off and placed them down onto the workstation at his side. "I could use an extra pair of hands."

"And I could use a bit of advice." Danny sighed.

"Perhaps we can help each other out at the same time." The scientist nodded knowingly and slipped his rubber gloves off. "Now, what seems to be the problem—is my boy coming to the revelation that romance is far from a straightforward, logical pursuit?"

"No." Danny shrugged. "That's going swell. It's *The Britannica Junior Detectives* that's the problem."

"I suspect," Dr. Oxford said, walking over to the lockers at Danny's side, "that the two are far more linked than you realize." He opened the nearest locker, then reached in and withdrew a yellow polyethylene suit. The scientist tossed it over one arm, then reached for another. "Balancing friendship and romance can be a tricky thing, Danny."

"I suppose." Danny twisted his mouth to the side. "But… you were a boy detective once, a long time ago."

"A lifetime ago." The man nodded as he shut the locker, handing one of the suits over to Danny. "It all began with an electric rifle—"

"I've heard this before, Pop," the boy said, yanking the zipper down and stepping into the familiar suit, "but I was just wondering… at what point did you decide to grow up and stop solving mysteries?"

"Stop?" Dr. Oxford raised his eyebrows, stepping into his suit. "No. I never stopped—I simply began to pursue mysteries of a different nature. As I grew, I found that the most intriguing questions of the universe were not human, but atomic." He zipped the front of his suit up, as did Danny. "But to answer your question, it was high school where I discovered my love of science. And speaking of…" He flipped his helmet up, then pulled the zipper closed, sealing himself into the suit. "Let's get to business."

Danny sealed his own helmet as the scientist gestured toward a large plexiglass box on a nearby table. There were two holes cut into the front, with a pair of black rubber gloves built into the chamber. A mass of tubes snaked out from the rear into an air tank on the other side.

"This cloud chamber," the scientist said, voice muffled, "is connected to that gas canister, which contains the atomized version of a crystalline compound which I've dubbed *Substance X*—until I've thought up a better name, that is." He walked over to the metal sphere, then pointed Danny toward a nearby control panel. "Your task will be to operate that console while I release this plutonium core."

"Plutonium?" Danny's eyes went wide.

"Yes, it does sound rather dangerous, doesn't it?" His father laughed and turned his hands out. "But I can assure you that the containment unit is perfectly safe. All that I require from you is to pull that red lever when I give the signal."

Danny nodded, then walked over to the panel. He looked down at the dials, buttons, and switches covering its surface. Many were labeled with rather alarming words like *gamma radiation*, *absorption rate*, and *alpha wave decay*. He looked back up to his father, who was placing the sphere inside of the chamber.

"What exactly are you building, here, Pop?"

"Despite your curious nature, despite having assisted me with many of my experiments over the years, I believe this is the first time you've taken an interest in the nature of my work," Dr. Oxford said, shutting the door and turning back to Danny. "Unfortunately, however, this time I'm afraid that the details are classified at the highest level—secret even from my own son."

Danny frowned, eyeing the small metal sphere

as his father slipped his arms into the chamber's in-built gloves. His mind wandered to Violet's words from earlier that afternoon—about the nature of power's influence, about questioning authority, and about, when the time came, who would have their finger on the button.

"Pop." He said. "I'm not quite sure that I'm comfortable with this…"

"Nonsense!" his father said, placing his fingers atop the sphere. "An experiment of this nature is necessary for the betterment of mankind."

"If…" Danny swallowed. "If you say so, sir."

"Now," the scientist said, "turn the dial marked 'release valve' all the way to the left."

Danny found the knob, then twisted it fully counter-clockwise. From the gas canister on the far side, a faint, high-pitched hiss began.

"Wonderful!" Dr. Oxford said. "Now, on my mark, pull the large red lever. Ready?"

"Ready."

"Three, two, one…" The scientist twisted the top of the metal sphere, unscrewing one half from the other. "Now!"

Danny pulled the lever and all the lights in the laboratory dimmed. The sphere immediately began to emit a strange blue glow, its particles of light dancing across the room in a frenzy of stippled light and shadow. The box slowly began to fill with a sickly yellow gas, causing the chamber to grow more and more opaque, obscuring the sphere and its light.

"P—pop?" Danny swallowed. "Is it—"

KER-TUNK! The overhead light suddenly turned back on, and all of the other lights in the laboratory began to flicker up. When Danny looked back to the chamber, the yellow gas had nearly dissipated and his father was screwing the top of the sphere back on.

"Incredible." Dr. Oxford slipped his hands out from the gloves, then turned to Danny with a wide grin. He pulled the zipper across his neck, then pushed his helmet back. "The most promising result so far!"

"What does it mean?" Danny shook his head.

"Well, I'll need to validate the results, but—"

BZZZT! a disturbing buzz rang out from the other side of the room, causing the scientist to whip around as a large television screen on the far wall blinked on, displaying a live, black-and-white image from the closed circuit camera atop their front gate.

Staring directly into it was a tall man in a black suit, hands folded behind his back. He was lit only by the bright hazard light on the top of the fence, also illuminating his dark Cadillac Impala parked at the end of the road. After a few seconds, the man turned and reached down to the keypad at his side and pushed a button. *BZZZT!*

"Curious…" Dr. Oxford furrowed his brow as he walked toward the screen. For a few seconds he studied the man, then looked back to Danny. "Are you expecting someone, son?"

"No, sir." Danny shook his head.

"When you met with Mary-Sue about her case tonight," he crossed his arms, "did she mention the Federal Bureau of Investigation?"

"No." Danny narrowed his eyes. "I don't think so."

"Hmph." The man reached up and stroked at his chin.

"Should I go and see what he wants?" Danny asked.

"Absolutely not," Dr. Oxford said tersely, turning and looking at the plutonium core. He studied the object, jaw clenched. "At this stage of my research, I can't be too careful. I think that it's best we wait for the man to leave, then send you on your way, too. I have a long night ahead of me in the lab."

Danny's eyes flicked back to the monitor, where the man was pacing back and forth in front of the gate. After a few seconds, he looked back to the camera and shook his head. He walked back to his car, got inside, and started the engine up.

"Yes, yes, good…" The scientist nodded, then turned to Danny with a forced smile. "Now—off with that radiation suit. And off to bed."

17   The Search for the Saucer

"Wake up!" Mary-Sue kicked at the leg of the picnic table where Ace was napping, hands folded contentedly behind his head. She gave a few more swift kicks until the greaser groaned, stirred, and opened his eyes, attempting to focus on her face.

"Mmh." He pressed his eyes closed, then blinked them open and sat up, rubbing at his stiff neck. "Back so soon, Red?"

"That's right," the girl said, digging through her bookbag. "I decided to accept your case."

"…you?" Ace looked around the campgrounds, then glanced back to Mary-Sue. "Thought you was comin' back with your partner?"

"Partner!" Mary-Sue spat the word. "Hardly—his ego is far too large to share the credit like that. No, I'm taking it on by myself."

"Yeah, well…" The greaser hopped down from the table, stretching his back out and twisting side-to-side. "Probably for the best ya learn that while you're young—can't nobody rely on nobody in this world, 'cept your lonesome."

"My thoughts exactly."

Mary-Sue pulled two flashlights out from her bag, then extended one to Ace. He eyed it as he pulled the pack of cigarettes out from his sleeve and slipped one between his lips, then grabbed his lighter, flicked it on, and held the flame up to the end of the cigarette.

"What's that?" he asked out of the side of his mouth.

"It's a flashlight." Mary-Sue rolled her eyes.

"Yea." He scrunched his face up, looking out at the clouds just above the treeline, the last fading sunbeams causing the edges to burn a brilliant orange against a deep blue backdrop. "But what's it gotta do with me?"

"You're going to take me out into the swamp," Mary-Sue said. "And you're going to show me where you saw the creature. Then, I'm going to solve this mystery and prove your innocence—to clear your name with the police and with the townspeople."

The greaser let out a long stream of smoke. "What—now?"

"Now."

He looked down to the flashlight, then back up to Mary-Sue.

"Clear my name?" He raised his eyebrows.

"Yes." She tightened her jaw.

Ace held his steely gaze for a moment, then reached out and took the flashlight. He studied it for a moment, getting a feel for its weight, then pushed the switch on. A bright, yellow beam shot out, and he waved the device back and forth in the air.

"Please." Mary-Sue gestured toward the woods. "Lead the way."

Ace nodded, then stepped onto the grass and began walking toward the treeline. Mary-Sue jogged to catch up to his side and together the two walked from the landscaped grass into the underbrush.

She clicked her flashlight on as they passed the treeline and scanned the beam across the forest floor, catching the edges of leaves and twigs in its soft light. The ground before them was littered with rotting logs, pine nettles, and other detritus. The way ahead was dotted with mushrooms, ferns, and scrubby bushes.

"Can you believe," Mary-Sue said, stepping over a lichen-speckled rock, "he called our mysteries childish. Childish! While he's out chasing girls— the nerve!"

Ace glanced back over his shoulder, cigarette hanging from between his lips. He narrowed his eyes and shook his head. "What?"

"My partner—or boss, or whatever." She shrugged. "He said he only wanted to solve adult crimes, as if he were some kind of a—"

"Look Red," Ace cut the girl off and turned his attention back ahead, grabbing a branch at the top of an incline, "this ain't a topic for me. I ain't your shrink, and I ain't your pal, get it?"

"Oh." Mary-Sue twisted her mouth to the side, then stopped behind him. "Yes, I see—I'm sorry."

"I just mean..." He frowned. "Let's keep it professional, yea?"

"Of course." She nodded.

The greaser led her down the steep incline with confidence, weaving around trees and brambles as if he knew the path well. For a few minutes the two navigated in silence as the last of the twilight faded, casting the woods into darkness beyond their swinging yellow beams.

"You know," Mary-Sue said as they reached the bottom of the hill, "I was reading that magazine of yours—*Sight*."

"Learn anythin'?" The boy paused and looked out into the darkness, scanning his flashlight to and fro.

"What else do you know about those men in black suits?" Mary-Sue asked. "I'd never heard of them before."

"Ah, there we are." Ace nodded toward the edge of a dirt trail, then took off in its direction. "Ever hear 'a Hopkinsville?"

"No." Mary-Sue shook her head as she ran to catch up.

"Then them guys did their job." Ace shrugged. "'Cause y'see, couple 'a years back, there's this meteor shower in Kentucky—lotsa respectable witnesses. But these folks livin' out in the sticks, the Suttons? They seen 'em, too. Yea?"

"Sure." Mary-Sue nodded as they reached the path.

"Well this one, Lucky, okay?" Ace took a left, she followed. "His dog starts yappin' up a storm, just ain't shuttin' 'er trap. So he and his buddy Billy-Ray, they head out 'n take a look, see if maybe a meteor hit nearby or somethin'." Ace hopped over a shallow ditch as the foliage began to thin. "So they follow that mutt way out there 'til they reach this clearin' in the middle 'a nowhere, when lo and behold, they see this flyin' saucer sittin' there, ramp down, little green men walkin' out."

"That's unbelievable." Mary-Sue caught up to his side. "First contact with an alien race!"

Ace stopped as they reached the edge of the

treeline, Mercury Marsh beyond. He gazed out over the wetland lit dimly by the stars above. Half a mile across, it was a sea of tall grasses and reeds dotted with large pools of water and small, boggy islands. Wisps of haze curled above the water, slowly drifting in the still night air as bullfrogs and crickets echoed off the surrounding spruce trees.

"I think it was…" Ace looked to his right, then left, then back again.

"Maybe…" Mary-Sue swung her bookbag around, then unbuckled the straps. The girl dug around inside for a moment, then withdrew her map. "Maybe this would help?"

Ace held his flashlight up to the map, tracing the path from the trail over to the old Civil War graveyard. He nodded, then took off to the left.

"You were saying?" She followed close behind. "About the saucer?"

"Yeah, well, this Billy-Ray guy, he ain't stupid," the greaser said as he parted a patch of reeds and walked into the marsh. "He sees these things, he lifts his shotgun up, 'n he blasts 'em. Well, they ain't like that one bit, obviously—chase them boys back to the house. Lucky and Billy-Ray, they board 'em-selves up with the whole family right quick."

"Golly!" Mary-Sue pushed into the grass, the

soggy ground beneath her feet gently pulling at her shoes. "Really?"

"Really," Ace grunted, nearly out of view as the reeds swung back and forth in his wake. "So these Martians try sneakin' inside—windows, chimney, vents, all 'a that. Well, these broke folks ain't got no phone, see, so three whole hours the family holds 'em off 'til Lucky makes a break for the truck. Starts it up, they all run out, pile in, head off to town to get the sheriff, right?"

"And what did he say when they arrived?" Mary-Sue asked. "Even if true, the story would certainly stretch credulity to an authority."

"Good thing this pig knows Billy-Ray, then—knows he ain't a liar. So he gathers twenty cops 'n a couple Army guys 'n they all head back out." Ace hopped over a muddy puddle and Mary-Sue followed suit. "When they get there, ain't no sign 'a them Martians. So Billy-Ray takes 'em out to that clearin' where they seen the things first. And that saucer? Gone. Buncha burnt grass where it used to be. But that whole crew? They look around, see tracks, shotgun shells, scratch marks all over the house. Tell Billy-Ray straight to his face they believe 'im. Then, local papers come out sayin' it's all true."

They pushed out of the grass and onto a muddy

bank. Ace shone his flashlight along the edge until he found a patch of grass in the middle of the water. He walked to the water's edge, sprung from the bank onto the island, then turned back and reached his hand out.

"What happened?" Mary-Sue shuffled to the edge of the bank, then leapt to Ace's side, grabbing his hand to steady herself. "How could the story be suppressed at that point?"

"That's where these men in black suits come in." The greaser turned, then jumped to the far bank. "See, few days later, black Cadillac pulls up at the house, coupla G-Men get out, insist on doin' a new search. Coupla minutes later they come back around, say they ain't seen nothin', call 'em a buncha drunks." Ace waited as Mary-Sue jumped next to him. "But the thing is, see, Ma Sutton? Teetotaler. Ain't let Lucky ever have no booze in the house—not on her watch. So they leave, and a coupla days later, AP runs a big story—calls 'em a buncha drunk rednecks, says they saw some owls 'n let their imagination go nuts. Suddenly the whole thing's a joke." He shook his head. "Owls! Ya believe that?"

He looked down to the map in Mary-Sue's hand, then back up to the treeline at the lagoon's edge. The greaser tilted his head sideways, nodded, then took off into the next patch of grass.

"Well, it's a swell story," Mary-Sue said, following him, "but before I believed it, I'd have to read the police report and look at the newspaper accounts. See if there wasn't some element lost to sensationalism. Put the pieces together for myself, rather than just blindly believing—"

"Here we are," Ace cut her off as the two stepped out from the grass. Mary-Sue raised her flashlight up, then took a sharp breath.

Before them was a crumbling gateway, its stone wall overtaken by a dark, green ivy which snaked up and around the cast-iron gate beneath a curved sign reading 'Cemetery.' Beyond it, a dense layer of fog obscured the two or three dozen headstones still standing, their inscriptions long since faded. Another handful of markers had broken apart or fallen to the ground, caked with thick patches of brown moss. At the far end were two large mausoleums, half-sunken into the bog.

Ace slowly moved the beam of his flashlight across the clearing, the shadows of the graves dancing back and forth as it crept along. Finally, he stopped the light at the far end near a stone burial vault.

"There," he said, voice low. "I saw it there."

Mary-Sue nodded, and without a thought found herself drifting past the gate. The girl wandered between the gravestones, drawn to the vault on the other side, barely conscious of her own steps.

"Around midnight, maybe a bit after," Ace murmured, remaining on the outside of the gate. "Moon up high, frogs croakin' out. Sittin' on that tomb, havin' a smoke. Peace and quiet—I thought. That's when I seen the thing, through the fog."

"Where?" She turned toward her companion, but despite only being a dozen yards away, the boy had nearly faded from view in the fog. The fuzzy halo of light around his dark silhouette was all that she could make out. "From the lagoon?"

"You got it," he whispered. "One look at them black eyes, orange space suit, 'n I hop jump down from that grave 'n take off this way."

Mary-Sue turned back to the vault, scanning her flashlight across the ground for clues; footprints, burn marks, anything at all out of place. She stopped as something was caught in the edge of her beam, then crouched down. Stuck in a patch of damp grass was a soggy cigarette butt.

"Checks out," she mumbled to herself, then stood up and swung her flashlight toward the lagoon, its beam pointed down to the muddy ground.

And there, just at the edge of the light, was a shallow impression in the mud. Mary-Sue walked toward it, and as she approached she noticed one more behind it. Then third, and fourth. Footprints—and they were fresh, not yet faded by the night tide.

A chill ran down the girl's spine and she swiveled around, squinting into the darkness in every direction. Seeing nobody, Mary-Sue crouched down and unbuckled the straps on her bookbag. She grabbed her small Brownie camera and pulled it out, then rooted around inside until she found a fresh flashbulb. She screwed it in, wound the film, then put her eye up to the viewfinder and pushed the shutter. *KA-PIFF!*

"What's goin' on?" Ace growled from the haze.

"It's just my camera," she said. "No need to be frightened."

Mary-Sue stood back up, legs quivering, and pulled her bag around. The girl slipped the camera's strap around her neck, then hoisted out the large, green box which Dr. Oxford had let her borrow that morning—the Geiger counter. She twisted the knob to the right and the needle on the dial immediately sprung to life. *TK-tk-TK-tk-TK-tk!*

Something in the area was radioactive. Or someone.

She forced herself to take a step forward, following the tracks. Then another, and another, until she reached the crumbling stone wall along the far side of the cemetery. The counter's needle began to jump back and forth, faster and faster.

"Red..." Ace's voice wavered from behind her, but Mary-Sue barely heard him. She stepped over the stone wall, her eyes drifting beyond the tracks and up to the treeline at the bank of the lagoon. And there, not thirty yards away, was an eerie, red glow, reflecting off of a huge, metallic disc. It looked exactly like a flying saucer.

Mary-Sue swung her bag back around and jammed her hand inside, desperately searching for a fresh flashbulb.

"Red!" Ace barked out. "We gotta go. Now!"

Mary-Sue tore her eyes away from the craft, whipping back around to look at the boy. Instead, her eyes were drawn to the campsite at the top of the hill where twin, yellow beams cut through the dense fog, scanning through the trees.

"I'm goin'!" Ace cried out, then began to run.

Mary-Sue looked back to the saucer, back to the campsite, then took off after Ace, dashing through the cemetery and following the sounds of his footsteps splashing through the water. The girl tripped and stumbled forward, trying to get to the hill as quickly as possible. When she finally arrived at its base, Ace was standing there, waiting for her.

"I saw it!" Mary-Sue ran up and grabbed his arm. "Over the water, I saw the red light. I saw the saucer! It's real!"

"Yea, I know!" The boy hissed, then gestured back over his shoulder. "But we got more important things to worry 'bout right now."

Ace grabbed her hand and took off up the hill, scrambling between the branches and thorns, scratching at their arms. But as they got closer to the glowing treeline he slowed his pace to a crawl, looked Mary-Sue right in the eyes, then put a finger up to his lips. He turned back to the camp, pulling her along as he crept to the trunk of a large tree, then released her arm.

The two pressed their backs up against the bark, breathing hard, and exchanged a terrified look. After a moment they each turned and peered out around the side of the tree. There, parked right in the middle of the campsite, was a jet-black Cadillac.

The twin headlights were pointed directly at Ace's motorcycle, and a shadowy figure moved about in their glow. As Mary-Sue's eyes adjusted to the light, she realized that she recognized the man as the government agent from Graham's Soda Fountain.

"Just pigs," Ace sighed, letting a breath out.

"No, he's not with the police, he's with the FBI." Mary-Sue shook her head, keeping her voice low. "I've seen him before—questioning people about what's going on up here."

"You don't think..." Ace's eyes went wide. "He's... one of them?"

"The... men in black suits?" Mary-Sue gulped. "If he's investigating the sightings, then he would be following up on rumors..."

"Them other campers musta reported it." Ace nodded, then looked around the tree once more.

"Yes." Mary-Sue's breathing was shallow. "Maybe he already knows about the saucer, about the extraterrestrial. Maybe... maybe he already knows about us."

"Now he does, anyway." Ace pulled himself back around, nodding out to the clearing.

Mary-Sue slowly leaned around the trunk to see Ford standing next to her bicycle, looking it up and down. She snapped back, eyes wide.

"Do you think," she said, pressing her back into the tree, "there's any chance that he could be here for another reason? Is there anyone looking for you, or… or—"

"Nah." Ace shook his head, eyes flicking to hers. "Ain't nobody cares 'bout me."

KA-TAM! the car door slammed shut behind them. A few moments later the Cadillac's engine roared to life, then the car pulled around the gravel circle, headlights slowly swinging through trees on either side of the two terrified teenagers. After a few seconds idling at the exit, it drove off down the hill and out through the park.

"It…" Ace broke the silence after a few seconds, stepping away from the trunk. "It ain't safe for me camp here no more."

"W—what are you going to do?" Mary-Sue pushed herself off from the trunk and turned to face him. "Skip town?"

"Nah," the boy murmured, staring off after the car. "I can find some place to crash—but I gotta know what's goin' on here."

"Me, too." Mary-Sue nodded, then reached into her bag. She pulled a walkie-talkie out and handed it over to Ace. "In the morning, we can use these to meet up in the marsh and solve this thing once and for all."

"Got it." Ace took the radio without hesitation. Mary-Sue extended her hand. "Partners?"

He looked her directly in the eyes and gave a firm shake. "Partners."

18   # Ignoring the Inevitable

Danny paced back and forth across his bedroom in a pair of striped pajamas, brow firmly knit. The young detective was attempting to avoid looking at the beige folder sitting on his desk—the one with a large, red *Top Secret* stamped across the front. The one which he had discovered in a box of his father's documents earlier that morning.

Instead, he stopped at his bedside table and looked through the stack of magazines before him. On the very top was *The Dissident*, Violet's radical, social-satire "zine" which the boy had stayed up late reading all the way through. Beneath that was *Nuts*, a humorous kids magazine with pop-culture parodies and off-color comic strips. Finally, there was *Them!*, a politically-inclined periodical to which his father subscribed.

On the front, it promised a shocking expose on the beat generation, above a smaller headline about the newly-discovered Van Allen radiation belt at the edge of space. Danny grabbed the magazine, hopped onto his bed, then flipped it open to the featured story. It read:

THE BEATS' WEIRD, WAY-OUT WORLD

by Aldous O'Neill

Unlike their fastidious and pragmatic forebears in the Roaring Twenties, the impossible hipsters of the Beat Generation give off a calculated obstinance, a rebellion carefully crafted to offend all who choose to live within our civilized society—whom they consider to be simply tragic squares.

Yet your average Beat hails from a well-off, middle-class family in middle-America. They take one look at the wealth of abundance their parents worked so arduously to provide and find the comforts of a coddled life too monstrous to comprehend.

The unwashed Beat withdraws from their community, turning to intravenous drug use and gang violence to get their fix of what they consider to be a real-world struggle. The fraud constructs an impersonation of the neurotic recluse, the nihilistic artist they so desperately wish to be, but lack the legitimate passion to embody.

They strive at all times for some authenticity just out of reach, they worship at the feet of the junkie and the jazz musician, they yearn for skid row, the roach-infested hobo jungle which so utterly represents the ideal of these self-imposed outcasts.

Then, brought to a willful hysteria by their dependence on dope and destruction, by their coffeehouse schemes of political anarchy, by their barbarous, bare-knuckle preposterations, the vulgar Beat must turn to carnal depravity to fulfill their quest for meaning and purpose in a world

                CONTINUED 116

Danny frowned and flipped the magazine shut. The article was pure fiction, with some sort of an agenda against youth culture. Against the act of rebellion itself. It seemed to the boy like uneasy projection, born more from fear than fact. He promptly dropped it into the wastebin.

BRRRZZZZT! the intercom downstairs rang out. Danny jumped up, dashed to his window, then pulled the latch and threw open the sash. He stuck his head outside, looking down toward the front gate, where Violet stood waiting next to the callbox.

"Good morning!" Danny called out, pulling her attention up toward the second story. He gave a vigorous wave, and she gave a cool nod. "I'll be down in just one moment! To get in, enter *8A3C-B259* on the keypad."

Danny slipped his pajama top off as he dashed to his dresser, tossing it into the hamper near his closet. He yanked the second drawer open and grabbed his most casual polo shirt, then pulled it over his head and shut the drawer. The boy quickly swapped his pajama bottoms out for a pair of shorts, then looked in his mirror and mussed his hair up as much as he could.

He dashed from his bedroom, flew down the stairs, then slid across the foyer's hardwood floor to the front door. He grabbed the knob and twisted, then yanked it open just as Violet walked up the steps, a funny look on her face. The girl jammed a thumb back over her shoulder.

"Paranoid much?"

"Oh, you mean the security?" Danny looked behind her to see the gate close shut and the warning light blink on. "Yes. Well…" He reached up and scratched at the back of his neck. "Pop's a man of science, you see—an inventor. Sometimes, well, he works on things for the government, so they require him to maintain strict measures."

"Things?" Violet raised an eyebrow. "Well, I'm sure he's just about cracked world hunger." She leaned up against the side of the door. "Or is it the common cold he's after? Or is the government prioritizing the cure for cancer over the Cold War, now?"

"I, uh…." Danny pursed his lips. "Yes, I've been thinking about that myself, lately. In fact, just this morning—"

"I like the look." She nodded down to his shirt and shorts. "A bit less uptight."

"Thank you!" Danny attempted to relax into a casual stance, at first placing his elbow onto the wall, then dropping his arm down to his side and leaning his shoulder against it, then crossing his arms.

"The very picture of hep." The girl laughed and shook her head, then glanced around his shoulder. "So, what, I need another secret password to get in the house or something?"

"Oh. Oh! No." The boy's cheeks flushed crimson and he leapt back, gesturing her inside. "Please, come in. You're most welcome."

Violet stepped past him into the foyer and spun around, taking in the tasteful furniture and chic decoration, then looked up to the elegant, modern chandelier above.

"I never knew science paid so well." The girl looked back down to Danny and smirked. "Guess I shouldn't 'a dropped out."

"Oh, right…" Danny gave a half-hearted laugh and looked around the room. "I suppose it must appear rather opulent to you, yes? I hadn't really thought about how it might look from the perspective of someone who… well, a person who doesn't have a, uh…"

"For such a smart guy," Violet said, wandering through the archway into the den, "seems like there's a lot you haven't thought about before."

"I was just thinking the very same thing…" Danny nodded, slipping his hands into his pockets.

The boy watched from the archway as Violet walked down the two short steps to the sunken conversation pit.

"So this is the American dream, huh?" Violet dropped down into his father's favorite Herman Miller lounge chair and put her feet up onto the ottoman. "Victorian mansion. Draconian security. Scandinavian design." Her eyes flicked over to Danny. "The bomb industry must be booming."

The boy frowned, then walked into the den and attempted to see the room through fresh eyes. There was a good amount of wealth on display, from the elaborate fish tank along the far wall to his father's Polynesian-themed bar covered in expensive-looking bottles of alcohol and intricate crystal glassware.

"Our conversation yesterday, about questioning authority..." Danny turned around to see the girl examining a pastel blue ashtray on the teak side table. "I can't stop thinking about it."

"Wanna go give the bird to some cops?"

"No." Danny frowned, serious. "Last night after I got home, Pop had me help with an experiment. With a rather... reactive substance."

"Baking soda and vinegar?" Violet raised her eyebrows. "I hear those volcanoes can get pretty messy."

"It got me thinking," he brushed past her joke, leaning back against the bar. "I never really questioned what Pop did. I knew that he worked in atomic science, but it never occurred to me that his experiments might lead directly to people getting hurt. I just thought..." He chewed at his lip. "Well, I guess that I figured it's what science was: knowledge for the sake of knowledge. And if someone wanted to build power plants with it, they could. And if someone wanted to build bombs with it, then, well..."

"Intent isn't the same as impact." The girl narrowed her eyes. "Even if you're trying to do something good, you always gotta consider the effect your actions have on other people. On the world."

"Last night, I attempted to ask Pop about the nature of his work, but he simply told me that it was classified. Then, an FBI agent showed up at the gate, and Pop seemed pretty on edge about it. Now, he's been out in the lab all night, so..." Danny took a deep breath. "I took the opportunity to go through a few of his boxes in the attic, to try and find out precisely what he's up to. And I found a recent file marked *Top Secret*."

"Oh?" Violet slowly sat up in the chair. "And what did it say?"

"I don't know." The boy shook his head. "It's upstairs. I haven't had the nerve to open it yet. I'm... I'm torn; wouldn't that be a betrayal of my father's trust?"

"You can't shut out the world." Violet moved to the edge of the seat. "Ignorance is no excuse for avoiding responsibility—willful ignorance, doubly so. You owe it to yourself to find out. You owe it to the world."

"But he's my father—"

"Exactly." Violet nodded. "All the more reason to figure out if he's a war profiteer—aren't you just dying to know why a government agent is sniffing around?"

"I don't know..." Danny looked down, nervously playing with his hands. "What if I find out that Pop's a bad man? What if—"

The front door suddenly swung open and the scientist strode in, a huge grin on his face. He spotted Danny through the archway and began meandering in his direction, hands cooly and casually jammed into the pockets of his lab coat.

"We've done it, my boy." The beaming scientist puffed his chest out proudly. "I've managed to thoroughly validate our results from last night and can officially declare *Substance X* a success." He passed into the living room and spotted Violet out of the corner of his eye. "Oh! Who do we have here, now— Violet, I presume?" He pivoted to Danny and gave a small wink. "I hope?"

"Oh!" Danny blushed. "Ha. Well—"

"You hope right, doctor," Violet said, pushing herself up from the lounge chair, then hopping up the steps over to Danny, leaning casually back against the bar and folding her arms.

"Well it's delightful to meet you, young lady." The man gave her a cheerful nod. "And it's quite the fortuitous timing! What do you say we celebrate the occasion. Waffles? Or perhaps this is the morning where I finally try out these European 'crêpes' I've heard so much about. Eh?"

For a moment, Danny just stared down at his hands. Then, he looked up and shrugged.

"Actually, pop," the boy said, "I'm afraid that we already have plans today."

"So if you'll excuse us." Violet grabbed Danny's hand, leading him toward the stairwell. "We've got some very important business to take care of."

"Well, okay then!" The scientist laughed as they darted up the stairs, calling out after them. "Just make sure to keep the door ajar!"

19   # Developing a Deduction

TK-tk-TK-tk-TK-tk! Mary-Sue placed her mother's egg-timer on the sink, then sat on the lip of the bathtub, bathed in a dim, red light. The foul smell of a noxious chemical bath filled the room, forcing her to breathe from her mouth as she waited for the photograph to develop.

She grabbed the copy of *Sight* from the tile floor and flipped it open to a dog-eared page. The girl then scanned her finger down the column, straining to read the small text in the dim light. It read:

❖

ABOMINABLE SNOWMEN BEHIND THE IRON CURTAIN

 This past February, the remains of 9 members of a Soviet skiing expedition were found torn apart by superhuman violence. While officials have reportedly ruled the cause of death as an avalanche, rumors have begun to circulate amongst nearby townsfolk that the injuries on the corpses appeared to be caused by Almas, a species of ape-man known to inhabit the area.

"They have faces like apes, are three meters tall, and are covered in hair," a local mountain guide was reported to have said. "I have yet to see them with my own eyes, but I have seen their tracks in the snow; forty centimeters long, stretching into the Ural peaks."

SIGHT MAGAZINE

Readers will of course be familiar with the ape-man phenomena as reported within the pages of this magazine since the inception of its publication. These elusive hominids go by many names across the globe: Sasquatch, Chuchunya, Abominable Snowman,a Swamp Ape, Yeti, Hibagon. One thing remains consistent across all: that stories of a bipedal, wooly ape-man exist in every culture and have since pre-history.

In recent years, scientists have begun to speculate that this primate may be a surviving member of gigantopithecus, a nine-foot tall relative of the orangutan thought long-extinct. Researchers of mystic phenomena have their own theories, however: that the ape-men are inter-dimensional shape-shifters, psychic sub-human wild-men, or that their origin is intergalactic in nature.

For now, however, communist authorities are sticking to their official story—that the complete and utter dismemberment of an entire party of experienced hikers could be the result of a little bit of falling snow.

Don't be so naïve, dear reader! This threat lurks not just in the Far East where it's been in hiding for a millennia, nor has its spread been limited to the cold, distant lands of the Soviet Union. This creature's deadly kin secretly stalks the whole of the Earth. Even now... it may be in your own back yard!

—R.A.P.

Goose-pimples shot down Mary-Sue's arms. The EARS believed that a Sasquatch had been responsible for the fleeing campers. Now she read that another name for the creature was "swamp ape"? Could it truly be a coincidence? Was it any less likely than an extraterrestrial? Or a mutant? Or, of course, there was always the possibility that it was a human being—she had to remain open to every potentiality, after all. But the metallic disc that she saw in the swamp…

DING-donnng! DING-donnng!

Mary-Sue tore her attention to the doorbell, then glanced at the egg-timer on the sink. Nearly five minutes remained—just enough time to get rid of whomever was at the door and get back to her investigation. She jumped up from the bathtub and cracked the door open, then slipped out of her makeshift darkroom, attempting to allow as little light as possible inside. She shut it behind her, ran to the entryway, swung the door open, then took a step back.

"Hello," Agent Ford said, jaw clenched. He glared at her through his dark aviator sunglasses. "Do you remember me?"

"Uh, w—well…" Mary-Sue floundered, lost for words.

"You and your friend Prescott gave me the slip at the soda fountain on Friday." He reached into his back pocket, pulled out a rolled-up comic book, then unfurled it. Mary-Sue's stomach sank—it was *Young in Love*, which she had left behind in her hurry to sneak out through the kitchen. He placed it down on a shelf next to Mary-Sue. "Luckily, the owner was able to provide me with your identities."

"G—gave you the slip? Golly, no sir! No," Mary-Sue lied, taking the comic and shaking her head innocently. "I was just trying to help out my friend—see, he'd gotten an awful stomach ache, and… and I didn't want him to be embarrassed in front of his crush, so—"

"Lying to a Federal agent is a crime, young lady." Ford reached into the inner pocket of his blazer and pulled his notepad out, then flipped it open. "I spoke with young Mr. Trowbridge earlier this morning and he informed me that you had been grilling him about an incident out in… Chautauqua Park?"

"W—well, that's true, too, sir." Mary-Sue nodded. "Maybe he didn't mention the stomach ache because he was embarrassed. But I'm a private detective, you see, and I was just following up on a lead."

"And what's your case, precisely?" The man reached up and took his sunglasses off, opening their case and slipping them inside. He placed it into his inner pocket, then withdrew a pen and clicked it on, looking her in the eyes.

"Truthfully, sir," she shrugged, "*The Britannica Junior Detectives* have no case at the moment. My boss, Danny, well, he told me right to my face that the case had no merit. If you can believe it, I'd pitched him on trying to find an atomic mutant living out in the swamp. How stupid, right?"

"And this is one Daniel Oxford?" Ford flipped to the previous page. "Residing at the end of Sunset Drive?"

"That's right." She nodded. "You can ask him yourself if you'd like, he'd corroborate my story."

"Mm." He made a note. "Now, what exactly were your whereabouts last night, around ten o'clock PM?"

"Last night?" Mary-Sue swallowed, thinking. Following the incident at the campsite, she had stashed her bicycle in the shed behind her house. But if the agent had somehow identified her as the owner of the vehicle, then he could be trying to lead her into a trap. "I—I was in Chautauqua Park, visiting a friend. We decided to go on a walk just around then."

"Would this friend be William Kuroki?"

"I—I'm not sure, honestly," Mary-Sue said with a shrug. "I'm afraid I only know him by a nickname: Ace."

"Mm." The man took a note, then looked up. "Quite the friend."

"He's… a recent friend." She tried to smile. "He's new in town."

"I'm afraid that I have some bad news for you." The man flipped his notepad shut. "This 'Ace' is a dangerous juvenile delinquent—a criminal wanted by the law." The man furrowed his brow. "A killer."

The knot in Mary-Sue's stomach tightened.

"K—killer?" she stammered.

"Of one Charles King, a teenage boy from Mendocino, California." The man glanced down the hallway behind Mary-Sue, where the dim red light was bleeding out around the bathroom door. "What are you—"

"I had no idea, sir. Honest!" Mary-Sue said, pulling Ford's attention back toward her. "I never would have made friends with him if I did! But I'm sorry, I don't know his whereabouts now—Scout's honor. He's not at camp anymore, something about a bear in the woods, I think? It scared the other campers off, too. I know he'd talked about splitting town at one point, so maybe he's already gone. You could always check the bowling alley—I know he was there on Friday night."

Ford narrowed his eyes, studying the girl, then flipped his notepad back open and scribbled something down. He shut it, put it back into his inner pocket, and pulled his billfold out, withdrawing a small, off-white card and handing it over to her.

"Well, little girl, if you just so happen to run into him in the course of some investigation," the man said, "please contact me immediately—my forwarding service should be able to reach me anytime, anywhere."

"Thank you, sir," Mary-Sue said. "If I can help in any way, I certainly will. I don't want to associate with dangerous criminals."

She looked down at the card. It read:

JONATHAN FORD

AGENT 517   K-4306

"You know, little girl," Ford said pulling his sunglasses back out and slipping them over his ears, "with your sly maneuvering, you could make a very good agent in my organization some day..." He turned and began to walk down the stairs, then paused and looked back up at her, pointing to her left hand where Mary-Sue was still gripping the issue of *Sight*. "But that stuff will rot your brain."

Mary-Sue looked down with dread. Somehow,

she had completely forgotten that she had been holding the magazine the whole time. Ford gave her a nod, slipped his hands into his pockets, then walked down the stairs and out of view.

D-D-D-RIIIINNG! the egg-timer rang out and Mary-Sue jumped. She turned and dashed down the hall, bursting back into the bathroom and yanking the photograph out from the chemical bath. The girl pulled a clothespin off from the counter, clipped the picture to the line of string, then grabbed her magnifying glass and leaned in.

There, dripping in crisp black-and-white, was a perfect image of the footprints in the mud, their trail leading off into the darkness—but the closer she looked the more ordinary the footprints seemed. Not the tracks of a three-toed Martian or a disfigured mutant. They were simply shaped like the feet of a regular human being.

20   Investigating the Investigator

"Well?" Violet asked, leaning over Danny's shoulder as he sat at the cluttered worktable in the A-frame attic, lit only by a small lunette window on the far side. "What's it say?"

The boy's eyes scanned down the document—a single piece of paper inside of a plain manilla folder.

It read:

ADVANCED RESEARCH PROJECTS AGENCY
WASHINGTON, D.C. 20330

ARPA

OFFICE OF THE SECRETARY

TOP SECRET

*The information contained in this document is classified TOP SECRET with
ARPA. No other government agency has access to this information. No notes, photographs, or audio recordings may be made of this briefing.*

To: DR. NATHANIEL H. OXFORD
From: ADVANCED RESEARCH PROJECTS AGENCY   November 27, 1958
Subject: COMMENCE PROJECT FINAL CURTAIN

1. Intelligence confirms USSR 'Project 7000' is well underway. Recent reports indicate 3-stage, 50-megaton weapon being developed.

2. Analysis of available materials proves largest, most intensive, most comprehensive program expansion ever—34 detected detonations between 1 October 1958 and 6 November 1958, 12 with yields greater than current US capabilities.

3. Research to begin immediately on 'Project Final Curtain' in response. Development phase to be accelerated to match or exceed Soviet advances.

DONALD A. QUARLES
United States Secretary of Defense

"It's…" Danny swallowed. "It's inconclusive."

"Get real." Violet rolled her eyes, leaning back against the worktable with a frown. She turned and tapped at the document. "It's from ARPA—those cats make weapons for the Army."

"Amongst other things!" He said, shutting the folder and pushing it away. "There's… nothing in there to say what this 'Project Final Curtain' actually is. For all we know it could be some… early detection system! Or a… a new type of radar satellite. Or… or—"

"You're grasping at straws, daddy-o." The girl rapped her fingers on the edge of the table. "Your dad's an atomic scientist in the midst of the Cold War—you think the military wants him building satellites or power plants?"

"What about nuclear submarines?" Danny asked, chewing at his lip. "He could be working to miniaturize them. Or, or make an atomic airship that could—"

"No." Violet gave him a look.

"I just…" The boy put his fingers on his temples and shut his eyes. "I just can't believe that Pop would build a device destined for destruction. For killing innocent people. It just… it doesn't make sense!"

"War never does." Violet looked out across the

attic at the cardboard boxes piled high in every corner.

"With..." The boy began, then stopped himself, attempting to think. "With the right evidence... I might be willing to accept such a possibility. But..." He gestured toward the folder. "But this isn't it. It isn't enough. It has to be conclusive!"

"Then just ask him." She shrugged. "Straight to his face."

"I tried!" Danny turned his hands out. "Last night. He told me it was classified, then refused to elaborate any further!"

"So let's sneak into the lab," she said. "Look for ourselves."

"Look for what, precisely?" He slumped his shoulders. "I'm not sure about you, but I wouldn't know the difference between the inside of an atomic bomb and the inside of an atomic satellite."

"Fair." She crossed her arms with a frown, staring out the window at the laboratory. "What about that G-man, from the FBI? You said he was sniffing around last night. If he's here about your dad's bomb—"

"Experiment." Danny shot a look her way.

"If he's here about your dad's experiment," Violet said, walking back toward him, "then he'd know for certain, right?"

"I…" Danny chewed at his lip. "I suppose so…"

"Then we investigate the investigator, daddy-o." Violet put her hand on his and gave his fingers a squeeze. "Scope out what he's looking for, all that detective jazz—I'll be your partner. We'll be just like Nick and Nora Charles. Except I'll be the only funny one. Yeah?"

Danny stared down at the folder for a few moments, then pushed his chair out. He stood up and walked over to the corner of the attic, found a box labeled *Scouts*, then tossed aside the wrinkled green sash dotted with embroidered badges. Underneath it were a whittled slingshot and a pan flute, his prize-winning pinewood derby car, a book of dried flowers and leaves, and a broken phantasmascope.

He pushed them aside to uncover a homemade quartz radio set—the same which had secured him the Adventure Scouts' coveted engineering badge. Its exposed interior was a mess of vacuum tubes, bulky metal-halide bulbs, and fraying wires. He pulled it out from the box and walked back over to the workstation, placing it down on top of the folder.

Violet hopped up onto the table next to it, studying the ramshackle device as Danny ducked down beneath the table and slipped its plug into the outlet.

"The little light came on," Violet said as he shimmied back out, "and it's hasn't caught on fire yet."

"Good," he said, sitting in the chair, "then it's still working."

Danny leaned forward, examining the transceiver. The pencil marks which had once labeled the tuning dial had faded, but otherwise the unit seemed fully operational. The boy flicked the broadcasting switch on and a burst of static crackled through the tinny speaker. He carefully turned the dial back-and-forth, searching for the eleven-meter band.

"Gonna... tell me what you're up to, or is that part of the mystery?" She leaned down in front of the radio. "Because I've gotta say—I'm only literally on the edge of my seat."

"Oh!" He laughed. "I'm sorry—I'm not used to explaining myself, I guess. You see, with this transceiver we'll be able to contact the Electronic Amateur Radio Society."

"To, what?" She frowned. "Pipe in some Perry Como as we come up with a plan on how to find this guy?"

"No, no," Danny chuckled. "They're a group of wireless enthusiasts who monitor the local airwaves."

Violet frowned and shook her head. "Why?"

"To spy on Martians, if you can believe it," Danny said. "But for our purposes, they've created an interconnected network of—"

"...so I finally cracked the pattern!" Hugh's voice came through loud and clear as the dial hit its mark. "It looks like Pierre was right."

"Great job, Hugh," Kat lisped through the tinny speaker. "I say focus all your energy on the cypher while Pierre starts the translation in parallel. That way we can—"

"I'm... sorry to interrupt," Danny cleared his throat, "but you've got Britannica on the wire—or should I make up some sort of fun call sign like you all have? Flatfoot? Gumshoe? Sherlock? Or, well, I guess Britannica is already a nickname..."

For a few seconds, the other end of the radio went silent. After a few seconds more, Danny gave Violet a puzzled look.

"I... hope that I haven't done anything wrong," the boy said. "Have I misunderstood the intent of this radio band? Based on our conversation yesterday—"

"It's fine," Kat said, curt. "We were just... discussing a new project. What do you want, Britannica?"

Danny looked back over to Violet, who just shrugged and shook her head. The boy turned back to the radio.

"Well, fellas, I'm on another case—"

"Mon ami," Pierre crooned, "I do so hope zat you discovered zis mysterious girl zat you were looking for—no zing is so unsatisfying as unrequited love."

A satisfied smirk washed over Violet's face. The girl slid down from the edge of the table, then wandered toward the other side of the attic as Danny's cheeks flushed crimson.

"W—well," Danny stuttered, "I have something a bit more pressing this time around. I'm looking for a car—a black Cadillac, to be precise. With government plates. Has anyone seen it around town this morning?"

"Wheels, here," the elderly milkman said. "Been keepin' eyes on that fella ever since he rolled into town. Just saw the thing parked at Flamingo Lanes not a half-hour ago—"

"Out of curiosity," Kat interrupted, "why exactly are you looking for a car with government plates, Danny?"

"Well, uh…" He frowned, cleared his throat, then turned to look at Violet who was rooting around inside of a cardboard box marked *Work Papers*. "I believe that it's the car of an FBI agent that I'm attempting to track down. Why is it of interest to you?"

"…no reason," Kat said after a moment. "But, unrelated, EARS? Let's meet up at HQ if you can. Radio silence 'til then. Pipsqueak out."

"Wheels out."

"Maquis out!"

"Rustbucket out."

"Oculus out."

"Buoy out."

And then, the radio went quiet. Danny flipped the switch off.

"That's funny," he said with a frown, swiveling around in his chair. "Yesterday they seemed so open with—"

"Where did you and your dad live?" Violet said, looking up from a second folder stamped *Top Secret*, pulled from a box of older files. "Before Bonnifield?"

"Albuquerque, New Mexico." Danny shrugged.

"And before that?" She arched an eyebrow.

"Los Alamos." He frowned. "Why?"

"What did your dad do there?"

"I—I never really knew," he said slowly. "Government work."

"Danny," Violet said, holding out the folder, "this refers to *Project Y.* You do know what that is, don't you?"

The boy shook his head, swallowing hard.

"That was the code name for The Los Alamos Laboratory, where The Manhattan Project was architected." She shut the folder. "Danny, I think your father is a war profiteer."

"But…" A chill ran down the boy's spine.

"If all this…" She gestured around. "Was built on the backs of dead civilians—wouldn't you want to know for certain?"

"But…" Danny frowned. "But, even if it was, more people would have died from a land invasion, so—"

"Eisenhower didn't think so. Neither did MacArthur. That's just propaganda that you're repeating—history rewritten by the victors." She stared right into his eyes. "So? What do you say?"

Danny nodded wordlessly.

"Good," the beatnik said. "Now, where was that Cadillac?"

21   A Paranormal Paranoia

"So then I twist this thing on. Get some, y'know, static," Ace said, holding his walkie-talkie up as he pushed his way through the tall marsh grasses, leather jacket flung over his shoulder. "Start playin' with that dial when all 'a sudden, I get these weird noises—*beep-beep, beep-beep-beep*. Like, might as well be a goofy sound effect in a Corman flick or whatnot. That's, y'know, a clue—right?"

"Mmph." Mary-Sue grunted, half-listening from a few paces behind the boy, leaning down in an attempt to get a good look at the treads of his boots. "Where were you sleeping, if you couldn't be up at the camp?"

"Out here," Ace said, nodding toward the treeline. "Stashed the bike behind the ranger's tower, pitched a tent over yonder."

"You camped in the marsh?" Mary-Sue narrowed her eyes. "Despite believing that a Martian is lurking in the area?"

"Hey, Red, if ya wanna put me up at the Dream Motel, I ain't gonna say no." He leapt over a puddle and the girl managed to get a look at the soles of his boots—quite different from the ones in her photograph. "But 'til then, I ain't gotta lotta options."

"I see." She ran to catch up to his side. "I was just curious, that's all."

The two pushed through the reeds to find themselves at the entrance to the graveyard. In the morning light, it was significantly less ominous— no fog, no shadows, and no gloom. A small, blue heron stalked across the clearing. It paused, looked toward the teenagers, then spread its wings and pushed away, flying off over the tall spruce trees beyond.

Ace stepped through the gate, then wandered toward the vault and hopped up to sit on top. He pulled his cigarettes out from his sleeve and stuck one between his lips. Mary-Sue took off the other direction, walking across the clearing to where the tracks had once been. In their place now, however, was simply a shallow pool of muddy water, the prints washed away in the tide.

Mary-Sue pulled her bag around and withdrew the Geiger counter, twisting its dial all the way to the right. The needle immediately sprung to life as she scanned the device back and forth across the area. *TK-tk-TK-tk-TK-tk!*

"Anythin'?" Ace asked from behind her, flicking

his lighter on.

"Nothing new," Mary-Sue mumbled, taking off toward the lagoon and hopping over the crumbling wall on the far side of the cemetery. She held her breath as the dilapidated dock came into view, but where the eerie red light and the strange metallic disc had been the night before, there was now only the still, calm water of the lagoon.

The needle jumped rapidly back-and-forth as Mary-Sue approached the lagoon's edge, indicating radiation. Her eyes scanned for anything at all unusual. But as the girl arrived at the dock, the only thing beyond was a line of box turtles sitting in a sunbeam on a half-submerged log. She frowned and leaned against a dry wooden post.

"Drag," Ace said as he meandered past the cemetery wall, releasing a long stream of smoke from his nostrils. The greaser stopped a few yards away from the dock, gazing out across the water and furrowing his brow. "Guessin' that sucker took off after all the commotion at camp." The boy jammed his hands into his pockets. "Maybe jumped into Dimension X. Or, never know, maybe out there with some cloakin' shield up, invisible, laser beams pointed at us right now."

"Or it was a boat," Mary-Sue said, crossing her

arms, "that rowed off when you had us go back to camp."

"Ain't never seen no boat looks like that." The boy stared her down as he took a drag of his cigarette. "Say, what's with ya today, Red?"

Mary-Sue looked back toward the boy, studying him for a moment. She looked at the dark bruise across his cheekbone, earned in a fistfight. At his wild, unkempt hair, messy from sleeping alone in the woods. At the grease stains on his jeans, from fixing a dangerous motorcycle. And at the tattoo on his bicep. Bad Luck.

"You haven't told me a single thing about yourself," she finally said. "Since the moment we met— not where you're from, not why you're here. You haven't even told me your real name."

"What, wanna see my papers or somethin'?" He scrunched his nose up.

"No, I'm serious." She narrowed her eyes. "You said you wanted to keep it professional, right? Well, I'm interested in a professional capacity. I don't think it's unreasonable for a detective to want to know a little bit about their client. I am trying to clear your name, after all."

Ace let a cloud of smoke slowly roll out from between his lips. After a moment, he flicked his cigarette out into the water.

"Alright." He crossed his arms. "Real name's Will—William Kuroki. I've always called my pop Sir, but Ace, well, that's what the squadron called 'im."

"I—in the war?" Mary-Sue furrowed her brow as he nodded. "For... which side?"

"Our side." Ace shot the girl a dirty look and tightened his jaw. "See, that's just the thing for us Nisei—loyalty's in question no matter what we do—still, now." He turned to look out over the water. "My pop, see, right when he walks through those camp gates, gets handed this... loyalty test, makin' 'im swear he ain't no traitor. Makin' 'im say he'd join the US military."

"Camp?" Mary-Sue tilted her head to the side.

"Internment." Ace nodded, looking back over his shoulder. "Never hearda it?"

She shook her head.

"Ain't shocked—nobody seems to like talkin' 'bout it these days." He looked down to the ground. "Was where they stuck all the Japanese folks livin' here. Citizens. Japanese-Americans born here—like my ma 'n pop."

"Like you?" She pushed herself off from the post, softening.

"Wasn't put in there." Ace shrugged. "Was born in there."

"Gosh," she said, taking a step toward him. "So, then, your father…"

"Never met 'im." The boy pulled the pack of cigarettes out from his sleeve and slipped another one between his lips. "Got shipped off 'fore I was born. First trainin' in Texas, where them recruits tried startin' fights with 'im." He lit the cigarette, then watched as the smoke slowly drifted out. "Pushed to see combat, got made a clerk in Louisiana. His outfit got assigned to Europe, tried leavin' 'im behind, but he pushed again—made it, barely. Trained as a gunner—temporary, 'course, 'til he proved 'imself an ace shot. Twenty-five missions over Spain, got released to come back. Turned it down, did five more. Last one, well…"

Ace paused, looking down to the ground. He leaned over and picked up a flat, smooth stone and tossed it back and forth in his hands. The boy looked out over the water, wound up, then skimmed it along the surface. *PSSH! SHH-Shh-shh…* The box turtles looked up, startled, then slid down from the log and ducked beneath the surface.

"I'm… I'm sorry." Mary-Sue walked up to him and placed her hand gently on his arm. "I didn't mean to imply—"

"Well, ya did." Ace kept his gaze out over the water.

"He sounds like a very brave man."

"He was."

"Ace." She twisted her mouth to the side, taking a deep breath. "I… I have to ask you. Who… who is Charles King?"

Mary-Sue felt the greaser's entire body tense up and he whipped his head toward her, eyes filled with fire.

"Where the hell ya hear that name?"

22   Peer Pressure Problems

Danny leaned forward on the bicycle, his athletic legs pumping with perfect precision, the summer breeze whipping his sandy hair to-and-fro. Violet was perched gingerly atop the spokes behind him, arms wrapped delicately around his chest, the warmth of her body against his back.

Two blocks ahead, a large fiberglass flamingo marked the entrance to Bonnifield's bowling alley. In the summer afternoons, teenagers gathered to roll a few frames, compete in a sporting game of foosball, or purchase ice-cold freezer pops and socialize with friends. It was also where the more blue-collar adults would come to drink alcoholic beverages at the John Wayne Bar tucked into the very back.

Danny pulled a left and weaved onto the sidewalk, then pushed back on the breaks and came to a stop directly next to the bike rack. After a tight squeeze, Violet hopped down to the ground and Danny wheeled the vehicle into the rack alongside a dozen other colorful bicycles.

The detective turned back toward the parking

lot and was met with Violet's outstretched hand, her fingers slipping between his. She pulled at his arm and led the way around the corner, but as the parking lot came into view, Danny's heart sank; there was no black Cadillac in sight. Only a handful of hard-top sedans and a few beat-up old trucks.

"Rats." Danny frowned.

"Mmph." Violet shrugged. "Bum lead, I guess."

The boy scanned his eyes across the parking lot until they landed on some high schoolers sitting in the bed of a truck, talking, laughing, and drinking from glass bottles wrapped in brown paper bags.

"I wouldn't be so sure..." Danny shook his head. "When it comes to mystery-solving, there's rarely such a thing as a true dead-end, just a new opportunity for outside-the-box thinking." He nodded toward the teenagers and started to walk their direction, pulling the girl behind him. "Come on, let's see what these people know."

The two teenagers walked across the parking lot hand-in-hand. As they approached the truck, Danny planted his feet and cleared his throat.

"Good morning, fellas!" He raised a hand in a friendly wave. "I was hoping that you would—"

All of the high schoolers jumped, then attempted to hide their bottles behind their backs, but as they turned around and recognized Danny, each of them relaxed. At the front was Jack Hardy, now cast-free.

"Hey!" Jack broke out into a broad grin and turned to the other high schoolers. "It's Britannica, that kid I was tellin' y'all about—the one from the drive-in. *Bam! Pow!*" He shadowboxed in the air, then chuckled and took a swig from his bottle. "Didn't know ya had that in ya, kid—figured you was just some square, y'know? But geez, man, you got a mean right hook!"

"Uh, thanks." Danny shrugged. "But—"

"Woulda cleaned that greaser's clock real good if ya hadn't 'a been stopped by that old man. Knocked his block right off!" He turned toward Violet and a sly grin came over his face. "Who's the new chick?"

"Oh!" Danny said. "This is Violet. We met—"

"Wanna drink?" Jack held his bottle out toward them. "It's the good stuff."

"I'm afraid that—" Danny began, then stopped himself. He looked over to the beatnik girl beside him, who had given him a sip of liquor the other night. She just looked back, eyebrows raised. Danny turned to Jack and reached out. "Uh, yes, actually. Thank you."

He took the brown bag, but didn't need to see

the label to discern its contents; the smell of cheap, stale beer wafted out, pungent in his nose. Danny cleared his throat, put the bottle to his lips, then swung his head back, taking a large gulp of the foul liquid.

"There we go!" Jack grinned, then reached out and grabbed the drink back, taking another sip himself. "Y'know, there's this big shindig out at Hunter's farm tomorrow. Y'all gotta come out and meet the whole crew, throw back a few brews. Yeah?"

"I… I'll give it serious consideration," Danny said, raking his tongue across the roof of his mouth, attempting to get rid of the awful taste. "But right now, I was hoping that you'd be able to provide some insight into a matter that I'm pursuing."

"Sure, kid, sure." Jack shrugged. "What's up?"

"Gee, that's swell!" Danny said, standing up straight. "In the course of my most recent investigation, you see, I've found myself in pursuit of a particularly peculiar puzzle wherein—"

"Was a black Cadillac here this morning?" Violet cut him off. "A few minutes ago, government plates?"

All of the teenagers nodded.

"Yeah. Drove on up 'round ten." Jack shook his bottle, the last sip of beer sloshing around inside.

"We freaked, 'course—thought for sure he was gonna bust us for drinkin'."

"Yes, I see." Danny nodded. "This was a tall man, thin, black suit?" They all nodded again. "And what did he do?"

"Didn't roll any rounds, that's for sure." Jack shrugged and finished his bottle off. "Got in, got out, like, five minutes. Figured he was in there crackin' skulls like in *Gang Busters* or somethin'."

"And this man, he didn't question you?" Danny asked. They shook their heads. He looked over to Violet, who nodded toward the front entrance of the bowling alley. "Thank you very much for your time, but I have to be on my way."

"Sure, sure." Jack nodded, chucking the paper bag over his shoulder without a second look. *KSSH-KKK!* the glass shattered as it hit the gravel. The boy grabbed another bottle from cooler at his side, then reached into his pocket and withdrew a small, black object.

KA-FTT! Jack flicked his wrist and a switchblade sprung out. He put it firmly against the cap then pushed down and popped the top off.

"Don't forget about that party, now, yeah? Lemme know."

"Sure thing. Will do, fellas." Danny nodded,

then turned and pulled Violet's hand as he quickly walked away.

"That was pretty slick," she said, voice lowered.

"What do you mean?" He glanced back over his shoulder, where the teenagers had returned to their animated conversation.

"That beer." She shrugged and jammed her thumb back toward the truck. "I could see you didn't want it—but ingratiating yourself so they'd loosen up? Creative. Unexpected. Surprisingly manipulative."

"Oh, uh," Danny said, forcing a chuckle, "yes, of course. That's why I did it. But inside, such… manipulations likely won't prove necessary."

Danny pulled his hand away from hers as they approached the door, pulling it open and gesturing her inside. The girl laughed and shook her head, then stepped through into the vestibule beyond. Danny joined her in the tiny room, covered floor-to-ceiling with private storage lockers for league bowlers and the more dedicated aspirants.

The next room over was the bowling alley itself, loudly bustling with dozens of teenagers and the explosive sounds of balls crashing violently against pins. *KA-KRAAK!* The two stepped though and were immediately hit with the powerful scent of buttered popcorn and all-beef frankfurters, popping and sizzling under a heat lamp at the front counter.

At the far end of the room were the bowling lanes, filled with groups of teenagers talking and horsing around. To their right were the foosball and pool tables, and to their left were the arcade cabinets where Prescott stood alone, hunched over a casino-themed pinball machine, his tongue jutting out over his lip, lost in concentration. He fumbled his last ball and growled, hitting the cabinet in frustration.

"I've been swindled!" He barked. "This infernal machine is fixed, a scam of the highest order!" Prescott turned to see them, then straightened up pulled at the lapels of his blazer. "Ah, Britannica—a favor? Might I be able to borrow a nickel for another attempt at besting the beast?"

"I'm afraid that I don't have anything on me," Danny laughed.

"And yourself?" Prescott turned toward Violet, cocking an eyebrow. "Also cash-poor, presumably?"

"But rich in personality." She shrugged.

Prescott huffed, then looked back to Danny. "Who's the bird?"

"Violet." She shot a dirty look Prescott's way.

"Uh, yes." Danny nodded. "Prescott, this is, my

uh, well, my... my girl, I suppose."

"Your girl?" Violet cocked an eyebrow, then gave an amused chuckle. "Okay, yeah. I'm his girl."

"Well, well, well..." Prescott gave him a sly, approving look. "Aren't we quite the Lothario? I'd suspected as much! However, might I suggest that in this particular venue, you keep that fact hush-hush? I suspect that Sondra over there might not take too kindly to the news."

He gestured to the other side of the room, where Sondra and Francine were sitting, waiting for a lane.

"Why?" The detective frowned. "Did she say something?"

"Well," Prescott said with a shrug, "by now, everyone's heard about your big date—and, naturally, your big fight. I rather regret my decision to attend soda fountain on the night in question. Seeing Danny Britannica clean some greaser's clock, so to speak, would certainly have been a sight to behold."

"I don't think it was so spectacular as all that." Danny scratched at the back of his neck.

"Regardless, it would have been the better choice." Prescott scowled. "Because if it weren't for your friend Mary-Sue that night, then I'd be in the Hamptons at this very moment drinking Shirley Temples."

"Why?" Danny narrowed his eyes. "What happened?"

"If you can believe it," Prescott huffed and crossed his arms, "the girl sicced an FBI agent on me—to expose my sneaking out to my parents. I'm forced to assume, anyway. In turn, they've made me stay with Aunt Gladys for the summer. When you see the girl, would you mind telling her to jump in a lake for me?"

"FBI agent?" Violet raised her eyebrow. "The same one who was just here?"

"I wouldn't know." Prescott shrugged. "I only just arrived myself. In order to sneak out, I was forced to wait until Aunt Gladys was asleep. It took three whole soap operas for the bag to doze off. Interminable!"

"What did he say, the agent?" Danny asked, narrowing his eyes.

"That's the worst part!" Prescott rolled his eyes. "He simply wanted to know if I had seen some youth in the course of my travels through the woods— someone named… William? It had nothing at all to do with me, yet I still get punished! A gross injustice."

"What else?"

"Only that the boy was dangerous," Prescott

said, narrowing his eyes. "A killer. That he was wanted by the law for the death of another boy."

"Nothing about a scientist?" Danny frowned. "Nor about a bomb, or, perhaps, my pop?"

"No," Prescott said. "Just after some delinquent."

"So then," Violet said, turning to Danny, "he wasn't after your father at all. He may have just wanted to talk to you about the fight—"

"Uh, Danny!" Prescott gulped, eyes flicking over the boy's shoulder. "You might wanna—"

"You have a lot of nerve showing your face here, Britannica!"

The detective whipped around to see Sondra and Francine standing behind him. And they looked more than a little upset.

The Big Break

"C'mon, out with it," the greaser growled at Mary-Sue, making her take a cautious step back. "Who told ya 'bout Chuck?"

"The... FBI agent," she said, holding her hands out. "From last night. The one who was looking around the campgrounds. T—this morning, he showed up at my house. He knew my name, he knew your name, and he said—"

"That I killed a kid named Chuck, yea?" the boy asked, looming tall.

"Y—yes," she gulped. "He seemed to know an awful lot about—"

"Everythin'! 'Course he did!" Ace kicked at the grass, then turned away and jammed his fingers onto his temples. "It's what these people, these... men in black suits—that's what they do. Change the story, drive folks apart. He's tryin' to confuse us, tryin' to split us up, throw us off the trail of the saucer. Didn't ya think 'a that?"

"Of course I thought of that!" Mary-Sue stood up tall and looked him right in the eyes. "And if that is the truth, then I threw him off the trail. I didn't tell him where you were—I said that you were thinking of splitting town, that maybe you were going to the bowling alley before you left. So he's miles away right now."

"Yea?" Ace frowned, backing away. "And why'd ya do that?"

"Because I didn't think he was telling me the whole story." The girl crossed her arms. "But I don't think you are, either."

"Don't go callin' me a liar, Red." Ace narrowed his eyes.

"But you did lie to me, didn't you?" Mary-Sue pursed her lips. "Last night, after the agent left, you said nobody was after you."

"So ya think they are?" Ace took a long drag of his cigarette.

"I think you are on the lam." She nodded. "And I think regardless of his true identity—FBI or man in black suit—he's got something on you. Something you're running away from."

"So, then, what?" The boy looked out past the dock. "Think I made it all up, now? Think I never saw no Martian in the first place? Think it's all some guy in a boat wearin' a spooky mask?"

"I'm…" She took a deep breath, looking back

to the water. To where she saw the disc the night before. "I'm open to any possibility—provided the evidence supports it."

"So that's that." Ace let out a long column of smoke, then flicked his half-spent cigarette away and shook his head. "Open to the idea I'm some kinda cold-blooded murderer."

"Unless you tell me your side of the story, that's all the information I have to go on. It's like I said: a good detective doesn't make up their mind until they have all the evidence in front of them—though I wouldn't have come out here this morning if I thought it was the whole truth," she said. "We both know there's some weird stuff going on out here in the swamp, stuff that someone—or something— doesn't want people to see. You saw the proof with your own eyes, and I've seen it, too. Now you and I need to figure out what's really going on out here— together."

"Even if my side of the story ain't so pretty?"

"I wouldn't be here right now if I thought my life was in danger."

"Then you're too naïve, Red." Ace sucked at his teeth and shook his head. "Can't believe I thought ya was different 'n the rest of 'em."

"What are you talking about?" she balked. "I

just told you I thought you were innocent!"

"Nah." Ace pulled his leather jacket down from his shoulder, then shrugged it on. "'Cause ya said '*full truth*.' But ya took a look at me and wrote me off—no matter what I said."

Mary-Sue paused for a moment, then looked into his eyes. "Ace, I'm sorry. I didn't mean to doubt you. I don't know what you did, but—"

"Nah." He shook his head. "Sorry don't mean nothin', Red. Way ya act's what matters. If ya was sorry—you'd change. "

"Ace, you're being—"

"Y'know, I been a lotta places the past year," the boy growled. "Kept sayin' this one, nah, *this* is the one things'll be different. And y'know, for a second there..." He took a deep breath. "But wherever I go, folks're the same kinda bad. So... maybe I really should skip town—or, maybe there ain't nowhere for me to run no more."

"Who is Chuck?" She pleaded. "All you have to do is tell me!"

"That's just the thing, Red." The boy studied her for a moment, then shook his head and sighed. "I shouldn't have to."

"You're just giving up?" Mary-Sue took a step forward. "What about the saucer, the alien? You saw something out there."

"Did I?" He glared at her. "'Cause ya don't seem to believe me 'bout that either."

"Of course I—"

"Said it yourself, coulda been a boat. And y'know?" Ace jammed his hands into his pockets and turned to the cemetery. "Lotta fog out here, 'n I saw that thing late at night. Coulda been anything. Anyone."

"That's an excuse." Mary-Sue narrowed her eyes. "You're just trying to justify running away, because it's all you know how to do anymore."

"Screw this." He shot a dirty look back over his shoulder, stared into her eyes, then stepped toward the grass. "Screw this podunk town, screw this lame-brain mystery—and screw you, too."

The boy stepped into the reeds. Mary-Sue's shoulders slumped as he disappeared from view. The girl pushed herself back up against the post, fighting the tears beginning to well in her eyes.

But no matter how hard Mary-Sue tried, she couldn't seem to push the mystery out of her head. Something was nagging at the back of her mind—something which Ace had said. Something about him sleeping out in the woods.

He had claimed to have heard strange radio signals, but her walkie-talkies had a limited range of only a few hundred feet—which meant that if he did hear something, then it must have originated from inside of the marsh.

At this point, she wanted to be done with it all—done with atomic mutants, with flying saucers, with extraterrestrial invasions and men in black suits and wild conspiracy theories.

But there was only one way that she could get it out of her head—and that was to exhaust every lead. To follow-up on every clue. To solve *The Mutant of Mercury Marsh* once and for all. And there was only one group of radio experts who could help her solve it: the EARS.

24   Fallout at Flamingo Lanes

"What's wrong with you, Danny Oxford?" Sondra growled, causing Francine, Prescott, and Violet to all turn his way.

"I…" The boy took a step back. "I'm sorry, Sondra, but—"

"Oh!" She raised her eyebrows in mock surprise. "Now you're sorry? But… certainly not on Friday! And not yesterday either, I suppose."

"I'm afraid that I don't understand." He frowned.

"Exactly." Francine narrowed her eyes at him.

"You don't—do you?" Sondra shook her head. "You have absolutely no idea why I might be upset with you? That's the worst part!"

"I—"

"Did you stop to think for one second," Sondra said, taking a breath, "about how your actions might have affected me? After I asked you out for my first date ever? After I picked you up—my father in the back seat? After you ditched me at intermission, after you started a fistfight out of insecurity, after my father drags me away and forbids me from going on another date until I'm sixteen?"

"That's awful." Danny turned his hands out. "I didn't know!"

"Of course you didn't," she sighed. "Because you didn't even bother to give me a phone call the next day and see how I was."

"Then you waltz in two days later," Francine said, "holding hands with another girl. So, Sondra can't date 'til she's an old maid, but you've already moved on!"

"No." Danny frowned. He turned to look at Violet, who had a blank expression on her face. He turned to look at Prescott, who was pulling at his collar. "I—I don't feel as if that's a... fair and objective assessment of the situation."

"Oh?" Sondra pursed her lips. "So, then, what is?"

"W—well, first off," Danny began, furrowing his brow, "that greaser started the fight, not me. And it wasn't insecurity, either. I was defending your honor, not—"

"Oh come on!" Sondra rolled her eyes. "Defending my honor from what? A conversation with someone who had mistaken me for somebody else? What needed defending—precisely?"

"He was being overtly aggressive!" Danny shook

his head. "I believe that you'll recall he immediately challenged me to a fight."

"A challenge you accepted of your own volition." Sondra narrowed her eyes. "Despite the fact that I begged you to just walk away—and then you threw the first punch, if you don't remember!"

"But starting the fight wasn't my intention." Danny crossed his arms. "Nor was getting you barred from dating. I was just trying to do the right thing."

"Ah!" Sondra nodded. "So that makes it okay, then."

"You made your own choices." Francine placed her hand on her hip. "And now you need to take responsibility for them."

"I'm…" Danny narrowed his eyes. "I'm not the bad guy, here!"

"So, then, you weren't ditching your best friend at the same time?" Francine chimed in. "Because I saw her at the soda fountain that night, all alone—stood up on the first night of summer after being so excited about her secret project that afternoon."

"We had… made plans, that's true," Danny blurted out, "but… then I canceled them in order to go on our date! You can't be upset at that."

"Gosh." Sondra shook her head. "Great defense, Danny."

"Come on." Francine tugged at her sleeve and nodded back toward the lanes. "Let's not waste any more time on *The All-American Boy*."

Sondra stared at him for a moment, then shook her head and turned to Violet, twisting her mouth to the side. "He's all yours."

And with that, Sondra and Francine turned and walked away.

"I, uh…" Prescott said, stepping backward toward the foosball tables and pointing over his shoulder, "I must obtain a nickel. If you'll excuse me…"

Danny barely heard the boy, focusing instead on the knot forming in his stomach. He took a deep breath, attempting to push the feeling away, but it only worsened. His eyes flicked over to Violet, who was looking at him with a strange expression on her face, chewing at her lip.

"I, uh…" Danny cleared his throat, reaching up to scratch at the back of his neck. He tried to smile. "I guess… the FBI agent was a bum lead."

"Danny," Violet sighed, "I don't think—"

"All that," he said, gesturing off after Sondra, "it's not what it—"

"Look, kid…" The beatnik girl frowned and looked down to the floor. "You clearly got a lot on your plate right now and I…" She looked back up and sighed. "I can't wait for you to grow up. Y'know?"

"But…" Danny tightened his jaw. "That isn't… isn't me." He balled his fists up. "And… besides, what about the mystery? My pop and Project Final Curtain? Isn't that worth looking past some minor indiscretion—"

"Seems pretty cut and dried to me, kid." She shrugged. "He's got a work order to build a bomb. Then you help him build the thing using some 'reactive materials'. And that FBI cat's after some kid—unrelated. What's the mystery?"

"But… maybe we can stop him? Maybe we can—"

"You can try to save the world your way, daddy-o." She took a step back. "And I'll try and save it mine."

She shook her head, then turned away.

"Wait!" Danny called after her. "Where are you going?"

"I'm a nomad." She shrugged. "There's nothing left for me here."

Violet gave him a look, then walked into the vestibule, out through the front door, and out of his life.

"Dames, hm?" Prescott meandered over and clapped a hand onto his shoulder. "Not to worry, my boy—I believe that you did the right thing. Playing the field is a noble pursuit! However, ideally next time you won't get caught."

VRRRRMM! RM-RM-Rm-Rm-m...

The heavy, choking rumble of an engine caused their heads to snap toward the window to the parking lot where a motorcycle had just pulled up. Sitting on the top, cigarette dangling loosely from between his lips, was Ace. The juvenile delinquent whose feet at which all the blame fell. Danny's blood boiled.

"Come now," Prescott said, "let's sneak out the back. I know a—"

Danny shook the boy's hand from his shoulder and charged toward the front door. He threw it door open just as the greaser stepped down, a look of ugly consternation on his face. As the door slammed hard against the brick wall, Ace's eyes flicked his direction, full of fire, and he plucked the cigarette out.

"If it ain't the square." Ace snarled and flicked the still-lit cigarette at Danny, who deftly dodged the projectile and planted his feet a few yards away.

"I am no such thing, you reprobate," Danny shot back, standing tall and puffing his chest out. "I won't let you bully me again—or any other person in Bonnifield, for that matter."

From the far end of the parking lot there was

a brief commotion as Jack and his friends became aware of the scene. After a moment, the older teen-agers hopped down from the truck and began to wander over.

"And I ain't gonna let some kid tell me what I can and can't do." Ace took a step toward Danny they stared each other down in tense silence.

"I told you," the boy growled, "I'm not a kid."

From the corner of his eyes, Danny noticed that a number of people inside had begun to gather at the window, Prescott, Sondra, Francine and the bowling alley's portly owner amongst them.

"Sounds like we got a rematch a-brewin'," Jack said, stopping a few yards away. He took a swig of beer and let a sly smirk spread across his lips. "Y'all gonna rumble?"

"Hell…" Ace growled, studying Danny. "Seems the guy I'm lookin' for ain't here, anyway. So why not?"

"I'm game if he is," Danny said through gritted teeth.

"Let's go." Ace shrugged. "I ain't got nothin' to lose."

"This time," the younger boy said, crouching and putting his fists up in the air, "you throw the first punch. Right here, right now."

Ace chewed at his lip, eyes drifting across the parking lot. He paused at the window, the owner glaring back, then shook his head.

"Nah." He looked back to Danny. "Not here. Ain't gonna let some ol' geezer break it up this time. But I know a place, real secluded-like. Where we can end this thing once and for all."

"Well, then," Jack said with a grin. "What're we waitin' for? Gather on up and hop in the truck!"

25   The Terrifying Transmissions

KA-TONK! KA-TONK! KA-TONK! Mary-Sue banged her fist against the knotted door at the entrance to the EARS headquarters. After a few moments the peep slot slid aside and a pair of sunken eyes ducked down into view. They went back and forth, seeming to study Mary-Sue's face with suspicion.

"Password?" A man barked out in a thick, French accent.

"Pierre, let me in." Mary-Sue crossed her arms. "I need your—"

KA-TACK! The slot quickly slammed shut. Mary-Sue jumped back in surprise, then and reached out and rapped at the door again. Once more, the slot slid open and Pierre glared through, eyes narrowed.

"Password?"

"It's me, Pierre, Mary-Sue Welles—"

KA-TACK!

Mary-Sue growled and stomped her foot on the platform. She didn't have time to play games—she was on a mission to solve her mystery once and for all. To be rid of it.

Besides, requiring a password didn't make any sense; Pierre knew her well. Just the previous summer, *The Britannica Junior Detectives* had helped the Frenchman to recover a stolen bottle of 1821 Grand Constance in *The Vexing Case of the Victorian Vineyard*. Pierre would surely trust her after she had helped to retrieve his prized possession.

WH-PAM-WH-PAM-WH-PAM!

This time, the peep slot did not pull aside.

"Pierre!" The girl yelled through the door. "I know you can hear me! I don't have a password, but you know the content of my character—I got that bottle of Napoleon's wine back for you and never asked for anything in return. So I'm asking now: let me in. It's an emergency!"

Nothing happened for a few seconds, but then from inside Mary-Sue heard an exchange of heated whispers and after a few moments more, the door unlocked and swung open. Standing at the entrance was Pierre, his arms crossed.

"For ze savior of my precious vintage?" He nodded and took a step back, gesturing her inside. "Anyzing, my friend."

Mary-Sue returned the nod, then stepped into

the clubhouse. Behind Pierre stood several of the other EARS members, glaring at the girl in front of a pile of hastily-packed boxes. The entire clubhouse looked ransacked, like they were packing up to leave in a hurry.

"What's the emergency?" Kat lisped. "This is a bad time."

"Then I won't be long." Mary-Sue stepped inside. Pierre closed the door behind her, turning the lock and leaning back against the door. She turned toward Kat. "You have powerful equipment here, right? Enough to pick up radio signals all across town, yes? Even faint ones? Even the ones you're not supposed to hear?"

"The girl's a snitch!" Gloria bared her teeth.

"I agree." Hugh frowned, placing his hand onto the elderly woman's shoulder. "I bet she's working for *them*."

"Them?" Mary-Sue frowned.

"Exactly what one of them would ask." Kat gave her a rueful look.

"Why'd you wanna get inside so bad, Welles?"

"Who sent ya?"

"What's it to you?"

"Spit it out!"

They all began stalking toward her, eyes narrowed. Mary-Sue took a step back and bumped into Pierre, who just stared down at her, cold. She whipped back around to find herself surrounded on all sides by scowling conspiracy theorists.

"Yes, my friend," Pierre muttered, stroking his mustache, "why have you come?"

"I—I'm pursuing a case!" Mary-Sue put her hands up. "I don't know who you think sent me, but I'm just following up on a lead of some radio signals that came from the swamp—that's all!"

"Radio signals?" Kat twisted her mouth to the side.

"The swamp?" Hugh scrunched his face up.

"Last night?" Gloria sniped.

"That's right—they were picked up at a very short distance." Mary-Sue cocked her head, her eyes drifting to the hastily-packed boxes. "Wait… do you already know about them?"

"Maybe!" Gloria pouted.

"A series of beeps, right?" Mary-Sue looked around at their faces, all eyes downcast. "They were Morse code, weren't they?"

"I am afraid not, my friend," Pierre said solemnly, stepping out from behind her. "Morse code, you see, is for ze English language."

"Not…" Mary-Sue took a step back and her

eyes went side. "In some sort of an… extraterrestrial language?"

"Worse." Gloria shook her head.

"Much worse." Hugh nodded along.

"Russian." Kat lisped. "Pierre just finished translating."

"Huh?" Mary-Sue scrunched her nose up. "The… Soviet Union? In Bonnifield? I don't understand. What did the code say?"

"Zat *Ze Britannica Junior Detectives* would not interfere," Pierre said grimly. "Zat ze sleeper cell's cover had been effective. Zat ze weapon would be stolen by mid-day. And zat tonight, zey would test it—set it off in Bonnifield."

"W—what?" Mary-Sue took a step back. "No, I… I can't…"

"Zis is why we wonder about your intentions." Pierre shrugged. "It seems zat you are somehow involved, whezer you are a spy or not."

"We…" She swallowed, shaking her head. "We need to tell someone! This is too big for *The Detectives*. We need to call the police, now!"

"We already tried." Kat frowned. "They didn't believe us."

"Called us nutty," Hugh sighed.

"Laughed at us!" Gloria tightened her fists.

"Said it was yet anozer conspiracy zeory." Pierre tightened his jaw.

"That's why we're leaving." Kat gestured to the boxes. "If nobody is going to believe us, at least we can save ourselves."

"Save yourselves? What about everybody else? What about warning the town? What about..." Mary-Sue placed her fingers on her temples, then closed her eyes. "There's a Soviet spy, hiding out in the woods! That's why the campers got scared away—to make sure nobody found out. And they're after..."

Her eyes went wide.

"Danny!" She yelped. "I need to find my partner!"

"On it!" Kat dashed to the radio console and pushed the microphone lever down. "Break one-one, this is Pipsqueak with an emergency request from HQ. Does everyone copy?"

After a moment, there was a burst of static.

"Copy, ten-four, Wheels here!"

"And Oculus!"

"You've got Buoy!"

"Treetop reading, loud and clear!"

"Great!" Kat jammed the lever down. "Anyone have eyes on Danny Britannica today?"

"Britannica? Funny you should ask," Treetop said. "Saw the kid not five minutes ago on his way up to the campgrounds, riding in the back of a truck. There were a few trucks, actually—and a motorcycle. Looked like a party."

"Wait, a motorcycle? Danny? No!" Mary-Sue's hand flew down her pocket and she pulled Ford's business card out, then handed it to Kat. "I need you to call this number right now, tell them Agent Ford needs to get to the campgrounds, as soon as he can. Then I need you call Dr. Oxford, have him look in his lab to see if his *Substance X* is still there—if not, he needs to get to the campgrounds, too."

Kat chewed at her lip. "What are you going to be doing?"

"Stopping an atomic bomb from killing us all," Mary-Sue said, then turned and sprung toward the door. She swung it open, slid across the platform, grabbed the rail, then started down the trunk.

"Bon voyage, mademoiselle!" Pierre called out behind her. "Bonne chance!"

26   ## The Reckless Rematch

Danny paced restlessly at the edge of the campgrounds as he waited for the greaser to finish his cigarette, fists balled up and knuckles white with rage. Surrounding him were two or three dozen teenagers who had piled into the back of their cars and trucks to witness the showdown—this time, free from the meddling of any adults.

On the other side of the gravel roundabout, Ace leaned coolly against his motorcycle, leather jacket flung casually over his shoulder. He stared off into the woods, as if the fight were the last thing on his mind—Danny, however, felt as if he could see a hint of fear hidden just behind the boy's eyes.

To Danny's left stood Sondra and Francine, looking concerned but saying nothing. To his right stood Jack and the high schoolers, flanked by Prescott and Phil—the latter of which was flipping through his notepad searching for a blank page, the former of which was dabbing at his damp forehead with a pristine handkerchief.

"My, uh... my good man..." Prescott cleared his

throat as he folded the cloth back into a neat square, then unfolded it with nervous fingers once again. "It's just occurred to me that this ruffian could be the very same that the FBI agent was referring to. We're in the woods, after all…"

"I handled him well enough the first time, Prescott," Danny said confidently. "This time, I intend to hold nothing back."

"Yes, yes, but…" Prescott began to pace alongside Danny. "The man said that he was a killer. A killer!"

"So, then," Danny said, smacking his fist into his other palm, "after I've defeated him, I'll hold him under citizen's arrest while the police are fetched."

"Mr. Oxford," Phil interrupted, looking up from his notepad, "as a representative of *The Gazette*, I must inquire: why have you chosen to employ these extrajudicial measures in your pursuit of justice?"

"Because every person is responsible for the impact of their actions," Danny said, narrowing his eyes as he watched the ember burn down on Ace's cigarette. "So if I chose to do nothing, then I'd be responsible for the reign of terror he enacted upon the next town, and the next. So, right here and now, I'm going to teach him a lesson in the only language that brutes like him understand: might."

"Yes, I see…" Phil jotted the quote down with a faint frown, then slid his pencil behind his ear and snapped the notepad shut. "Thank you Mr. Oxford. And while it's my sworn duty as a reporter to remain as objective as possible, I do wish to convey that my readership would surely hope for you emerge victorious."

"Thanks." Danny nodded. "I think that I know what you mean."

"Hey, folks!" Jack barked out. "We doin' this thing or what?"

Danny turned to see the high schooler taking a swig from a bottle of beer, then looked over to Ace, whose cigarette was nearly out.

"You know," Danny said, placing his hands onto his hips, "studies show that smoking kills."

"Funny," Ace said, squinting, "they say the same thing about me."

"Are…" Danny frowned. "Are you finished, yet?"

"Enough." The boy plucked the cigarette out from his mouth, looked at the end, then flicked it down to the gravel. "Ready when you are, kid."

"Cool." Jack grinned, then held his beer out toward Danny. "C'mon, have a nip. It'll calm the nerves."

"Danny," Prescott said, "shouldn't you try and

keep a clear—"

Danny grabbed the bottle without a second thought, then took a large swig of foul concoction. Across the lot, Ace stood up and tossed his leather jacket onto the seat of his motorcycle, then cracked his neck and twisted around to stretch his back.

"I must admit," Danny said, head fuzzy as he stepped forward, the other teenagers quickly gathering into a loose circle around the two boys, "that I'm not sure how to begin. Do we... touch gloves, as it were? Or is this the moment to decide on some sportsmen's rules? Say, nothing above the chest or below the belt? That sort of a—"

Without warning, the other teenager charged forward, covering the distance between them in no time, his fist careening directly toward the younger boy's face. Danny, caught off-guard, attempted to duck but was just a second too late—*KA-KRAAK!* the blow connected to the side of his head causing a daze of stars to dance before his eyes.

"Hot damn!" Jack yelled. "That's what I'm talkin' about!"

A cacophony of hoots and hollers burst from the crowd as the boy stumbled backward, barely hearing them through the sharp ringing in his ears. He shook his head and the fog began to clear.

"Danny!" Sondra cried out from the crowd. "Look out!"

His head whipped back toward Ace, who was charging his direction. On instinct alone, Danny dropped down to the ground and rolled to his side, forcing the greaser to leap over him, losing his footing as he landed. Danny jumped to his feet and swung a wild uppercut. Ace leaned back at the last moment and watched the fist fly by, sending Danny stumbling to the other side of the crowd with his follow-through.

"Knock his block off, Danny!" someone called out.

"Yeah, cream that greaser!" Someone cried.

"C'mon, hit the Jap!" Jack hollered. "Right in his slant-eyed face!"

Ace's head whipped to the side, scanning for the source of the slurs.

"Just what I thought…" He bared his teeth at Jack, then hoisted his fists up into the air and turned to Danny. "Let's give these folks a real show."

"The only thing that I'm going to show them," Danny said, licking his lips and tasting copper, "is that villains like you can only run for so long. That sooner or later, your past always catches up with you."

He raised his fists to match Ace's.

"Villains?" The greaser began to pace along the rim of the crowd. "What is this—grade school? C'mon, now, kid, ain't no good guys here." He smirked. "Just us."

"Oh yes?" Danny raised an eyebrow as he began to circle. "How do you figure?"

"I'm a wanted man." Ace eyed him as they stalked the circle. "You? An insecure little boy— petty, jealous, scared. Started a fight, challenged me to a rematch, brought all your little bigot friends to cheer ya on. Why? All 'cause your girl dug me more at the drive-in."

He turned and spotted Sondra in the crowd, then gave her a dirty look.

"You're a liar!" Sondra growled. "I never said anything of the sort! I only had eyes for Danny— until I saw his true character, that is."

"Stop lyin', doll, ya know ya said—"

Danny charged forward, slamming his shoulder into the distracted boy, sending them both careening down to the gravel in a tangle of limbs, dust kicking up around them and sharp pebbles slicing at their exposed arms. Danny was first to get a real blow in, punching Ace hard in the ribs, the other arm wrapped tightly around the greaser's torso. Ace responded by slamming his elbow into Danny's back over and over again.

For nearly a minute the boys scrambled desperately on the ground, neither able to gain any sort of advantage over the other, nor able to pull away. Finally, Ace managed to jam his boot heel into a clump of grass, then gave a hard shove, flipping Danny over onto his back. The younger boy yanked his arm free and rolled a few yards away.

"Come on, get up!" Jack yelled from his other side.

Slowly, Danny pushed himself onto his feet, breathing hard, his arms bleeding, his back aching. He looked around the circle, attempting to get his bearings, wobbling slightly back and forth, a fog in his head. Across the way Ace was still on the ground, his white t-shirt stained with streaks of red. All around them, the older teenagers clapped and cheered at the spectacle, a sea of faces lusting for blood and violence.

"Hit him!" someone sneered. "Hit him while he's down!"

"Finish the dirty Jap off, Danny!" Jack screamed.

The only faces that Danny could focus on, though, were those of his peers—Prescott's concerned expression betrayed his aloof and arrogant nature. Phil, ever austere and controlled in his emotions, gazed on with a tightly-knit brow. Francine looked frightened. Sondra, disappointed.

"C'mon!" Jack growled as Ace pushed himself to his feet. "Fight!"

"Fight! Fight! Fight! Fight!"

Danny pulled his gaze away from Sondra, then looked down at his arms, covered in cuts and bruises. Then at his shirt, streaked with red—his or Ace's, he couldn't tell. Danny took a deep breath, then turned his back to Ace.

"I'm done," he said, putting his hands up into the air. "It's over. This isn't going to solve anything."

"What?" Jack balked. "Just when it's gettin' good."

"It's a draw." Danny shook his head. "Or maybe I lose. I don't care—there isn't any point in continuing. We're just a couple of children, rolling around in the dirt—nobody is proving anything, here."

"C'mon, kid." Jack shook threw his hands up into the air. "You're just gonna let this—"

"Don't bother." Danny scowled. "I'm done."

"You may be done." Jack shrugged, a dangerous glint in his eye. The high schooler reached into the pocket of his jeans and pulled something out, then tossed it casually at Ace's feet. "But him?"

"A fight takes two people," Danny said, walking toward the far edge of the circle. But as he approached, Jack took a step forward, blocking his path, eyes fixed on Ace. *KA-FTT!*

Danny slowly turned around to look at the greaser, his eye pulled by something gripped in the boy's right hand. It gleamed in the evening sun as he waved it back and forth, considering the thing. After a moment it dawned on Danny what he was looking at: a switchblade knife.

Jack placed his hand on Danny's chest and gave him a shove back into the center of the circle.

27   Stopping the Senselessness

For just a moment Mary-Sue's bicycle left the ground as she crested the hill leading to the campgrounds. When the tires touched down the girl pushed back hard on her brakes, bringing the bicycle to a skidding stop behind the trucks parked at the entrance. As the dust settled, she spotted a crowd of teenagers standing in a circle nearby, cheering madly.

"Mary-Sue—over here!" Sondra called out from the fringes, waving her over. "It's Danny, he's in trouble!"

Mary-Sue pushed the bicycle down to the ground then charged past Sondra, plowing through the crowd without a second thought. She burst into the makeshift arena, causing all heads to snap her way. At the center of the circle was Ace, brandishing a knife at her best friend.

"Stop!" The girl yelled as she dashed toward them, sliding to a halt directly between the two bruised and bloody boys. "Drop it!"

"No—watch out!" An exhausted Danny yelped,

attempting to jump between the girl and the knife. Mary-Sue, however, dug her heels into the gravel and thrust her arms out to hold him at bay.

Ace snarled and took a step back, his grip tightening on the knife. He held it out, arm steady, eyes narrow, staring directly into her eyes.

"Scram, Red," he growled. "This is between me and the kid."

"I don't know what happened in your past, with Chuck," Mary-Sue said, voice steady, "but it's not too late to do the right thing—you have a choice. Just put the knife down."

"Already sang that song." Ace took a threatening step forward, but Mary-Sue stood in place, unyielding. "Tried playin' by the rules, stuck my neck out, played detective. Got screwed. Ain't nothin' changed. Or don't ya remember?"

"Ace—"

"Save it." The greaser took another step, waving the knife back and forth, blade glinting in the evening sun. "'Cause I ain't through with the kid. And if I gotta go through you, well—"

"Then you're going to have to," Mary-Sue said, "because I won't let you hurt my best friend."

"What, this kid?" Ace gave a cruel laugh and nodded. "Yea, okay—makes sense, now. You two deserve each other, Red."

"I got myself into this." Danny put a hand on her arm. "And it's my responsibility to face the consequences. I won't let you—"

"You ain't doin' nothin'—"

"Shut up! Both of you," she growled, shaking Danny's hand off. "If you two don't listen to me then none of us are going to be around to care about your personal drama very, very soon."

"What are you talking about?" Danny narrowed his eyes.

"Ace and I," Mary-Sue said, "we've been investigating a mystery in the woods." She locked eyes with Ace. "Or don't you remember?"

"Nice try," the greaser sneered, tossing the switchblade back and forth. "But it's like ya called it, Red—ain't no saucer, ain't no conspiracy. FBI man's after me, 'n that's that."

"You're half right," Mary-Sue said softly, "there isn't a saucer—but there is a conspiracy."

Ace hesitated, lowering the knife a few inches.

"I looked into the radio signals. They were the biggest clue yet," she continued, "but it's not Martians—it's Soviets spies. And…" She turned to Danny. "They've stolen your dad's secret weapon and they're going to test it in Bonnifield tonight."

Danny took a step back, the color draining from his face.

"So it is true," Danny gulped. "Violet, she was right. How could I be so naïve? I... I just didn't want to believe it! That my own father could..." the boy stuttered. "I—I saw the plutonium with my own eyes..."

Everyone in the crowd began to murmur amongst themselves.

"Everyone needs to head back to town." Mary-Sue called out above the rising din. "Get to safety—a fallout shelter or a basement. Any kind of safe place. Just in case."

And without another word, they all broke into a panic, shoving each other as they ran toward their respective vehicles, terrified groups of high schoolers piling in as doors slammed shut.

In the confusion, the younger kids seemed lost. Having tagged along with the unfamiliar high schoolers, they were unsure of which vehicle to head toward in the chaos. And as engines roared to life, they each bolted in a different direction.

Prescott attempted to scramble into the bed of Jack's truck, but was knocked back when a panicking high schooler took his place. Sondra and Francine tried the door handles of the next car, but they were locked. Phil headed toward the farthest truck, but couldn't reach it before it peeled out, spraying him with rocks and gravel. One by one, each vehicle pulled away, speeding down the hill and leaving the youngsters in their dust.

Mary-Sue turned to the boys, a grave expression on her face.

"There's a chance we can stop it, but I need you—both of you, to set aside your personal problems and do what I say. Are you in?"

Danny nodded, but Ace took a step back and shook his head.

"This is my chance. My only chance, wipin' the slate clean."

"Ace?" Mary-Sue raised her eyebrows. "Please! You can—"

"Don't try it, Red." The greaser shook his head, backing up toward his motorcycle. "This FBI guy, he placed me. He knows I been campin' in the woods. He got it on record, yeah? So this thing blows…" He grabbed his leather jacket and slipped it on. "Then I'm a ghost. Ain't nobody even knows I exist no more. A real second chance."

"No!" She cried out as he swung his leg over the seat. "Your second chance is saying, helping us stop the bomb. Please—consider all the good you can do!"

"Only good I got left..." He flipped his kick-stand up and turned the key. *VRRRRMM! RM-RM-Rm-Rm-m...* "Is savin' my own hide."

Ace looked up, giving Mary-Sue a sad look, then hunched over and hit the gas, peeling out and rocketing away down the hill.

"W—what are we to do?" Prescott squeaked through rapid breaths, pacing back and forth, wiping at his brow with his handkerchief. "What did Mrs. Applebaum say? Duck, then cover, yes?"

"Is it..." Francine looked toward Mary-Sue, wide-eyed. "I mean, are we going to be okay?"

"How can we help?" Sondra asked, voice steady.

"Well," Danny began, "if we all—"

"Danny and I are going out into the swamp," Mary-Sue interrupted. "We're going to find the spy and stop them from blowing the bomb up. I contacted Dr. Oxford and the Agent Ford—they should be on their way now." She swung her bag around, unbuckled the straps, then yanked her map of Mercury Marsh out. She plucked the pencil from behind Phil's ear and marked a large X next to the old dock. "When they arrive, give them this map and tell them to head to this mark. Then find a low area, crouch down, and cover your heads. Got it?"

"Got it." Sondra reached out and took the map.

Mary-Sue turned to Danny. "Are you ready to take my lead?"

Danny nodded. "Ready."

Mary-Sue turned toward the swamp.

"Then let's go solve *The Mutant of Mercury Marsh*."

28   # Stalking the Specter

"I didn't get a chance to thank you," Danny said, scanning the beam of his flashlight across the muddy forest floor, "back at camp. For putting yourself in harm's way. For saving me."

A few yards ahead, Mary-Sue stomped across the dense underbrush, sure-footed despite the rapidly-growing twilight.

"Mm-hm," she grunted.

"And," Danny said with a sigh, "I'm also very sorry."

"Oh yes? For which part?" Mary-Sue shook her head, ducking under a prickly blackberry bush as they approached the lip of the hill.

"For not believing your mystery, of course, at the soda fountain." He jogged to catch up to the girl's side. "You were right—I let my judgement become impaired by my romantic entanglements. And I let my priorities get out of order. But now that's been corrected."

"Uh-huh." She began to shuffle down the side of the hill, steadying herself on the trunks of the sturdy spruce trees.

"But really," he said, following her down, "it was only two days that we weren't pursuing your case, so in the grand scheme of things—"

"Actions speak louder than words, Danny," Mary-Sue said, stopping at the bottom of the hill and turning to glare at him as he shuffled to catch up. "Apologies are meaningless—unless they're followed by a change in behavior, an awareness of what was actually done wrong. And over the last two days, you've shown a pattern of poor decision-making and a lack of judgement in a whole lot of areas. So, no—I don't forgive you. Not yet, anyway. Not unless you alter the pattern."

"I see." He reached her side. "Then I hope to earn that forgiveness in time and prove that I do understand—that I have changed my ways." The boy looked out over the marsh as the twilight gave way to dusk, then directed the beam of his flashlight toward the tall grasses of Mercury Marsh beyond, a thin mist beginning to rise above them. "Perhaps I can begin by lending my insight to the facts as-known?"

Mary-Sue gazed silently across the marsh, eyes narrowed, then took off across the path, disappearing into the grass. Danny ran to catch up, the suction of the boggy mud pulling at his shoes as he went.

"What I mean to say is, if I understood the timeline, then perhaps—"

"Dale Brown saw a mutant. Ace saw an extra-terrestrial. And I saw a flying saucer, all by the old Civil War graveyard," Mary-Sue whispered harshly, leading them deeper into the marsh. "Campers got scared away, they all blamed Ace for no reason, and it put the FBI back on his trail. We couldn't find the saucer, but we did find traces of radiation out near the old dock. Ace heard radio signals coming from somewhere in the swamp, and the EARS confirmed that they were Soviet in origin. Their plan was apparently to neutralize us, steal your dad's secret weapon, and blow it up sometime tonight. All in the past two weeks, while I was investigating this and you were doing... well, whatever you wanted. Got it?"

"Y—yes." He nodded. "Got it."

"No clever insight?"

"I—I..." Danny cleared his throat. "I think that you have a fairly firm grasp on the situation."

A few yards ahead, the girl stopped at the entrance to the graveyard. As Danny jogged to her side, his foot plunged into a gap in the peat moss and soaked his shoe and the bottom of his slacks. He scowled, shook his leg off, then joined the sure-foot-ed girl.

In the cool night air, the mist had grown more dense and the graves and crypts were cast in abstract shadows. Mary-Sue stepped through the gateway, then scanned her flashlight around the grounds. Clear, the girl began walking toward the far side of the cemetery, fading more and more the farther she went. In the distance beyond, he could barely make out a slowly pulsing red light through the fog.

"Now," Mary-Sue said, voice wavering as she lost herself in the glow. After a moment she turned and pointed at a limestone burial vault on Danny's other side. "I need you to sit there."

"Why?" Danny narrowed his eyes. "What's the plan?"

"Do you trust me?" She ran back over and swung her bag around.

"Yes…"

"Then we need to split up." Mary-Sue pulled the walkie-talkies out and handed one over to Danny. Together they clicked the power dials on. "And you need to serve as lookout."

"I think that we would be better served by—"

"This is where Ace saw the extraterrestrial. And where Dale saw the mutant. The radiation trail went

right through here, as did the footprints. Which either means that I'm going to sneak up on the specter over there," she said, gesturing toward the red
light, "at that saucer, or disc, or bomb or whatever it
is—or its going to sneak up on me through here. If
you're the lookout, you can give me ample warning."

"Don't you think we should—"

"This isn't *The Britannica Junior Detectives*," she
said firmly, "and I'm not *Rocket the Wonder Dog*. This
is my mystery, you got it?"

Danny took a deep breath, then nodded. "Got
it."

Mary-Sue turned, jumped over the crumbling
wall, then disappeared through the haze. Danny
hopped up onto the burial vault and clicked his
flashlight off, not wanting to risk giving his position
away. He scanned his eyes back and forth, but there
was nothing outside of fog, shadow, and the sounds
of frogs and crickets in the uneasy darkness.

He felt sick. Everything that Violet had said was
true—his father was a war profiteer, who had built
atomic bombs for the United States government.
And now, the scientist's newest and most powerful
weapon was in the hands of the Soviets, and the only
thing standing in the way of them blowing a bomb
up in Bonnifield was him and Mary-Sue. And he

was stuck sitting watch.

Lost in thought, the boy barely noticed a slight movement out of the corner of his eye, at the far end of the cemetery. It was only as the figure began to stalk toward him that he became fully cognizant of its presence. Danny slowly slid down from the vault and took a large step back, a chill running down his spine.

Through the haze and darkness, the specter looked just like Mary-Sue's drawing: a horrible atomic mutant with two massive, black eyes. It was wearing a protective orange suit with a bizarre breathing apparatus. And it was holding the canister of *Substance X*.

"Mary-Sue!" Danny raised the walkie-talkie up to his mouth. "Mary-Sue, do you copy?" He turned around and leapt over the wall, then took off into the reeds, jamming the call button down as the specter pursued close behind. "Mary-Sue it's after me!" He cried. "*The Mutant of Mercury Marsh* is after me!"

29   # The Secret of Suicide Hill

Mary-Sue pushed through a final patch of reeds to find herself at the edge of the lagoon, two hundred yards away from the metal saucer, faint through the murky fog. Above it, the eerie red light blinked on and off, over and over again.

Despite reassuring herself that there was nothing supernatural afoot, the girl's arms were covered in goose-pimples and the hair on the back of her neck was standing up straight. If she had found the idea of a flying saucer frightening, then a covert Soviet mission to set off an experimental atomic bomb was far more chilling.

The metallic disc sat there, motionless and ominous. Whatever *The Mutant of Mercury Marsh* really was—man or monster—the Soviets had yet to execute their final plan. If the saucer was its escape vehicle, that meant it was still around, lurking somewhere nearby. But if the object was instead some sort of a bomb, then the Soviet agent could be miles away, ready to set it off at the touch of a button.

sshhSSHHSFF! There was a sudden rustling in

the grass behind her, and Mary-Sue jumped back, whipping around and raising her flashlight up to reveal Ace, standing coolly at the edge of the grass.

"You!" The girl slapped her hand onto her chest, catching her breath. She glanced back over her shoulder at the saucer, then grabbed his arm, pulling him back through the reeds. "You scared me half to death," she whispered. "What are you doing here? I thought this was your chance to get away."

"Yeah, well." The greaser shoved his hands into his pockets and cast his eyes down to the ground, voice lowered. "Farther I got, more I knew I gotta turn back."

"What made you do it?"

"Funny thing a little freckled redhead said to me once." Ace gave a shrug and lifted his eyes to hers. "Sometimes ya gotta do the right thing, just to do it. And I ain't ever done a damn thing right."

"Well, it's now or never," Mary-Sue said, studying the boy. "But if we're going to put our lives on the line, I need to know what I'm getting into." She frowned. "I still don't know what precisely is going on here. When the bomb is going off, if the creature is connected to the Soviets, what the saucer truly is... anything! For all we know, you could be right—Agent Ford could be lying about who he is and why he's here. He could still be one of the men in black suits, throwing us off the trail. So I need to know the truth: is he after you for killing a boy?"

Ace stood silent, gazing out into the fog. After a few moments, he nodded then mumbled, "Suicide Hill."

Mary-Sue tilted her head to the side. "What's—"

"Every kid in town heard 'a Suicide Hill—out on 'Thirty-Four, past that ol' Hickenbottom place." The boy shoved his hands into his pockets. "Highway curves 'round the top, can't nobody see what's comin'."

Mary-Sue nodded and slowly crossed her arms. "Okay."

"After Pop died in the war, well… Ma had a rough time raisin' me." He closed his eyes. "After them camps let us out, we moved 'round a lot, never quite settled down, never quite fit in. Everywhere we went, nobody seemed to trust us—always givin' us the side-eye, y'know? Never givin' us the benefit of the doubt. All the other kids, well…" The boy gave a wry laugh and shook his head. "We didn't get along too well. Soon, I get a bad rep, get a record—get in a fight here, break a window there. So Ma, yea? She gets me into shop class, fixin' stuff instead 'a breakin' it. By the time high school rolls 'round, I'm best in Ukiah Valley, I figure. 'Til one day this new kid shows up at the shop—Chuck. A real knack for engines, y'know? Lives 'n breathes the stuff. But he likes hot rods 'n I like bikes. Work side-by-side two years, pushin' ourselves to be better 'n the other, always tryin' to one up each other. Rivals through-and-through."

"Friends?" Mary-Sue pushed her mouth to the side.

"Maybe." Ace shrugged and kicked a patch of grass. "Somethin' like that, anyway. Then, see, summer 'a junior year he meets a girl, real sweetheart. At first he's just showin off his rig, but when he talks 'bout it she sees he got somethin' special inside 'im. Could be an engineer, she says, design 'em instead 'a fixin' 'em. Turns him 'round right quick 'n now he's gettin' straight As, runnin' with the brainy crowd. Ain't showin' up at the shop on the reg' no more, dig?"

"Sure." Mary-Sue nodded.

"So one day, Chuck, he shows up 'n tells me he's gettin' a gig at that factory on the edge of town—not on the line, mind ya, but fixin' up the machines. Ain't got no time for 'rods no more, droppin' it to focus on the engineer thing." Ace cast his eyes down. "So I goad 'im, y'know? Run my mouth. Tell 'im that skirt made him go soft. Tell 'im he sold out, ain't got it no more."

Mary-Sue took a step toward him. "You were afraid of losing your only friend."

"He laughs 'n says ain't no way." Ace quickly brushed past the girl's comment. "But I call 'im out in front 'a all 'a his new square friends. Tell him he ain't no good, say I coulda got that job if I wanted, but I ain't no sellout—say my bike could beat his rod any day." Ace tightened his jaw. "Well, he ain't take kindly to that, not in front 'a his girl, especially. So I say let's race, rod against bike. He just asks me when 'n where. All eyes on me, I say Suicide Hill. Right now."

"No." Mary-Sue laid her hand on his arm. "You don't mean…"

"Yeah." Ace yanked his arm away and turned to look out over the marsh toward the campgrounds. "Half the school comes out, all rootin' for him. Chuck 'n me, we get side by side on that ol' highway. His girl begs him not to, 'course, but neither 'a us can back down. That flag flies and so do we—neck 'n neck down Thirty-Four. He pulls ahead, then me, then him. We reach that hill 'n I start gainin' on him, engines gunnin' so hard we ain't payin' attention to nothin' else. And when we get to the top of that hill, another car comes around the bend and…"

He stopped and stood silent as a tear fell from the corner of his eye.

"I am so, so sorry, Ace." Mary-Sue tenderly took the boy's hand. "It wasn't your fault. It was just a freak accident, bad timing. It was—"

"Those brains, they don't see it that way." Ace wiped the tear from his cheek with his other hand. "All them got it 'gainst me, sayin' I killed their golden boy, ran 'im off the road on purpose. Tell the pigs the same, fingers pointin' right at me, callin' me a killer. They says it adds up 'cause I got a bad record, say I'm a juvenile delinquent—gonna make an example outta me, throw the book at me. So I skip town before they can grab me. Been on the run ever since." He shrugged. "Guess crossin' state lines made it Federal."

"But if you knew they were after you, then why cause any trouble?" Mary-Sue asked. "Why draw attention to yourself at the Co-Ed and start a fight with Danny if you already had a record?"

"Told ya once already," Ace huffed, tightening his jaw, "I ain't the one that started it—I was off mindin' my own business between a coupla monster flicks when this chick comes up ta me, points to her little blonde friend yonder, tells me she's a nice girl with a thing for bad boys. Now, ain't no girl ever pay me no mind. Not no sweetheart, 'specially. So I head over, start talkin to her, then POW! Your little friend gives me one across the jaw."

"Wait." Mary-Sue frowned. "So that means—"
BLEEP-BLEEP!

"—Sue! Mary-Sue, do you copy?" Danny's desperate voice crackled out from the radio at the girl's side. "Mary-Sue, it's after me! *The Mutant of Mercury Marsh* is after me!"

Mary-Sue snapped her head over to Ace, eyes wide. "Do you still have that knife?"

He nodded and pulled the switchblade out from his pocket, flicking it open. Mary-Sue raised the walkie-talkie to her mouth and jammed the call button down.

"I read you Danny!" she yelled. "Head to the saucer, to the red light, then wait for my signal. Over. And. Out."

30   Beneath the Black Bayou

Danny scrambled through the grass, tripping and stumbling over the unfamiliar terrain. He burst out through a patch of reeds to find himself at the edge of a deep pool of water. Eschewing his usual careful planning, the boy allowed his blind panic to take over and gracelessly leapt to the other side.

Only as he landed on the far bank did Danny dare glance back over his shoulder. A few dozen yards behind him, the specter crashed through the grass in close pursuit. Attempting to remind himself that nothing supernatural was afoot, Danny took off toward the treeline, where Mary-Sue was waiting for him at the flying saucer.

The closer he got to the lagoon, the more difficult navigation became. The ground beneath his feet, once-firm, had quickly turned into muddy, water-logged peat moss as the tide came in. His pace had slowed to a crawl. But just as Danny felt the creature gaining on him, he pushed through the grass to find himself at the water's edge.

All around, the dense fog was cast in a chilling

red glow. There was a deep, unsettling hum emanating from somewhere nearby, reverberating in the boy's chest and causing the hairs on the back of his neck to stand on end. Slowly, he turned to find its source, then froze.

There, not a dozen yards in front of him, was a huge, metallic disc at the very end of a dilapidated old dock. But instead of a flying saucer from another world, as Mary-Sue had described, all that Danny could see was the curved, rivet-lined surface of an atomic bomb—just like the ones his father had helped drop on Japan.

Danny took a step in its direction, but before he could reach the dock there was a rustling behind him. The boy whipped back to see the creature slowly emerge from the tall reeds. He tensed, instinctively attempting to come up with some sort of a plan. But Mary-Sue had told him to stay put and wait for her signal—and he had agreed that it was her case.

Carefully, he took a step backward toward the bomb as the creature lurched forward, holding the canister of *Substance X* in front of it. As it stalked closer and closer, the monster's gloved hand reached up toward the release valve at the top of the canister. The terrified boy took another step back, then another, and another until his heels just touched the edge of the rickety dock as the monster was nearly upon him, hand slowly moving toward the valve until—

KA-PIFF! A blinding light exploded all around, illuminating the fog as Danny fell to his knees, ducking for cover and throwing his arms back over his head as he had been instructed to do so many times before—but instead of a terrible, burning pain as he had expected, the boy simply felt a cool splash of swamp water against his skin. *KER-SPLSH!*

After a moment he opened his eyes and attempted to blink the bright after-image away. As his vision adjusted, he saw Mary-Sue emerge from behind a nearby stump, her camera in hand, unscrewing a flashbulb. He spun back to where the creature had been, only to see it half-submerged in a bog-hole cut into the peat moss. It struggled hopelessly, trapped in a tangle of reeds, giving off muffled grunts. More importantly, though, the *Substance X* lay safely on the ground a few feet away, thrown clear in the confusion. Unopened.

"What…?" Danny looked back to Mary-Sue, who had a huge grin on her face, deep dimples pushed into her freckled cheeks. The boy tilted his head to the side. "Did we do it?"

"We did it." She nodded.

Danny looked back to the creature. With his vision returned and his panic subsided, he was now able to see it for what it truly was—the large, black eyes which had seemed so alien through the dense fog now looked to be a pair of protective goggles, built into a rubber orange suit. The boy could even see the stitching on the fabric and the mechanics of the breathing apparatus built into the mask. Not a space suit at all—but a diving suit.

His attention was pulled away by a rustling in the reeds on his other side. A dark figure emerged. As the eerie, red light blinked on once again, he realized that it was none other than Ace—and he was holding a long line of reeds tied together into a makeshift rope. Danny looked at him, at the creature, then at Mary-Sue.

"A tripwire?" he asked. "For a trap... in which I was the bait?"

"Ya really are sharp, kid." Ace sneered, then gestured to the water. "Next you'll be telling us that thing ain't no flyin' saucer."

Danny turned to the disc, sweeping his flashlight across its smooth, rivet-lined surface. Free from superstition, the young detective could see that it was no flying saucer at all—nor was it an atomic bomb. Through the fog, the thing had appeared to be a huge, floating orb, but in reality it was the tip of something much larger beneath the surface, reflected in the lagoon's calm waters.

"A submarine!" Danny's eyes went wide. He stepped onto the dock and walked carefully along its old, creaking boards. In the dim red light, he could just make out the Cyrillic letters. "I've seen one just like it before, in *Popular Mechanics*. But that was a November class—this is much too small to be the same. Though... perhaps it's an experimental model, designed to be helmed by a skeleton crew, or a new classified—"

"Look!" Mary-Sue called out as a pair of twin yellow beams cut through the fog in the sky. Danny followed her gaze out across the marsh and up the hill toward the campgrounds, where two sets of headlights had come to a stop. "That'd be your dad, Danny," the girl said, then turned to Ace. "And Ford. You'd better go, once he gets here he'll—"

"Go?" Danny balked. He marched back down the dock and out onto the grass, putting himself between Ace and any escape route. "And let a fugitive evade justice once again? Not while I'm here, we won't!"

"You don't understand," Mary-Sue said, walking up next to Danny and gently placing a hand on his shoulder "He's innocent. He didn't kill anyone. It was all just an accident—a misunderstanding exacerbated by ignorance and bigotry."

"And from whom, precisely, did you hear that story?" Danny glared at Ace, eyes narrowed. "An objective witness, I'm certain?"

"He came back," Mary-Sue growled as the two hot-headed boys took a step toward each other. "Even knowing the risk, knowing that he could be arrested for a crime he didn't commit, he decided to do the right thing; to put his life on the line to save our home. And in the process..." The girl paused and looked down to the *Substance X*. "Maybe even the world. So... the least we could do is let him get a head start. Right?"

"And do what?" Danny crossed his arms. "Head to Burlington, or to Mt. Pleasant, or to Libertyville, off to bully the good people there?"

"He didn't bully anyone—"

"He pulled a knife on me, Mary-Sue!" Danny whipped back around, furious. "And on you. You saw it yourself: he's a menace!"

"He didn't—"

"Kid's right." Ace said, causing the two to turn toward him. "'Bout one thing, anyway: I'm stayin' and that's that."

"W—well," Danny stuttered, uncrossing his arms. "Good."

"No!" Mary-Sue cried out and ran to the greaser, taking his hands in hers. "If you stay, you'll be arrested for certain. If you go, if you run, then maybe… just maybe you get a second chance, somewhere out there."

"Ain't no more runnin' for me." The greaser stared into her eyes and a weary softness came over his face. "Gotta own up to what I done 'n take responsibility. I ain't done it on purpose, but Chuck's dead 'cause 'a me. So I'm settin' it straight, seein' it through to the end."

"Then it's decided." Danny said, looking out over the marsh where a set of flashlights bounced their way. "There's nothing to do but wait."

"Yes." Mary-Sue turned to the Soviet, still struggling in the bog hole. "And I think it will all make a lot more sense just as soon as we find out who *The Mutant of Mercury Marsh* really is."

"Let's see who's really behind The Mutant of Mercury Marsh."

31   The Radioactive Reveal

"It all began with a phone call," Mary-Sue said, standing at the edge of the dock.

To her left was Danny, to her right was Ace, and directly in front of her was *The Mutant of Mercury Marsh*, tangled hopelessly in the bog hole. A few yards ahead of them was a small group of onlookers; Dr. Oxford, Agent Ford, Sondra, Francine, and Prescott each watched on with eager anticipation. Even Phil, ever the austere journalist, looked intrigued as he yanked the pencil out from behind his ear, notepad at the ready.

"Dale Brown called the police to report a strange sighting out in the swamp: a bug-eyed mutant, lurking near the lagoon," Mary-Sue continued. "Due to his poor reputation in the community, his report was dismissed. Then, a Japanese-American boy reported an extraterrestrial being scaring campers off," she said, gesturing to Ace. "But due to bigoted minds, his report was also dismissed. Then, a group of conspiracy theorists reported a coded Soviet transmission. They, too, were dismissed. Finally, when a detective's sidekick put the whole pattern together and realized that there really was something going on—her report?" She looked over to Danny. "Dismissed."

He reached up and scratched at the back of his neck.

"I've been told," the girl continued, beginning to pace along the edge of the dock, "that too often I let my imagination get the best of me—that I've been prone to fantastical thinking. But if I'd listened to those words, if I hadn't pursued my own curiosity, then none of us would be here right now—and this fiend would have gotten away." The girl looked over and examined the unusual orange diving suit which had terrified so many. "I began my investigation with a flaw: because I was hoping for a fantastical explanation, I looked only for evidence that supported that conclusion. It wasn't until I discussed the scientific method with Dr. Oxford that I knew I'd have to push back on my assumptions and apply critical thinking, that I'd have to pursue the evidence objectively.

"So I challenged my preconceived notions and found Ace," she said. "An outsider to our community, someone born into bias, looking to find anyone who would believe him. Our first clue was a set of prints leading through the old cemetery—where he'd seen *The Mutant of Mercury Marsh* before. That established a pattern. Our next clue was the location of this." She gestured back toward the metallic disc behind her, its eerie red light still blinking on and off. "Witnessed by us and by Prescott. Searching the area later, however, proved fruitless. We were at a loss until my partner found our third clue: a series of coded radio signals, emanating from the same area. I followed the clue to the EARS where they told me the same thing they had tried to tell the police: that there was a Soviet spy amongst us, who had deliberately broken *The Britannica Junior Detectives* up—and who had stolen the canister of Dr. Oxford's *Substance X*. In the meantime, though, I'd made another big mistake: not trusting in my partner."

On her other side, she saw Ace straighten up.

"Who was mistrusted and driven out by his own community, only to come face to face with the same ignorance here in Bonnifield. Blamed for scaring the campers away, hassled by the police, pursued by the law for a crime that he didn't commit. But despite all this," she said, looking Agent Ford directly in the eyes, "Ace decided to do the right thing—the selfless thing. He came back to help me catch the real criminal. But it wasn't until he told me how he'd been manipulated into raising Danny's ire that it all clicked and I realized who the culprit truly was." She took a step forward onto the grass. "And right now, right in front of us, is the proof. Not of an atomic mutant, nor of a Martian from outer space, but of a Soviet ploy to steal secrets, uncovered by the dismissed at the fringes of society. Now," Mary-Sue said, leaning down and grabbing the diving suit's zipper, "let's see who's really behind *The Mutant of Mercury Marsh*."

She yanked the mask off.

"My word!" Dr. Oxford exclaimed.

"Gol-ly!" Sondra shook her head in disbelief.

"No kiddin'," Ace chuckled.

"Interesting." Phil scribbled furiously. "Most interesting…"

"No…" Danny took a step back, reeling. "No—can… can it be true?" He rubbed at his eyes. "Is—is that you, Violet?"

"I am afraid so," the raven-haired girl answered in a thick, Russian accent. She turned her head to look at Danny. "But my name is Anastasia Dimitrov."

The boy just stared back in shock.

"Now there's just one thing," Mary-Sue said, "that I couldn't figure out: why—"

"How could you do it?" Danny cried out, his face red and contorted. "Was everything you said a lie?"

For a moment, Anastasia was silent. Then, she took a deep breath.

"I come from a village in Southwest Siberia," she said stoically. "Papa was killed in the Great Patriotic War, Mama raised me alone. All my life I was told, like her, that I would grow up to work in the factory. But after the accident that took Mama's life, I left home, chasing dreams of a better future. I stowed away on trains until I arrived in Moscow. There, I lived on the street, first as a pickpocket, soon as a con-artist. After I was caught, I was put in a state orphanage for children of soldiers where I excelled in my studies. Due to my record, after the Supreme Leader died, I was put in a boarding school run by the KGB to learn espionage tactics, trained to pass as an American."

"My... God!" Agent Ford whipped his glasses off. "Children, trained as spies? The Reds are truly barbaric!"

"While you may have prospered from the war," Anastasia narrowed her eyes at Ford, "we were thrown into crisis—nine million lost in battle, twenty-six million total with starvation, famine,

disease. We did what we had to in order to survive."
She turned to look at Dr. Oxford. "So when our intelligence discovered you had been asked to build a weapon deadly enough to end the Cold War, the KGB made a plan to steal it. From your newspaper articles, we knew that your son was a renowned detective—a complication in the mission."

"So that's why you had to break up *The Britannica Junior Detectives*," Mary-Sue said. "Because you knew that we would uncover your plan."

"Correct," Anastasia said. "It would be dangerous, with little hope of success, and much need for improvisation. I volunteered immediately, knowing that I was the best suited for the mission. I was given a dossier and trained to operate an experimental nuclear submarine which would allow me to infiltrate Bonnifield undetected." She looked at Danny. "The dossier contained a psychological profile. It told me all I needed to know about you: high intellectual skill, but low emotional intelligence. Naïve, but well-liked. Wound too tight. No romantic experience. So we created a persona we knew would intrigue you—your opposite. A bohemian girl, unafraid to break the rules, to challenge your worldview. Distracting you from your detective work, putting your guard down. So when I arrived in the swamp,

I scared the witnesses away from the campgrounds, then watched you from the shadows, waiting for the right moment."

"And that's when you lied to Ace, told him that Sondra had a crush on him," Mary-Sue mused. "You were eliminating any competition—it was a honey trap! You endeared yourself to Danny so you could get the access codes to the laboratory and steal the *Substance X*."

"And hopefully," the Soviet nodded, "rid myself of the best witness in the process, getting him arrested."

"You dirty rat," Ace growled. "You were framing me!"

"Incredible..." Danny swallowed his words, eyes cast to the ground. "All of it was lies."

"Nyet." Anastasia's eyes shot toward him. "It was the plan, yes, but..." She looked to the *Substance X* and furrowed her brow. "Researching my beatnik cover story, I was exposed to radical new ideas. In school, we had been taught all Americans were the same—selfish, greedy capitalists. And while I saw where these stories came from in the excesses of Americans, in the writings of youth I found anger at the system, passion for new ways, humor and humanity. I realized I had been a victim of government propaganda, that my mission was flawed. That all I would be doing was handing the power from one corrupt system to another."

"Yet you still were going to go through with their plan." Danny scowled.

"Nyet." Anastasia sighed, her face softening. "I stole the *Substance X*, true. But I planned to take it to the middle of the ocean and drop it where nobody could ever find it."

"So why didn't you?" Mary-Sue arched an eyebrow, skeptical. "You had stolen the *Substance X*, broken up the *Junior Detectives*, and gotten away without anyone knowing your identity. Why try to scare us off?"

"When I got back to my submarine, the engine had stalled—it is an experimental prototype, after all. So I put on my diving suit one last time, to frighten you all away so I could fix it and make my escape." The girl gave a huff. "And I would have gotten away with it, too, if it weren't for Mary-Sue Welles."

"You underestimated me." Mary-Sue crossed her arms.

"This is true." Anastasia sighed. "The dossier contained little on you, only that you were not the brains of the operation—that you would pose no threat once separated from Danny. But you discovered my plan, and it was because of that mistake that the United States government now has the biggest bomb in the world."

"Well…" Dr. Oxford said, striking a match and bringing it up to his pipe. "Not exactly."

"You can't deny it, Pop," Danny said, glaring at his father. "I saw the contract myself, and the plutonium. Plus, I know that you worked on the Manhattan Project."

"That's right, sir," Mary-Sue said, joining Danny's side, "you told me yourself you were making something for the military. That it would end the arms race once and for all."

"And I hope that it will, truly," the scientist said, shaking the match out and tossing it onto the ground. "It's true that the military hired me to build an atomic bomb more powerful than anything that the Reds could produce—but ever since the second World War, I've been haunted by my part in the atrocities." He took a series of short puffs from his pipe, then blew a long stream of smoke out. "I realized that I had been justifying my participation under a guise of scientific objectivity. But with the weight of all of those lives at Hiroshima and Nagasaki heavy on my shoulders, I realized that I had to take responsibility for my own actions. I put myself to the challenge of creating a new type of nuclear deterrent. One that was truly peaceful, one that wouldn't require the specter of mutually assured destruction. So you see," Dr. Oxford said, gesturing to the canister, "this doesn't create atomic radiation—it destroys it. Absorbs it and neutralizes its effects."

"The submarine!" Anastasia gasped. "Why it would not start!"

"Exactly." The scientist nodded. "The radiation from its atomic core would have been rendered inert by the proximity of the gas, as will every atomic weapon on Earth, once I release it into the atmosphere."

"You mean..." Danny stared at his father, wide-eyed. "You found a way to end the nuclear arms race through peaceful means?"

"Indeed." He took a puff from the pipe. "When you helped me with that experiment, we were testing the effects of MAP on the plutonium with which the government had supplied me in order to build a bomb. After you pulled that lever, its radiation had become nearly undetectable."

"MAP?" Danny shook his head.

"The name I've come up with for *Substance X*." The scientist beamed. "It stands for *Mutually As-*

sured Protection."

"You fool!" Ford growled. "You've disarmed us! Leveled the playing field between Uncle Sam and the Reds!"

"And perhaps," Anastasia said, face softening, "saved the world."

"I hope so, for now, at least," the scientist said with a nod. "Until our governments devise some new super-weapon, our nations will be forced to negotiate, to attempt to understand alternative perspectives, to work together." He turned toward the submarine and stared into its pulsing red light. "'*For the word is sharper than the two-edged sword, piercing soul and spirit, joint and marrow, illuminating the intent and desires of the heart.*'"

"Don't think that I won't be reporting this to my higher-ups," Ford rebuked. "It's our national security that you've violated. I could have you arrested!"

"You and I both know that I would win that case in the court of public opinion. Let the public decide if the elimination of impending doom was a positive or a negative choice." He gave a shrug and turned his pipe over, tapping the ashes out. "I believe that everyone needs a reminder every now and then that challenging the government is their personal responsibility. I plan to publish an article on the incident in several scientific journals, myself."

"We had war before the bomb," Ford said, jaw clenched, "we'll have war after the bomb."

"True." Dr. Oxford nodded, slipping the pipe back into his pocket. "For now, though, the strongest and most destructive nations on Earth will no longer be able to hold the rest of the planet hostage just for minor, fleeting political squabbles. I, for one, think that's a very good thing."

For a moment, everyone on the bank of the lagoon stood silent as the red light pulsed. Then, Agent Ford pulled a pair of handcuffs out from his pocket and began walking toward Anastasia.

"Well." He reached down and grabbed her shoulder. "I suppose it's my responsibility to take you in, now, young lady."

Ford planted his feet and pulled hard, yanking the girl out from the muck and onto the grass. He quickly moved her wrists behind her back, slapped the handcuffs on, and raised her up to her feet. He then turned to Ace, reached into his blazer, and slowly pulled his revolver out. The man pointed it directly at the greaser.

"You're coming with me, too." He narrowed his eyes. "Killer."

32   The Detectives Disband

"Wait, sir!" Danny cried out, causing Ford to pause, gun still pointed at Ace. "I can't claim to understand the details of your assignment, but I can vouch the boy's character—which I saw in action earlier tonight." He looked at the greaser. "Ace had a chance to get away—not just from you, but from what we all thought to be an imminent atomic explosion. Instead, he came back to help, to catch Violet…" He paused to look at his former sweetheart, covered in mud, her hands in cuffs. He swallowed, a lump forming in his throat, his cheeks burning red. "A—Anastasia. And he said that he was going to face up to what he did. To turn himself in—which I know grants leniency within the court system."

"Him?" Ford scoffed. "Planning to surrender voluntarily? Ha!"

"It's true." Mary-Sue said, stepping between Ace and the gun. "And furthermore, I believe that he didn't run Charles off of the road. That he's a victim of small-town mistrust against the Japanese, bias left over from the war. But without his help, we may never have captured Anastasia."

"Is that so?" The government agent eyed Ace.

"That's so," Ace growled, then paused and cleared his throat. "I, uh, I mean, yes, sir. I'm ready to stop runnin'."

"After how I've seen our town treat Ace without good cause," Danny said, "and after how I've treated him, without good cause—I'm willing to bet that the witnesses in his case were biased and that, as he claims, the incident was an accident. A misunderstanding. So if my reputation and good standing in this community can in any way lend to the boy getting a fair and just trial, then I'd like to volunteer myself as a character witness."

For a moment, the man stared forward, gun pointed at the teenagers. Then, he lowered his weapon, reluctantly slipping it back into its holster.

"So you really didn't know about the Soviet plot?" Mary-Sue asked. "You were just after Ace the whole time?"

"That's right. And I hope, for your sake," Ford said, flatly, turning back to the greaser, "that the judge takes your actions today into consideration. With enough good will, he may even try you as a minor." The G-Man looked up the hill toward the campgrounds, then pulled at Anastasia's handcuffs.

"But for now, there's much paperwork to be done before morning. Let's go, Kuroki."

"One last thing before you do," Mary-Sue said, slipping her down to Ace's and intertwining her fingers with his. She looked him in the eyes, stood up on her tip-toes, then planted a tender kiss on his lips. "There—now you've had a sweetheart get a crush on you, too."

Ace looked deep into her eyes, and for a moment the two seemed lost. Then, Agent Ford cleared his throat and nodded toward the hill. Ace gave Mary-Sue's hand a squeeze, let go, and followed the Agent Ford and Anastasia toward the grass. The young Soviet girl glanced back over her shoulder, gave Danny an inscrutable look, and disappeared through the reeds. Both off to an uncertain fate.

A tear rolled down Danny's cheek. He reached up to wipe it away.

"I'm really sorry," Mary-Sue said.

"For what?" Danny gave a wry chuckle, staring at the submarine, a knot in his stomach. "I'm the one who mucked the whole thing up; I let myself get manipulated, I was a bad friend to you, I was a bad friend to Sondra, I was awful to Ace, and I nearly let a Soviet spy steal my father's secret invention."

"Everyone," Mary-Sue said, turning toward the

onlookers. "Would you give us a moment?"

"Of course." Dr. Oxford smiled. "Kids?"

Phil looked up from his notebook, then slipped his pencil behind his ear. Sondra and Francine each smiled sadly and gave Danny warm looks. Prescott gave Mary-Sue a respectful nod. Then, the scientist reached his arms out, shepherding the kids away toward the cemetery. Mary-Sue walked over to Danny.

"I meant that I'm sorry about Violet." She reached out and gave him a tender hug. After a few long seconds she pulled away, keeping ahold of his arms. "Are you okay?"

"I don't know what to think." The boy let a few more tears fall down his cheeks before wiping them away, giving a small sniffle. "If everything we had was a lie, then why do I still feel sad? Aren't I supposed to… hate her, or something?"

"No," Mary-Sue said, shaking her head. "She was a victim, too."

"Was she?" Danny frowned, brow knit. "I… I suppose she was a little like George Hudson, in a way. *The Phantom of Prom* and *The Mutant of Mercury Marsh*—casualties of two cold and uncaring systems. Of two governments with crass political agendas they strove to achieve regardless of the human cost."

"That's right." Mary-Sue gave a sad smile. "Violet was just a child when her government recruited her. Before she was capable of understanding the ideology she was taught. They indoctrinated her, trained her as a spy, gave her a mission no child should have had, all alone. And despite all of that, in the end she chose to do the right thing. Which means that what you two had was real."

"But she didn't make me dismissive," he said, "and she didn't make me abandon you—three times. She didn't make me fight Ace—twice. All that she did was use those things that were already inside of me." Danny looked Mary-Sue in the eyes. "But I'm going to work on changing those things, on breaking the pattern. I'm going to take responsibility for the impact of my actions, and I'm going to prove that I've changed through behavior rather than words."

"Thank you," Mary-Sue said, giving him a sad, sweet smile.

"And I was thinking." Danny twisted his mouth to the side. "About our detective agency."

"I figured something like this was coming." She frowned. "You want to disband *The Britannica Junior Detectives*, don't you?"

"I do," he said, putting his hand on her shoulder. "But not because I want to stop solving mysteries with you, but because it isn't my agency. You're not my sidekick, and you never have been. You're my partner, and I want to finally start treating you that way. If you'll have me."

"Really?" Mary-Sue looked up, a smile pulling at the edge of her lips.

"Really." Danny nodded. "So together we can decide what we want to be called—and what mysteries we want to pursue."

"Well, I don't think it'll be ghosts or ghouls," she said, twisting her mouth to the side. "Or aliens from Mars, or shadowy government agents. I think the real difference that we can try to make is in helping the people who really need it—victims of uncaring governments, communities, and police departments. Those at the fringes of society who have nowhere else to turn. That's where we can make our real impact."

"I'm in if you are." Danny smiled, extending his hand. "Partners?"

Mary-Sue broke out into a wide grin, dimples pushing deep into her rosy apple cheeks. She reached out and grasped his hand, giving it a firm shake.

"Partners."

THE END

Danny and Mary-Sue will return in...

THE CURIOUS CASE OF THE CLAIRVOYANT CULT

BY GREGORY R.E. GALLAGHER

Autumn, 1959. As Danny and Mary-Sue settle into high school, they meet the disciple of a mysterious guru who has founded a "School for the Dawn of Enlightenment" on the outskirts of Bonnifield. As this movement gains traction, the two teenage sleuths must investigate rumors that members of the growing cult have the power of extra-sensory perception.

DIXON & KEEN, LTD.

The Junior Detective Secret Code Dial

Do you want to be a junior detective just like Mary-Sue and Danny? Just cut out
the two dials, insert a brad, and turn the inner dial with the regular alphabet and
match it up with the outer dial that has the scrambled code alphabet! They say:

"NUYDU Y SKKV HUDQUC!"